ONCE UPON A FEVER

Chicken House

2 Palmer Street, Frome, Somerset BA11 1DS
www.chickenhousebooks.com

Text © Angharad Walker 2022

First published in Great Britain in 2022
Chicken House
2 Palmer Street
Frome, Somerset BA11 1DS
United Kingdom
www.chickenhousebooks.com

Chicken House/Scholastic Ireland, 89E Lagan Road, Dublin Industrial Estate,
Glasnevin, Dublin D11 HP5F, Republic of Ireland

Cover and interior design by Micaela Alcaino
Typeset by Dorchester Typesetting Group Ltd
Printed and bound in Great Britain by CPI Group (UK) Ltd, Croydon CR0 4YY

1 3 5 7 9 10 8 6 4 2

British Library Cataloguing in Publication data available.

PB ISBN 978-1-912626-98-4
eISBN 978-1-913696-91-7

For Callum

Also by Angharad Walker
The Ash House

CHAPTER ONE

I t was a night like any other at King Jude's Hospital. Steam filled the Invisibility Ward to make its fading patients visible. Muffled groans came from the Department of Dreams, Delusions and Disturbed Thoughts. Nurses and methics began their night shifts. None of them knew that on the other side of the quad, through stone corridors and sleeping wards, the Darke sisters stood on the threshold of a secret passageway.

'How did you find out about this?' Payton asked.

'By exploring,' Ani replied.

'And this is the only way to the old laboratory?'

'The only way without getting caught. You can go back if you're scared.'

'I'm not scared.'

'Are you sure you still want to go?'

Payton squared her shoulders. 'If it's the only way.'

The Methics Hall was empty but oppressive, with

its wood panelling and stern oil paintings. Only methics – the doctors who committed their lives to the care and healing of the city's people – were allowed in. The black eyes of the paintings stared into space, capturing nothing of the sitters' great minds. Payton's nervous breath brushed Ani's hair.

Ani marched across the hall without hesitating and stopped midway. She curled her fingers into a groove in the wood panelling and, with force from her shoulder, a section of the panelling bent inwards, revealing a door and stone steps. The sound of rushing water came from the darkness below.

Payton joined her and looked over her shoulder.

'Wow.'

'I told you.'

Ani went first, pulling a gwaidlamp from her pocket.

'How do you have one of those?' Payton demanded.

'Lost and Found.'

'There isn't a Lost and Found at King Jude's.'

'Well, somebody lost it and I found it.'

Ani balanced the glass orb in the palm of her hand. As it warmed with the temperature of her blood, it gave off a green glow that illuminated the steps, their faces and the awkward shape of the masks that hung unused around their necks.

Payton closed the door behind them and they descended.

At the bottom of the stairs was a basement filled with large wooden waterwheels, which gave the hospital its electricity. The water foamed pale in the gloom, thundering around each wheel before disappearing through the channels under a wall.

'This way,' Ani shouted over the din.

She leapt deftly over the narrow channels and Payton followed, holding up her hands to stop the water from splashing her face.

'We need to go through here.'

Payton looked where Ani was pointing. One of the channels had run dry; only a trickle fell from the bricks to join the rest of the underground stream. The wheel in front of it was still.

They clambered up the unmoving waterwheel, close enough to the others to feel the noise rattle their teeth. They crawled along the channel, their masks swinging from their necks and bumping their elbows. Cobwebs sagged overhead, and the bricks were cold and wet under their hands and knees.

Soon their way was blocked by a metal grille. Ani bashed it open with the heel of her hand, and it fell to the floor with a clatter.

'Careful!' Payton hissed.

Ani rolled her eyes.

They climbed down and found themselves in a corridor. Ani held the gwaidlamp aloft until she found a light switch. The lights were old – some of them sputtered, while others didn't turn on at all. Curved walls bent and disappeared from sight at both ends.

'Where are we?' Payton asked.

'Underneath the operating theatre. It's locked every night, but I found this way in,' Ani said with pride.

She walked a short distance and pointed. Payton saw that there was an alcove, about as wide as double doors, built from a different colour brick.

'In there?'

'Yes. Did you bring the stuff?'

Payton reached into the pocket of her dress and brought out a wooden tub labelled MOINTOTHE in neat lettering. She clicked the lid off to reveal a thick white paste.

'How long will it take?' Ani asked.

'I once saw Methic Gilchrist use it on a crystallized patient. A minute or two.' Payton jerked it away from the inquiring reach of her younger sister. 'Careful! It's a chemical. Not for kids.'

'You're a kid. You're thirteen.'

'And you're eleven, which makes you more of a kid than me. Besides, I know as much as any of the methics. Now hold up the light.'

Using the wooden stick inside the tub's lid, Payton began to smear the paste on the mortar between the bricks of the alcove. When she'd finished, she leant against the opposite wall, shoulder to shoulder with Ani, and waited. They watched the flickering green shapes Ani threw on the wall with the gwaidlamp and her fingers. Soon crumbs of mortar started to fall to the floor.

'Now?' Ani asked.

'Not quite.'

When Payton decided they had waited long enough, she instructed Ani to put her mask on.

'Do I have to?'

'It's an old lab, Ani. No one has set foot in it since the Turn. I don't know what's in there, but the methics will have closed it up for a reason. Put it on. Don't touch anything when we're inside either.'

'How do we get in?' Ani's voice echoed in her mask as they approached the wall, the mortar grainy under their feet.

'I guess we just bash it.'

'Brilliant!'

Ani flung herself at the wall. She cried out with pain, then laughed straightaway when she felt the bricks give a little. Payton began to push too and soon they had created a dark, gaping hole in the wall. Their breath was warm inside their masks, which gave each of them the ludicrous look of an adult's head on a child's body, with round, unblinking glass eyes and rasping breath.

They got mortar under their fingernails, and the grey, practical pinafore dresses that Nurse Wheeldon made them wear became covered in dust. They paused and inspected their handiwork. The hole revealed nothing beyond but darkness. They looked at each other. Payton nodded. Ani went first, the leafy glow of the gwaidlamp thrust out in front of her.

It became clear the dust-laden laboratory had been closed in a hurry. Notebooks lay open on the workbenches. Some had been abandoned mid-sentence. Beakers and test tubes were strewn about, and the girls winced at the sound of broken glass crunching underfoot as they entered. Ani held the gwaidlamp a little tighter.

'Stay here. Stand still. Keep the light shining.' Payton's voice was muffled by her mask but lost none of its imperious tone.

'Can't I help look?' Ani begged.

Payton ignored her. Something about the room made the hairs on the back of her neck stand up. She could hear rustling, just beyond the gwaidlamp's glow. The inside of her mask smelt stale, and she imagined the whole room around her rotting and releasing diseases it had stored like a tomb.

The chemical cabinet was old. There were small craters in the surface of the wood where some sort of acid had been handled carelessly. The wooden door creaked as Payton opened it. It was stocked full. In their hurry to leave and never come back, the methics hadn't even taken their most precious ingredients. She wondered what could have happened to make them abandon such valuable chemicals.

'Look at all this . . .' She scanned the long, complicated words on the labels. 'I don't even know what some of these are . . .'

'Maybe it's possible you don't know *everything*,' Ani jibed.

'I know my medicines.' She slapped Ani's hand as it reached out to touch the glass vials. 'And I know not to touch something if I don't know what it is. You're lucky I let you come tonight.'

'You *let* me? You didn't know this was here. If it weren't for me—'

'It's here!'

'What?'

'Bring the light closer.'

Payton's hand became bathed in green; she was holding a small vial of clear liquid. Ani tried to read the scientific label on its side.

'Thi . . . Th'eiraaa—'

'*Th'eiraudur*,' Payton whispered with awe. 'Unspoken Water.' She cradled it as if it was a rare gem. Her heart pounded with excitement. 'I wasn't really expecting to find it. This place was my last hope. *This* right here is my last hope.'

'Hope for what?'

Payton turned away from Ani. 'An experiment.'

'You mean like homework?' Ani felt that only Payton could turn a mission to the secret laboratory into something so dull.

'Advanced medicine that your tiny brain wouldn't be able to understand.'

'Fine. I don't care about your stupid experiments anyway.' Ani was already wandering away from the cabinet, holding the green light up to the chalkboard and workstations. A large glass box stood in the corner of the room. Its door was ajar.

'Payton, what's that?'

'It's a fume chamber. You put dangerous chemicals into it in case—'

'No, I mean, what's *that*?'

Something inside the fume chamber dripped. The girls drew nearer and saw that the insides of the glass were splattered with a thick, dark liquid.

'I don't know . . .'

Ani took half a step closer so she was standing on the threshold. She brought the gwaidlamp as close as she dared. The congealed sludge had a brown hue. Something seemed to move under its surface.

'Ani . . .'

'What the—?'

A droplet of the brown liquid burst from the surface of the glass, as if aiming for the warmth of the gwaid-lamp, and landed on Ani's mask. Payton screamed. Ani started to yell too, and the sisters locked arms and ran away from the fume chamber and out of the lab, bumping into the workstations, knocking over stacks of paper, and stumbling over the loose bricks. When they were through the hole in the wall, Payton yanked off her mask. Her usually neat hair was ruffled and chaotic. Ani removed her own mask and tossed it inside the lab without pausing to look at the liquid that had struck her. She started to giggle.

'What's so funny?' Payton demanded.

Ani did an impression of their screams within their masks, and Payton found herself laughing too. Soon they were bent over, clutching their stomachs, each whoop inspiring a louder one from the other.

'Stop, *stop*!' Payton rubbed her eyes with her shoulder. It had been years since she'd laughed like this with her sister. 'We shouldn't be so . . .'

'Happy?'

'It's not good for us. Feelings are the—'

'Start of all disease.' Ani recited the boring warning that the methics and nurses gave them every day. 'I know. As if you'd let me forget.'

The sisters were silent and awkward again, looking

at the hole in the wall.

'What do you think it was?'

'I bet it was a feeling.'

'A pure one?'

Payton nodded. 'Back then, methics did a lot of experiments trying to capture pure feelings so they could study them. Sometimes it went a bit wrong. I bet that's why they blocked it up. Come on. I found the Unspoken Water. Time to go.'

'What are you doing?' Ani asked.

Payton had picked up a brick.

'We have to rebuild the wall. Whatever that stuff was, it needs to stay in there. It won't take long.'

She set about methodically stacking the bricks back in place, brushing aside the crumbling mortar that had held them together. Ani started to help, but her approach was haphazard and none of her bricks seemed to slot together. Payton waved her away, so she drifted down the corridor, her hand trailing along the damp stone. With each step the sound of Payton stacking the bricks grew quieter and was replaced by the *pluh-plink* of dripping water. Spiders poked their crooked legs out from behind the lamps.

Ani carried the gwaidlamp in front of her and wondered what made her blood produce green light. Not much at King Jude's was green. There was a knitted rabbit made of faded green wool on the windowsill of the bedroom she shared with Payton. It was a present from the Head of the Hospital's wife when they first arrived at King Jude's five years ago, shivering and disoriented at the sight of the grand hospital, so different from their cottage in the Isles. Payton had declared herself too old for toys and Ani did too at the time, though she hid the rabbit under her blankets anyway.

She made a low whistle, which reverberated off the walls. It was one from the secret language she had made up with Payton when they were small; they had needed a series of sounds and gestures during the weeks they refused to speak to or in front of their father. This one, a lilting low noise that swept up into a higher note, simply meant: *Let's play a game.*

A whistle drifted back along the corridor.

'That's not it,' Ani called. Payton didn't reply, so she walked back to her. 'Payton, that's not it. It's –' Ani did their *yes* and *no* whistles.

'What?' Payton turned from the wall, now nearly bricked up again.

'You didn't do our language right.'

'I didn't do it at all.'

'But . . .'

'That was for when we were little, Ani.' She dusted the mortar from her hands. 'There. All done. Now let's go before Father notices we're missing.'

'I definitely heard something.'

'It was probably an echo.'

'No . . .' Ani turned and peered back down the gloomy corridor. 'Somebody whistled back.'

CHAPTER TWO

The next morning, Payton skipped breakfast and rushed straight to her desk in the Methics Lab. Like the hall, it was supposed to be a place where only the blue-robed methics could go. Most of them made an exception for Payton, who was as studious as any methic, and much better behaved than her sister.

She was bleary-eyed and electric with excitement, but tried to push the feeling down, as she knew a good methic should. Even with all her practice, it was hard this time. There were only two methics in the lab and no sign of her father. She noted with disdain that she hadn't seen him in the lab for some weeks.

She placed the Unspoken Water next to a stand of test tubes that ranged in colour from deep purple to lavender. She consulted her notes and was careful with her measurements, but it was just a formality. She knew what she was doing. She added two drops of the

Unspoken Water to one of the test tubes, and put all the others in the corner for chemical disposal. Nobody gave her a second glance as she pocketed the remaining test tube and headed out of the lab into the sporadic sunshine, running over the quad's cobblestones towards the Inertia Ward, her heart dangerously full of hope.

The Inertia Ward was in one of the hospital's oldest wings: the Sanatorium for Hysteria, Despair and Melancholy. It was less thrilling than working with poisons and explosions, and not as bizarre and fascinating as the Department of Dreams, Delusions and Disturbed Thoughts. Because of this, it didn't attract the most ambitious methics. It had wards where entire days passed with nobody uttering a word. The methics there mostly dealt with various forms of heartbreak, a few terrorized patients whose sharp shrieks were the only break in the dull routines, and a young woman who was slowly going people-blind – her ability to see other humans was retreating slowly but surely as her world became filled with kind, disembodied voices.

The Inertia Ward was in a windowless corner of the sanatorium. Its patients had no need for sunshine or fresh air. They simply lay and waited. Payton's footsteps echoed around her as she made her way there, the test tube in her pocket growing warm in her anxious grip.

The lights were supposed to resemble natural sunlight, but they were too white and constant, and dim enough that one could look at the outlines of the bulbs. To Payton they seemed like lacklustre suns. There was a lot she'd change about the ward if she was in charge.

She was pinning her hopes on the test tube. If her plan worked, she wouldn't have to visit that ghastly room many more times.

The beds nearest to her weren't hospital beds – they were stone tombs. She'd never seen the patients within, and didn't know what terrible afflictions kept them trapped. The other beds on the Inertia Ward weren't beds either – they were glass chambers filled with water where the patients lay submerged, sound asleep. It was where the hospital placed their worst cases of water fever.

Payton and Ani's mother was one of them.

Water fever was a fast-moving and terrible disease. The chamber kept Iona Darke alive, but asleep, unable to be a part of the world and unable to leave it. Her skin looked waxy and dull, like a painting. There were tiny bubbles on her lips. The patient who had been on the ward the longest was Mrs Coleman, an elderly woman whose chamber was at the far end of the ward, almost in shadow. Payton had never seen anybody visit her.

She shuddered at the thought of her mother being here for decades.

'Ready to take a chance, Mother?' she whispered, pressing her hand to the glass. Her throat tightened – feelings of love and fear and hope swirled and threatened to become too much, so she forced herself to remember her mother when she was awake and smiling, before the fever struck. Payton found it helped to soothe the bad feelings that threatened to bubble up inside her. She had always been proud that she was able to control herself, like the methics, while Ani needed medicine to calm her down.

The water chamber's glass panes were held in place within a metal frame. Underneath the patient, under a metal grille, a tray of aquatic plants swayed in the greening water, providing vital nutrients that held the disease at bay. They were known as 'breathers', because many people mistakenly thought that they allowed a person to breathe underwater, but Payton knew that one of them – a frilly, blue-green isoetid – was in fact a mild poison that froze the body in time. Her mother had no heartbeat, no need for breath. The only way to stop the illness was to stop everything. She floated closer to death than life, unconscious, in a watery jail cell that may as well have been a grave, until a cure could be discovered.

Payton's father had been working on a cure since they arrived at King Jude's. As a little girl, Payton had been full of admiration for her father and had absolute faith in him. Every time she saw him in his blue robes, she'd felt certain that she wouldn't have to wait long, and soon they'd be heading back to the Isles with their mother, alive and well. They would leave the city, and go back to days filled with laughter, salt-swept hair and looking for shells on the beach.

But every year he had disappointed her. As Payton taught herself medicine, stealing books and notes, hiding in lectures, assisting the nurses and methics on the wards, she took to following his progress with interest, only to find his research was filled with errors and dead ends. For the last year he'd been stuck entirely.

After reading her father's research, Payton came up with her own idea for a cure. The only catch was sourcing the Unspoken Water. Now there was nothing to hold her back.

Payton clicked the drain latch on her mother's water chamber, and it began to gurgle. The top half stayed full, while the liquid in the lower chamber, where the breathers were planted, started to drain. She took a deep, steadying breath and took the test tube out of her pocket. The pale liquid suddenly looked alarmingly bright next to the water. The top half of the chamber was sealed, so the only way to administer the medicine was by planting it among the breathers. As the tank filled up again, it would enter the water, and eventually reach her mother the way the poison did. It was a careful balance. If the medicine wasn't strong enough, it wouldn't have any effect. Too much and . . . She couldn't think like that.

The chamber stopped gurgling; Payton opened the breather drawer and pulled the tray of plants towards her. She wrinkled her nose – they smelt like a clogged gutter. She parted some leaves grown soft and mulchy with water and nestled the test tube in the gap. She chewed her lip. Part of her didn't want to tell her father or Ani if it worked – she wanted to take her mother's hand and run away, just the two of them.

Payton wasn't a child prone to fantasies, but this particular one made her eyes sting.

Some minutes later, she was still kneeling before her mother and the tray of breathers, paralysed by the enormity of her decision.

'Miss Darke.'

She spun round, trying to wipe her eyes.

It was Methic Gilchrist. He was the Head of the Hospital, a quiet, elderly methic who always spoke softly and stepped lightly, and Payton hadn't heard him enter the Inertia Ward.

'There's no need to hide it, child.' He held up his hands soothingly. 'As long as you haven't administered anything?'

Payton was dumbstruck with fear, embarrassment

and the awe she felt for him. To her, Gilchrist seemed as old as King Jude's itself. Nobody could remember the place without him. She shook her head.

He started to walk towards her. 'Because to do so without having earned your robes is a grave crime. One that would have you tried before the Guild of Medicine itself. Wouldn't it?'

She nodded.

'I would hate to see a bright future extinguished in such a way.' He held out a hand. His skin looked thin and pale in the unnatural light, every vein traceable. He suffered from a mild, ever-present tremor. Payton thought he was going to help her up, but then he said, 'I think I had better take care of that.'

He meant the test tube.

She gulped and plucked it out of the breather tray, carefully stoppered it, and gave it to him. His fingers wrapped around it and he drew it towards his heart.

'How did you—?' she began.

'Your little research station in the Methics Lab is no secret. I told them to leave you be. I played similar games when I was your age.'

Payton felt her ears begin to burn, but she didn't reply.

'However, when I began to believe you might actually attempt something, I kept a closer eye on you. I must say the Unspoken Water was an inspired idea. But wherever did you get it?'

'I . . . I found it.' Payton wasn't a practised liar. She kept her secrets by keeping her head down, studying hard and never getting caught. But it was too late for that.

Gilchrist gathered his robes around him and took a seat on the water chamber next to her mother's with an inappropriate casualness.

'Water fever is a very cruel disease,' he mused. 'So drawn out and draining . . . and since it always begins with grief in the first place, it's often a tragedy upon another tragedy.'

'Grief . . .' Payton repeated.

'Disease begins with a feeling, Miss Darke. It has been this way ever since the Turn – when people's feelings first started making them ill. Every emotion we feel alters our bodies. But when these emotions are thrown off balance – when we experience their extremes – disease takes hold. Sadness, anger, jealousy, greed, fear . . . they affect the body in endless, fascinating ways.'

Payton knew perfectly well what caused diseases; she didn't need Gilchrist to explain to her what she'd known all her life.

'We were supposed to have a baby brother,' she told him, glancing at her mother. 'When he died, that's how the water fever started.' She remembered her mother's tears at first. Then the sweating, the clear streams running from her mother's ears and mouth, the dry, rattling breaths. Holding a jug of water to her lips during the long journey south to Lundain, to King Jude's, where her father promised they would find help. 'But we were all sad. Father was sad. I . . .'

'You were all grieving.'

'Yes.' The question she couldn't stop asking herself continued to nag. 'So why her? Why was she the only one to get sick?'

'We do not know why some feelings turn into illness, Miss Darke. That is the mystery of the Turn. Medicine is only a small light, shining in the darkness of the mysterious human condition.'

She shook her head with irritation.

'I'm fed up with people not knowing. You're methics. You're supposed to know. How can anyone be fine with this?' She gestured at the rows and rows of water chambers in the ward.

'We aren't. That is why we work here.'

'Well, you should work harder.' Her anger made Payton forget her manners. 'All the methics should be down here, all the time, trying to bring her back.'

'You are angry with your father.'

'He's useless.'

'He is doing his best. There is nothing he wouldn't do for your mother. I remember when you arrived here. Your father wouldn't eat or rest until she was taken care

21

of. It was pouring rain, do you remember? You came to my house. My wife took you and your sister to the top floor so you could see the Tamesas Wheel.'

'She gave us Lundain cakes.'

Payton looked down. Mrs Gilchrist had been a kind lady; she'd died several years ago, but Payton had never given much thought to what it was like for Methic Gilchrist to live all alone in his big house on the edge of the grounds, with its impressive views of the river.

'It's all so horrid,' she said.

'It is,' he agreed.

'That's why the methics should try everything. *I* would try everything.'

'Very well, then. Here.' He held out her cure. 'Administer it.'

'Really?'

'If it works, I'll never tell a soul. If it doesn't, I will take you to the guild and let them decide your punishment. Certainly, you will never be allowed to become a methic.'

She took it back. 'Do you . . . do you think it will work? With the Unspoken Water?'

'You must answer that question yourself.'

'If you did . . .' she reasoned, 'you would have given it to her by now.'

He bowed his head at her correct answer.

'But *I* think it will work.'

His blue eyes watched her closely beneath his white brows.

'But you . . . you . . . Oh, I don't know,' she said hopelessly. 'I want it to work more than anything.'

'Sometimes, in science, you must have the courage to do things properly. That's why we have a guild in the first place. Confirmation bias is a scientist's worst enemy.'

'Confirmation bias?'

'It's where we want to see an experiment produce a particular result, as you do with your mother here. And we can want it so badly that we ignore other evidence that might prove us wrong.'

'But surely all methics want their cures to work.'

'Not every methic is as desperate as you are. Desperation comes from fear. Methics cannot be afraid. We must be hopeful, responsible, patient.'

'But being a methic means being daring sometimes too, doesn't it, Methic Gilchrist? To find cures and to help people you sometimes have to risk everything you have.' This idea spurred her into action. She shoved her cure into the tray of plants.

Beyond the breathers, Payton saw her mother's outline waver with the ripples in the water.

'Are you risking everything you have, Miss Darke?' Gilchrist asked. 'Or risking something that doesn't belong to you at all?'

Payton ignored him and slammed the breather drawer into the chamber.

In the same movement, she pulled it out again.

With a shout of frustration, she swiped the test tube from the tray and let it smash on the floor.

Gilchrist left her to pick up every shard.

CHAPTER THREE

Ani returned to the corridor outside the old laboratory a little after midnight, when most of the
hospital was moonlit and sleeping.

She knew King Jude's as well as any of the methics,
nurses, servants or ambulans drivers who had worked
there for decades. When she and Payton reopened the
old laboratory, the hospital became fresh with the
possibility of new secrets. Any friendship she and
Payton rebuilt that night had evaporated by morning,
but that didn't matter to Ani. She was used to it.
Besides, Payton hadn't heard the whistle. It was Ani's
secret to investigate.

She retraced her route from the Methics Hall, past
the waterwheels and down the curving corridor, listening intently, holding the gwaidlamp in her hand. She
whistled, but this time there was no reply.

Ani passed a stone staircase leading up. She

assumed it led up to the operating theatre – which these days was a lecture hall for the methics – through some back entrance not many people used.

She was about to climb it to go and see, but then, finally, she heard it: the whistle. This time it was so close it felt as if it was in her ear.

Ani whistled back: *Let's play a game.*

The response sang through the air back to her, and Ani whipped around. In the wall opposite the stairs there was a door with a small opening. A pair of bloodshot eyes were staring through the bars.

Ani jumped back and suppressed a scream. Her skin flushed hot as fear jolted through her. A dirt-streaked face was pressed against a small opening in the door. This was the sort of room patients stayed in when they had a more dangerous illness, with just this window to pass food, water and medicine through until they were safer. With a shaking hand, she lifted the gwaidlamp higher. The boy looked about ten – a year younger than herself. The light reflected gold flecks in his brown eyes.

'You're not a nurse.' The boy spoke strangely, as if there was food in his mouth. He pressed closer to the window and clutched the bars – his hands were covered in thick mittens.

'No,' she replied. 'I'm Ani.'

'I'm Kristofer.'

'What's sort of illness do you have?' Ani couldn't imagine what disease would banish him to this room, far away from all the other wards and patients.

He looked at her, then pulled at one of the mittens with his teeth. Something glinted, then he turned his bare hand so she could see. It was covered in a layer of gold.

'Wow,' she breathed.

'I don't know the fancy methic word for it,' he said. 'But at the market where I used to work, they called it Midas-fingers.' He gripped one of the bars and then let go so she could see how the gold smeared unevenly across the metal. He put the mitten back on.

'But why are you down here? Why aren't you on a ward?'

'*I* don't know. Nobody tells me anything. They just grabbed me while I was sleeping and put me in here.'

'Do they ever let you out?'

'Nope. The door's locked.'

He rattled the handle to prove it.

'You must be bored.'

'You have no idea. The methic says once I have this test, I'll be sent away to be cured. But it's been days and nothing . . .' His eyes fixed on Ani as if seeing her for the first time. 'What are you doing here? Are you a patient?'

'No. I live here.'

'Nice place to live.'

'I suppose. I like the people. The nurses are nice and there are always the patients to talk to. Especially the invisibility patients, because they've got so used to people ignoring them . . . But before, I lived in the Isles. That was the best.'

'I live in Leadenhall.'

'A hall?'

He laughed. 'It's not a hall! It's a place. Leadenhall. You know, the market in the centre of the city?'

'I've never been out in Lundain. I'm not allowed.'

The boy watched her for a moment, then he said, 'My friends call me Kitt.'

'I'm Ani. That's just my name. I don't really have many friends. Just the patients. And my sister. But she wouldn't want to be my friend.'

'I'll be your friend,' said Kitt.

She smiled at him. 'Really?'

'Promise.'

'Promise on the gwaidlamp!' She leapt closer to the door and held the gwaidlamp up to the window. Kitt flinched, scared for a moment.

'It's OK! It's just light. Every person makes a different colour. Touch it.'

Kitt took off his mitten again and his fingers passed through the bars. Ani pressed the gwaidlamp against them. After a moment, beams of gold light shone through the waves of green.

'You're gold!' she said with delight. 'We should have guessed.'

He pulled his hand away. The golden light disappeared, but there was a smudge of his Midas-touch gold on the lamp. Ani tried to wipe it with her sleeve, but it wouldn't come off.

'Sorry,' said Kitt.

'I don't mind. It makes it more special.'

'How does it do that?'

'I don't know. The wilders used them, years ago.'

'The what?'

'The Guild of the Wild.' Ani moved the gwaidlamp through the air to make shapes and patterns with the light.

'There's no such thing,' said the boy. 'There are only two guilds: Medicine and Finance.'

'Now, yes. But before the Turn, there used to be hundreds of guilds. A guild for everything. I always thought being a wilder would have been the best – they lived in forests and on mountains and beaches, and they let their animals run wherever they liked, and they had adventures climbing and sailing—'

'That sounds made up.'

'Maybe.' Ani felt deflated. 'Some of the older patients tell stories about the other guilds sometimes. I don't know if they're true. What's Leadenhall like?

Does it have stories like King Jude's?'

Kitt began to tell her about life in Lundain, running errands in the market and sleeping under stalls and building camps with the other parentless children who lived there. About the boats on the River Tamesas; the giant waterwheels that powered the city, just like the wheels that powered the hospital; the financiers, who wore their clean, golden robes the way methics wore blue.

Ani was enthralled. Kitt's stories were filled with *real* places and people, a world that was only on the other side of the hospital walls, but out of reach for her. The only way out of King Jude's was through the porter's lodge, which was always manned by hospital staff who were well aware of her father's rules.

Ani sat next to the door, leaning against the cool wall. Kitt did the same inside his cell, so for the rest of the night they couldn't see each other, even though their voices were close.

Kitt told her a funny story about trying to catch some rich lady's pet fox to get a reward. As Ani's giggles bounced off the damp brick, he sighed deeply.

'I really wanted that money,' he said. 'I could have spent the whole winter in a nice guesthouse instead of the market. You should see some of the houses in Lundain. Anyway, I think that's when my Midas-fingers started.'

'Does it hurt?' she asked tentatively.

'No. Mostly it just feels like . . . wanting. When you want something so much you ache. Do you ever get that feeling?'

An image of her mother flashed into Ani's mind, and she stubbornly pushed it aside.

'I don't know about that, but . . . I have to take medicine too. I'm not sick, not like the patients, but it stops me getting that ill.'

'What's the medicine for?'

'Since we came to King Jude's, I get very angry sometimes,' she whispered. 'Like when the methics tell me off, or when Payton ignores me, or when one of my favourite patients gets discharged. My father makes me take it.'

'Is it horrible?'

'Oh, no. It tastes better than sweets.'

'I mean feeling too angry.'

'I don't know . . . The medicine sort of takes it away. It makes me sleepy for a while. I just keep taking it until the thing I was angry about doesn't matter as much.'

Above their heads, at the top of the stone staircase, there was a creaking, grinding noise, like a heavy door being pushed open.

'What was that?' Ani asked.

'It must be the nurse bringing me breakfast. It's morning.'

'What! Morning? I have to go.'

Ani scrabbled to her feet and grabbed the door handle to pull herself up. As soon as she touched it, she shrieked. The handle felt cold yet somehow scalding as well. She staggered back, clutching her hand to her chest.

'What is it?' Kitt was wide-eyed, peering through the bars.

Ani peeled her fingers open and looked at her palm. A bright red stripe, hot and blistering, was taking shape.

'The door burnt me!'

'Are you hurt?'

'There's something on the handle . . . like a chemical or something. Why would they do that?' She looked up. There were footsteps coming down the stairs. She didn't have much time. 'Kitt. Which methic locked you in here? Do you know their name?'

His gold-flecked eyes were full of concern behind the bars.

'I think his name was Darke. Methic Darke.'

CHAPTER FOUR

Ani returned home, her mind racing.

The Darkes lived at the top of the East Wing, in an old apartment that had once housed student methics. The living room was long, with sloping walls under the roof. Ani and Payton shared a small bedroom near the front door, their beds so close they could reach out and touch each other mid-dream. Ani liked their bedroom – it was one of the highest rooms in the hospital and had a deep-set window with a comfortable seat from which she could see the tangled green of Battersea Meadows and the bustle of the street corner below. The windows were fogged with condensation so often that a thin ridge of moss grew on the window frame, which Ani lovingly tended, sprinkling water on it and stroking its soft green surface.

She closed the front door quietly behind her. Her father's room was at the opposite end of the apartment, near the kitchen. She paused to look at the closed door, Kitt's words in her ear: *Methic Darke*. Why would her father keep a patient – a child – locked away in a secret cellar? And guarded by . . . She flexed her fingers and pain shot through her hand. She couldn't think straight. She crept into the kitchen and opened several cupboards until she found what she was looking for: a tub of seal-fat salve, gathering dust. She twisted off the lid and scooped out a fistful of the meaty-smelling grease with her burnt palm, then crept back to her bedroom and wriggled under the covers fully clothed.

Payton woke when Ani came into the room. It wasn't unusual for Ani to come and go at strange times, but the smell of the salve was new.

'That's for burns,' Payton whispered, still half asleep.

'I know.'

'It stinks.'

'Shut up and go back to sleep.'

'Imagine having to get it out of the seals.' Payton shuddered dreamily.

Ani did imagine it. She imagined being a wilder, and far away from King Jude's, in the vast, freezing desert of the Icelands in the north, fighting sea monsters and polar bears and ice storms to find the seals, glistening and dangerous as they lounged on their floes. She used to think that just one day of a wilder's life must have been more exciting than an entire lifetime trapped within the walls of King Jude's. But now that she'd found a boy with Midas-fingers behind a burning door, she wasn't so sure.

When she woke later in the morning, Ani tried to be brave, but by the afternoon it was clear that she needed Payton's help. It was too risky to explain the burn to one of the nurses – they would want to know how it had happened, and with each passing hour it was becoming clearer to Ani that she couldn't pretend she'd scalded herself on a kettle or steam pipe.

Payton tended to go to the Inertia Ward in the afternoons, but Ani never went with her. She hadn't visited her mother since the methics put her in the water chamber when they arrived at King Jude's. She couldn't stand that sunless room. Even the thought of her mother in the liquid coffin made her face flush and her throat tighten.

But today Payton, red-eyed and even grumpier than usual, hadn't gone to the Inertia Ward, but to one of the smaller labs where the junior methics often studied. When the stinging and burning in her palm became too much, Ani sought out her sister. She found her with her head bent over an old exam paper, chewing on the end of a pencil in a tense, distracted way.

'Payton?'

'Working,' she mumbled.

'But I have a medical question.'

'Ask one of them.' Payton waved vaguely at the quiet methics at their workbenches.

'This is something I can't tell a methic. Only you. And you're just as good as any methic,' Ani begged.

The flattery, combined with curiosity, was enough to make Payton pay attention.

'What is it, then?'

'This.'

Ani put her fist over the exam paper and slowly opened it. The burn still streaked across her palm, only it was spreading, and the burnt skin was now a violent turquoise colour.

Payton stared at it with astonishment before she collected herself and said: 'This is why you shouldn't play in the labs when you go out at night.'

'I don't! And even if I wanted to, they lock them.'

'Like that would stop you.'

Ani grinned, though she knew her sister didn't mean it as a compliment. The medicine cabinet was thrown wide open, and Payton scanned it expertly, pulling out containers made of glass, crystal, metal and wood, assessing different options.

'That's a cloirias burn, Ani. It's serious.'

'What's cloirias?' Ani cradled her hand to her chest. The bright colour of the burn was alarming and un-natural, and the pain it caused was more intense than she would let anybody know. It moved like water under her skin, smarting and stinging in waves. It worsened with each passing hour, and the colour of it was growing brighter too. It looked like her hand had been brushed with paint.

'It's a very dangerous substance. A compound that methics can use to lock things.'

'Lock?'

'Yes. It jams mechanisms, locks metal in place, that sort of thing,' Payton explained. 'The methic who makes the compound can decide who can touch it without getting burnt.'

She came back to the workbench where Ani sat. She brought a pestle and mortar and three containers. She laid them out methodically and started to open the containers and mix them. One was a thin thread of dense white smoke that sank to the bottom of the mortar as if it was heavy. In another was a mossy-looking plant that Payton picked up with tweezers, carefully avoiding touching it. The last contained a bright-blue liquid, similar in colour to Ani's burn.

'So cloirias makes metal hot?' Ani asked, watching the chemicals get ground together by the pestle.

'It certainly does. This won't help the scarring, but it will stop the pain. Pass me those bandages. I'll put one on now and make you a spare for tomorrow.'

'It's going to scar?'

'The whole point of using cloirias is for the bright scars. It makes it easy to spot someone who's tried to break in . . .' Payton stopped talking and looked at Ani's hand again. 'What on earth were you trying to unlock that had cloirias on it?'

'A door.'

'A door?'

'A locked door.'

'A door someone didn't want you to even touch.' The chemicals were now a steaming blue paste which Payton smeared on one side of the bandage. She held it out, ready for Ani's hand. 'Which door?'

'I . . .' Ani chewed her lip. 'I can't tell you.'

'Fine. Don't tell me. You can forget this. Wait until the pain gets worse and worse and your whole hand shrivels up and falls off.' She turned away with the waiting bandage.

'Payton, please!'

'Nope.'

Ani couldn't resist the promise of the healing paste. Anything to make her hand stop feeling like it was stuffed full of angry bumblebees.

'Near the old lab,' she said, 'where we were the other night. *Please*, Pay, it hurts.' She held out her hand and puffed her bottom lip out childishly. Payton relented, and started to wrap the bandage around it. The relief for Ani was instant.

'Your hand was never going to fall off,' Payton confessed.

'There's someone down there.'

'In the old lab?'

'No, down the corridor! In a locked room.' Now she had started to confess, Ani found the story tumbling out in a confusing jigsaw of facts. 'It's a prison cell, really. There's a boy there. He's called Kitt. I wasn't even trying to open the door – I just grabbed the handle when I stood up—'

'Hang on—'

'He's sick with Midas-fingers. He made the gwaid-lamp glow gold.'

'Midas—?'

'He said that Father—'

'Ani, there aren't any patients down there. Patients stay on the wards.'

'But he is there!'

'And there aren't any Midas-fingers patients in King Jude's. It's extremely rare. I don't know where you read about it—'

'But—'

'That's enough.' Payton tied the last curl of bandage tight, making Ani wince. 'Don't mess around in the labs any more, do you hear me? It's getting you overexcited and it's not good for you. You'll make yourself ill with these imaginary games. Have you taken your medicine today?'

'*Have you taken your medicine?*' Ani mimicked her cruelly as she hopped down from the workstation. 'You're not a real methic. And Kitt really is down there. You may think I made that up, but I didn't make up *this.*' She waved her bandaged hand in her sister's face.

'Girls! There you are.'

They both jumped at the sound of Nurse Wheeldon, who stood in the doorway. She was taller than most men, stern and precise in her neat, navy nurse's uniform. Many found her intimidating when they first met her, but there was a warmth behind her strict rules and hard glare that made vulnerable people seek her out: the most homesick nurses, the most frightened patients. Nurse Wheeldon had never been asked to look after the Darke girls during their mother's sickness, but it hadn't occurred to anybody at King Jude's that the job would fall to anyone else.

Payton glanced guiltily at the medicine cabinet, but Nurse Wheeldon had more important things on her mind.

'You're dining with your father tonight in the Small Dining Room.'

'Tonight? Do we have to?' Payton asked.

Payton usually ate on her own, hunched over a book in the cramped kitchen in their apartment. Ani's meals were more sporadic; she often followed the nurses or ambulans drivers and ate what they shared with her. She would steal treats from the kitchen and go and hide in the stables, her favourite part of King Jude's. Family meals were a rare occurrence.

'Yes. And I know it's not the Methics Hall, but it's still a place for hospital staff, so you're to put on clean dresses. *Smart* dresses. Ani, what happened to your hand?'

'She scalded it,' Payton half-lied.

'Then you'll have to help her get a brush through that hair, Miss Darke.' Nurse Wheeldon looked sternly at Ani's tangle of dark hair, and then left.

Payton folded up the spare bandage lined with the wet, healing paste and passed it to Ani.

'Let's go, then,' she said to Ani. 'And you're brushing your own hair.'

CHAPTER FIVE

Payton didn't know why their father had summoned
them, but she wasn't looking forward to seeing
him. She worried that Methic Gilchrist had told him
about her gamble with the Unspoken Water.

Her failure stung. She longed to be alone to mourn
the hope she'd lost and come up with a new plan.
She didn't want to sit through a meal listening to her
father's promises.

He hadn't always been that way. Payton remembered what it was like in the Isles – her mother so full
of life, quick with a joke, opinions that could change in
a flash, a sharp eye. *Look, darling* – Payton could still
remember her voice, clear as a bell – *look at this wonder*.
It was always something small: the spiral of a seashell,
the matrix of a crushed bird's egg. Her father was quiet
then, always in the background, not a part of the
private jokes and stories the girls shared with their

mother. He changed when she fell ill.

In the hurry to reach Lundain, Neel Darke swore to his daughters that he would make her better and take them all home. But with each passing month, and then year, his failures grew into a broken promise that could never be repaired. Payton watched him become lost in the politics of the hospital and the guild. Promotions came, and power, but never a treatment to cure their mother.

Methic Neel Darke was standing by the fireplace when Payton and Ani arrived in the stuffy dining room. He straightened his robes as they took a seat.

'Girls,' he murmured. He spoke to them in the same way he spoke to the junior methics. 'Ani, that's not dinner attire.' He was talking about the baggy pink cardigan Ani wore over her dress. It had belonged to their mother. She was rarely without it.

'Sorry, Father,' Ani said lightly.

She and Payton sat elbow to elbow and ate the soup brought up from the hospital kitchens. When Neel asked about her hand, Ani told him she had burnt it changing the sheets for a fire-breath patient.

He looked at her sternly.

'What?' Flecks of soup left Ani's mouth as she spoke with her mouth full.

'Why were you changing a patient's sheets without a

nurse or methic there?'

'I was trying to be helpful! Payton does it all the time – you never tell her off.'

'Your sister knows how to do the more basic procedures.' Payton narrowed her eyes at the faint praise. 'She applies herself.'

'I was applying *myself*.' Ani glared at him fiercely, ready to defend her lie further.

Neel turned to Payton.

'Is this true?'

Payton took a mouthful of soup and nodded.

He looked from one daughter to the other and decided to abandon his line of questioning.

'Are you being good? Playing nicely and keeping out of the methics' way? Are you taking your medicine?' He glanced at Ani with this last question.

Ani bobbed her head and murmured, 'Yes, Father.'

'And you, Payton? Are your studies going well?'

'Yes,' she replied stiffly.

'You are making progress?'

Payton raised her dark eyes to meet his. 'Are you?'

She saw the corner of his jaw bulge as he tensed it.

'Of a sort.'

'You aren't any nearer to a cure?' she asked with careful innocence.

'The water-fever question is very complicated,' he muttered. 'The kitchen has not prepared enough courses to give me time to explain it in a way a child would understand.'

It was Payton's turn to grind her teeth.

'But, if you must know, I currently have a new project in mind. One that could take us to Queen Cleo's Hospital.'

Payton couldn't help but feel a twinge of curiosity. Queen Cleo's was the most prestigious of Lundain's seven hospitals. It was by far the richest, the grandest – the opposite of King Jude's in so many ways – and, because of this, it attracted the very best methics. The sort of methic she wanted to be.

'Queen Cleo's?' Ani blurted. 'But we live *here*.'

'This is a chance for something better.' Neel's eyes glittered with excitement. 'This new project—'

'But what about Mother?' said Payton.

'We can have her transferred . . .'

'But her treatment—'

'I am still working on the water-fever cure—'

'How can you—?'

'This is a very rare opportunity—'

'I don't *want* to live at Queen Cleo's!' Ani complained.

'Father, I don't think you should split your focus—'

'Enough!' he snapped, then smoothed a hand over his hair, a calm methic again. The grey strands caught the firelight from the hearth. Around them, methics and nurses glanced up from their meals. 'I am the head of this family and the only methic at this table. I will decide what is best for my work, and for you two. All you need to know is that tomorrow I will be hosting important guests from Queen Cleo's. It *must* go well. This is a big opportunity for our family. I need my most charming girls.'

His eyes strayed to Ani's tangled hair and Payton's stony gaze.

'And, no, I haven't given up on my search for the water-fever cure. In fact, I'm closer than ever. If all goes well, our friends at Queen Cleo's will be able to accelerate my work – give me the resources I need to complete it.'

'And Mother will wake up?'

'Yes, Ani. We'll wake her up.'

'And we'll go back to the Isles?' Ani asked hopefully.

Neel avoided her gaze as he pushed his food around his plate.

'You and Mother will,' Payton promised her. 'I'll have to stay in Lundain a little longer so I can attempt the Trials and join the guild.'

Neel speared a piece of meat on his plate with his fork.

'You have work to do yet.'

'I know more than most junior methics!'

'Father, I have a medical question.'

'Ask away, Ani.'

'There's this patient. He has Midas-fingers.'

'Not this again.' Payton rolled her eyes. She didn't notice Neel Darke's gaze snap on to Ani's face.

After a moment he said, '*Bysaur.*' He produced the medical term with a flourish.

Ani hesitated. 'Right. Well, he's in a room underneath the operating theatre. Why is he down there?'

Neel chewed his food for a long time, before answering.

'There are no patients under the operating theatre, Ani. And there is no patient in King Jude's with that condition.'

'Told you,' said Payton.

'But—'

'Hospitals are full of rumours and stories, and no doubt this is one you've heard, but I will ask you not to repeat it. In the past there have been people who have taken advantage of patients with the affliction.' He smoothed his hair once more. 'Now, back to tomorrow's visit. You'll be excited to know that Methic Blake will be joining us from Queen Cleo's.'

Payton sat a little straighter at this news. 'Really?'

'Oh, yes. It's actually her project—'

'LIAR!'

The methics turned to stare at the sound of Ani's outburst.

'Ani!' In a flash, Neel gripped his daughter's wrist, turning his body so nobody could see, and spoke with a quiet ferocity: 'Clearly you are unwell.'

'I feel fine,' she said.

Through clenched teeth, he suggested, 'Perhaps I should double your medicine?'

Payton's heart beat hard. She always felt an inexplicable thrill run through her when Ani talked back to their father, but she had no idea why she was clinging to her story of a Midas-fingers patient. Something wasn't right. She glanced at her sister's bandaged hand and thought of the turquoise burn splashed across her skin. Then she saw Ani's hand lash out.

Their plates smashed on to the floor. Gravy oozed from under sharp porcelain edges. Everybody in the Small Dining Room was staring.

'You're a liar,' Ani repeated, calmly this time.

Neel stood slowly and leant over the table. 'Go to your room. You too, Payton. Make sure she takes her medicine.' Then he hissed: '*Three* doses.'

CHAPTER SIX

Back at the apartment, Ani slammed doors to show what she thought of her father. Payton went into the kitchen to fetch her medicine.

'You can't expect to shout like that and not be punished,' she said in what Ani thought of as her annoying, grown-up voice.

'I – don't – care!' With each word Ani opened their bedroom door and slammed it shut.

Payton caught the door before she could slam it again. Ani saw the medicine bottle in Payton's hand – pearly white liquid glistening.

She had taken the medicine – she didn't know its name or what it really was – ever since her mother had fallen ill. Her father had told her that her angry outbursts couldn't go untreated. A drop of the medicine on the back of her tongue would send a cold, soothing feeling down her throat, into her stomach, and then into the rest of her body. That bit wasn't unpleasant. It was the feelings that came after it: apathy, sleepiness, the sense that she didn't care about anything or anyone in the world.

'Do I have to?' she asked Payton.

Payton touched her hand to Ani's forehead. 'You feel warm. And that was quite an outburst. You have to learn to calm down.'

'He really is lying, Payton. Kitt told me: Father is the methic who put him down there. He's locked in – it's cruel.'

'You think Father is secretly locking up patients? That's ludicrous.'

'I'll take you there and you'll see for yourself. Tonight.' Ani wanted Payton to believe her more than anything.

'Look, breaking into the old lab was fun. But it was just that one time. No more midnight adventures.'

'I'm not making it up.'

Payton ignored her, unscrewed the lid of the medicine bottle and filled the glass stopper.

'I'm going to give you a one-and-a-half dose. Fair?'

'Nothing's fair. I don't want to go to stupid Queen Cleo's either. I just want Mother . . . well, you know.'

She stopped. She and Payton never really spoke about their mother. Both of them were too lost in their own hurt.

'I know,' said Payton quickly to change the subject. 'Here.'

Ani stuck out her tongue. Payton squeezed out three sticky-sweet drops. She went back into the kitchen to put the medicine away.

'Queen Cleo's wouldn't be that bad, you know,' she called. 'We could learn a lot there. And we'd probably have a nicer place to live. Maybe we'd be allowed out into the city for once.'

Ani didn't reply. The second Payton was out of the room, she ran to the window, yanked it open, and spat as hard as she could.

Ani spent the night flushed with anger, her fists balled under her pillow. Her fury at her father kept welling up until she pictured Kitt in the sad cell guarded by a cloirias lock, then it turned into despair.

By the morning, she had a plan.

Everybody in the hospital was distracted when the methics from Queen Cleo's arrived that afternoon. All Payton could talk about was meeting Jenipher Blake, the woman who was not only Head of the Hospital at Queen Cleo's, but Guild Master for the entire Guild of Medicine. Methics gathered around the operating theatre where the lecture would be held, so, to carry out her plan, Ani had to go through the Methics Hall and take the secret passage.

Her quick footsteps echoed horribly but went unnoticed, and soon she was back in the dark curving corridor. She knew the way, and had no problem getting to Kitt's cell. The first thing she noticed was that the shutter was drawn across the opening. Ani pressed her ear to it. She couldn't hear anything.

She looked up and down the corridor, but there were no other doors, only the damp walls. She turned back to the door and raised her fist to knock, but before she could do so, the shutter snapped open and Kitt was staring at her.

'You came back!' he said.

'I wasn't going to leave you here.'

'Is your hand all right?'

'Just a scar.' Ani took pleasure in shrugging as she said this. 'What about you?'

'My test is today.' She saw fear flash across his face.

'Test?'

'The nurses say I have to take a test. Methic Darke's orders.'

'That doesn't matter. I'm getting you out.'

'How? The door—'

'I have a way.'

Ani glanced up the dark stairway. She could hear feet shuffling and the murmur of voices overhead. The operating theatre above them was filling up.

'You can't,' Kitt insisted. 'You got burnt last time.'

'Not this time,' Ani insisted. 'These nurses, do they use a key?'

'No, they just open it,' said Kitt.

'Good. That means they think the chemical lock is enough.'

Ani pulled the spare bandage Payton had made her from her pocket and began to remove her old one. The flesh on her palm was still a sickening, bright blue.

'I think it's better if I'm quick,' she warned Kitt.

The paste on the new bandage was still soft. She smeared it on her burnt palm – it numbed her skin, but she didn't pause to enjoy it. She grasped the door handle. There was a sound like steam escaping through a narrow opening. Something smelt sour, and she felt the hot burning sensation under her palm, but it was made almost tolerable by the cooling cushion of the paste. It was enough to let her pull the door open.

The room was smaller than she'd expected. It was strange to see Kitt as a whole person, rather than a sliver of a face. The first thing she noticed was the gold – on the walls, on the floor, on the hospital pyjamas he wore. It was streaked in his dirty red hair, lodged in the gaps between his teeth, and the corners of his eyes, where other people get sleep dust.

'How did you—?' he began to ask.

'Shh!'

They fell silent. There were footsteps – not the

shuffling of methics overhead, but someone coming down the stairs.

'We have to go!'

'They'll come after us.'

Ani grabbed him by the mitten and dragged him towards the door. When they reached the doorway, she heard the footsteps closer than she thought.

'We're too late,' he said with despair.

Ani cursed.

With no time to think, she pulled the door closed, then shoved Kitt into the corner of the cell behind the door. She hoped that if the door opened, he'd be hidden.

'If you get a chance to run, do it, all right?'

Seconds later the door opened. Two nurses, a man and a woman, were silhouetted by the sputtering lights.

They weren't King Jude's nurses. They wore grey, not navy. Ani had never seen them before in her life.

The nurses looked at Ani standing alone in the cell, with a gold smear on her unbandaged hand where she'd touched Kitt. She stood as she always did: with her chin jutting out, her cheeks tense as if she was biting her tongue. The woman took her by the crook of her elbow. Ani knew that if she resisted, they might come into the cell and spot Kitt. They clearly didn't know they had the wrong child, so she stepped out of the cell with them. The door clunked shut behind her. She risked turning around and caught the concerned glint of Kitt's eyes watching her go up the stairs with the nurses.

'Come along, sweetheart,' said the man in a cheery voice that didn't match his expression. 'It doesn't hurt at all.'

Payton watched the crowd from the doorway of the Elemental Disruption Ward. Methic Blake's lecture was the most popular talk ever to take place at the hospital. A sea of blue robes clustered around the entrance to the operating theatre. The sky was iron grey, and the first drops of rain were starting to spit down, streaking brown lines on the golden Lundain brick. Payton had a lot of experience sneaking into lectures, but this one would be tricky. She saw the crowd part slightly, and two methics walked towards the entrance: her father and a young woman who wore a heavy gold medallion over her blue robes. Methic Blake. She was the most successful methic in Prydein: she had discovered some impressive, ground-breaking cures that led to her becoming the youngest Guild Master in history. She was everything Payton wanted to be when she grew up. She had to hear her speak.

The operating theatre was a grand circular building with a magnificent glass-domed roof. Methics were beginning to move inside, their books tucked inside their robes to keep their notes safe from the rain. Payton joined the throng and ducked between the waves of blue fabric, scurrying to one side once she was through the door.

The seating was also built in a circle. It rose in steep wooden tiers separated by bannisters that the methics would lean on as they looked down at the small stage. Ani had been the one to tell Payton that the tiers were hollow. She hurried up the stairs. A loose panel was held in place by a metal latch that she spun open. Inside, there was a roomy space that offered a view of the stage through a latticed partition. As the methics began to break from their gossiping groups and take their seats, Payton ducked inside and pulled the panel closed behind her.

Her hiding place was littered with empty ink bottles and old pages of notes that had floated free and drifted through the gaps in the panels years ago. The murmur of methic voices began to fill the room. Their damp robes made the theatre smell like winter.

'They think they're better than all of us,' she heard one of them say, a man with a hairy neck. 'Those Queen Cleo's methics. Like they're in a guild of their own.'

'Apparently Methic Blake is on the lookout for new research assistants there,' said the woman next to him.

'Really?' the man asked too quickly.

A temporary hush rippled through the room. Payton pressed her eyes to the lattice and saw her father walk on stage with Methic Blake next to him. She was shorter than any of the methics hovering around her, but there was no denying that she was the centre of attention. Her blue robes were stained and rumpled, as if she had come to the lecture straight from treating patients, and her hair was cut as short as a boy's. She ignored her audience – her attention was on a structure that had been placed in the centre of the stage, hidden under a cloth cover.

'Methics!' Methic Darke's voice had everybody's attention. Payton shifted into a more comfortable position and took out her notebook, ready for the lecture to begin. 'It is a delight to welcome Methic Blake to King Jude's. These round walls have witnessed many innovations over the centuries. I have no doubt that today they will witness another. Without further delay, I will let Methic Blake introduce her work, and this mysterious contraption.'

He took a seat in the front row as the methics gave a brief round of applause.

Jenipher Blake paused at the front of the stage, unruffled by the rapt attention of her audience.

'Methics,' she began. 'How wonderful to be back here. I spent my student years here at King Jude's.' She smiled at them all. 'What a special place. A place that has been an important ally in my latest work.' There was the imperceptible sound of an audience leaning forward as she went over to whatever was hidden under the cloth. 'Work,' she said, 'that begins right here.'

She tugged the cloth away in one strong movement. The methics gasped. Payton pressed harder against the lattice until its intricate pattern was imprinted on her nose.

The machine was as tall as Jenipher. Its case was made of dark polished wood, and its front was open, filled with glass tubes. Some of the tubes were as thick as an arm, others fine as a hair, and each one was filled with a different substance – red liquids, electric-pink vapours, dull crystals, dark jellies. Each tube was labelled with a feeling. Payton held her breath to press closer and began to read them: fury, grief, sadness, envy, greed, disgust, anxiety . . . Every feeling that could cause an illness was represented on the machine.

A tiny waterwheel was exposed at the top, and Jenipher poured from a jug of water to start it. It began to spin.

'A gwaidmesur,' Jenipher said to a silence thick with curiosity.

'A blood-reader,' the woman in front of Payton gasped. The room glanced disapprovingly at her and her ears turned red.

'Yes, known also as a "blood-reader",' said Jenipher.

'This machine has been created by my team at Queen Cleo's Hospital. And it hasn't come a moment too soon. I know that "blood reading" is seen in an unfavourable light by the guild. Goodness knows, methics of the past made some mistakes with the practice. But my new research will show why we must use it, not fear it. Ever since the Turn, we lose more and more patients to the diseases caused by the terrible feelings that swirl through their blood. I am proposing a scheme that will see the end of anger, hurt, sadness, envy and despair. And this machine is where it all begins.'

Payton's knees were pressed painfully against the screen, but all she could think about was the meaning behind Jenipher's words. They stirred something in her. She wanted to be one of those methics who put an end to those terrible feelings.

'A gwaidmesur, for those of you who have trained at this hospital under its more *limited* resources, is a way of diagnosing illnesses. It can see the diseased feelings that lurk in our blood. Bad feelings. Feelings that my team and I will one day eliminate from our society so we can have a safer, brighter future. We will put things back to how they were before the Turn.

'Like any bright future, it begins with our children. The machine is best at reading younger people. Their feelings are so much stronger than grown-ups'. Methic

Darke here has found a very special, very rare patient to help us demonstrate what this machine can do. Bring them in,' she said to a woman wearing grey who was waiting at the edge of the stage. Payton recognized the uniform of a Queen Cleo's nurse.

In the lull, Payton picked up one of the loose pages of forgotten notes in her hiding spot and began to read. She was one of the last to see who joined Jenipher on stage. She only looked up when she heard the gasps.

There, twisting in the grip of a Queen Cleo's nurse as she was dragged on to the stage, was Ani.

CHAPTER SEVEN

When Ani saw the wash of blue robes, relief mixed with embarrassment. The methics sat in orderly rows, gazing down at her. Her own father was in the front row, his face ashen. The nurse made her sit on a stool next to a curious machine, and the woman methic with short hair stood next to her. She started to speak.

'Using the gwaidmesur is a fine art – its results are not easily read and should only be attempted by the most experienced methics.'

Ani heard her father make a strangled noise. She didn't want to imagine how much trouble she would be in later.

'Our blood contains our feelings,' Jenipher continued. 'Being able to read blood allows us to see a person's feelings clearly. Terrible feelings that no child should have to live with. I believe that by helping our most unwell children, we can make a new generation, free from all the flaws we have. As you can see, this little girl has a case of *bysaur*, more commonly known as Midas-fingers. Although –' Jenipher looked at Ani's gold-dusted hand critically – 'this is not quite as severe a case as you promised, Methic Darke. But I think we can see here . . .'

Some methics had started to mutter.

'Isn't that . . .?

'Methic Darke's . . .?'

Jenipher paused.

'Is something the matter?'

'My . . .' Neel half-stood, hovering over his chair as if desperate to sit down again. 'My daughter.'

Jenipher glanced from Ani to Neel.

'This is your child?'

'Yes.'

'Not the *bysaur* patient we were promised?'

'She . . .'

Ani couldn't understand why her father was struggling to make himself understood.

Beneath the seats, her breath hot against the lattice, Payton watched the back of her father's head closely.

Jenipher touched her Guild Master medallion, then broke the tension with a sudden smile.

'Well, it's only a demonstration. It will work on a healthy child too. We'll see her feelings all nice and level, as they should be. And you're here now, aren't you?' she said to Ani. Ani could tell that this was a woman who wasn't used to speaking to children. 'I'm afraid it's not the same if we use a grown-up.'

Ani looked out at the crowd of methics. Her father still hovered; his hand was slightly raised as if wanting to reach for her, but he couldn't do anything while every important person at King Jude's was watching them.

Ani looked at the strange machine with its tubes and chemicals. 'What is it?' she asked.

Neel sank back into his seat.

Jenipher poured more water into the machine. Its wheel spun faster.

'You'll see,' she said. 'We just need a drop.'

She turned back to Ani. 'Your hand,' she said briskly.

Ani hesitantly held out her unburnt, gold-stained hand. Jenipher grabbed it with a strength that surprised Ani and pulled it towards her. She produced a tiny needle and a glass thimble. Ani didn't flinch when Jenipher pricked her finger and squeezed two ripe drops into the glass thimble, bright red in the spotlights.

Once Jenipher had the blood, it was as if Ani didn't exist. Near the top of the machine was a tiny door, so carefully carved a person wouldn't know it was there unless they looked for it. It popped open, and Jenipher fitted the thimble inside it. After a pause, in which every breath in the room was held, it made a noise. There was the chink of glass on wood. A thin hiss of steam. The waterwheel spun faster.

A drop of blood inched down a long glass tube. When it hit the bottom, the other tubes came to life. The chemicals rose and fell in their chambers – it was mesmerizing.

'The gwaidmesur works by harnessing the power of pure feeling,' Jenipher explained. 'Of course, the guild prevents us from extracting pure feelings these days – too many things went wrong in the experiments done here at King Jude's in the early days of the Turn. But luckily our vast Feelings Library at Queen Cleo's had enough samples to help us finish the machine.'

Ani watched the substances in the tubes. The idea of having her feelings trapped in there, for all to see, made her squirm. The liquids and vapours and jellies and sands didn't obey gravity. They moved as if they were alive. Soon they began to find their levels, sinking to the bottom of the tubes. All except one.

One of the levels was climbing.

It was a burgundy liquid in a wide tube. The surface steamed, and flames flickered from it. Its level rose and rose, never stopping, nearer and nearer to the top of the tube and its label: ANGER.

Ani didn't know what it meant, but her palms started to sweat.

The machine stopped.

The room was stunned into silence.

'So nearly a perfect score . . .' Jenipher murmured. Only Ani heard her. 'If only it weren't for –' she walked up to the machine and touched the tube with the burgundy liquid – 'such rage.'

She seemed to gather herself and turned back to her audience.

'This demonstration is full of more surprises than I could have imagined. What we have here is something unique, rarer than Midas-fingers. See how the child has minimal amounts of toxic feelings.' She pointed at the tubes where the levels were right near the bottom. 'Even in a healthy child, we expect to see some bad feelings. A little envy, for example, or perhaps a slight increase of terror. As long as they are within a healthy range –' she gestured towards the lower ends of the tubes – 'it's not a problem. But this child's feelings are *exactly* where we'd want them to be. Every single one. Her shame, her fear, her inertia, her bitterness . . . This almost never happens. The result is perfectly balanced blood. Well, almost. Until we look here . . .' She drew their attention to the ANGER tube. 'Here we have something truly toxic. Terrible. An irrepressible rage that the child has been pushing down. Thank goodness she was brought forward to be read so I could catch it before it's too late.'

Ani thought of the sweet, milky medicine she'd spat out the window and felt dread sinking in her stomach.

'This kind of rage makes this child not just ill, but wild, even dangerous. Without treatment, there's no knowing how it will explode, and who it will hurt when it does.' Jenipher looked down at Ani as if she was a fascinating yet hazardous puzzle.

'She needs treatment straightaway. I will work on her case myself. Until she is fully healed, she must be kept safe. Separate.'

She looked meaningfully at Neel.

'Locked up.'

'No!'

Ani screamed and sprang up out of her chair, but the Queen Cleo's nurses immediately surrounded her, pinning her down. The man scooped her hands behind her back and held them tight. The methics were on their feet – some fascinated, some horrified – while Neel sat still, an unreadable statue.

'You can't do that!' Ani shouted.

Jenipher waited for the noise to subside and suppressed the small smile that was growing on her lips.

'Yes,' Jenipher continued, 'the gwaidmesur shows us the problems in our children that need correcting. This girl needs to join our treatment programme to set her on a better path. Once she's healed, she will truly have a perfect score. Isn't that what anybody would want?'

Jenipher's eyes met Neel's. He stared back. His heartbeat was a flutter at his throat.

Something passed between them.

He nodded.

In her hiding place, Payton had been sitting perfectly still, taking deep breaths to keep her anxiety at bay. But something about her father nodding while the nurses pinned Ani down made it impossible to stay silent and hidden any longer. She scrabbled towards the entrance to her hiding place.

'Hey!'

'What the—?'

'Somebody's in there!'

The loose panel was yanked open by the methic sitting in front of her.

'Payton!'

Somebody peered in, but she sprang out like like an apparition, flying down the stairs towards the stage and her sister. The methics on the aisle seats recoiled. Even Jenipher seemed taken aback.

'Payton!' her father shouted.

'I just wanted to listen!'

The sight of her sister made Ani feel strong, ready to fight. She sprang to her feet again, catching the nurses by surprise. 'I'm not sick, I'm *not*!' she shouted.

Neel was on his feet too, rushing to the front of the stage to subdue his daughters.

'Payton – out of the way. Ani, Methic Blake is going to help you.'

Ani started to fight the nurses like a wild animal, scratching and clawing at them as they tried to hold her. Neel seized Payton's wrist and tried to pull her from the stage, but she shook herself free.

'The girl needs treatment.' Jenipher's voice rang sharp over all their heads. 'Look at her, she's burning up.'

It was true. A redness was rising in Ani's cheeks. Her sweating palms were getting hotter and hotter. She looked down at her hands. The tips of her fingers were bright pink, becoming smooth, as if they were burning from the inside. Was it to do with the anger the machine had found in her? The thought made her panic more.

Ani wrestled with the nurses, and Payton shouted at them as they pinned her sister down so hard that she cried out in pain. Payton tried to pull them off, but they were too strong.

'Let me help her!' she insisted. 'She needs her medicine.'

They started to drag Ani from the stage. She reached out her hand for her sister.

'Payton!'

Payton lunged forward. Her hand wrapped around Ani's fingers. The spot where Jenipher had drawn the blood was scorching hot . . .

As soon as she touched Ani's blood, Payton felt dizzy. The whites of her eyes became patterned with red. Then they rolled back into her head and she keeled over. The side of her face smacked on to the floor.

Jenipher's voice cut through the fugue.

'And this one has a phobia of blood. Your daughters are quite the pair, Methic Darke.'

CHAPTER EIGHT

When Payton collapsed, Ani knew she could use the distraction to get away, or she could stay to help. She had seen her sister faint at blood before. She could see the network of delicate purple veins on Payton's closed eyelids, which were fluttering as if she was trapped in a dream.

Ani twisted her wrist from the nurse's grip and hurtled for the staircase that led down to Kitt's cell.

Her breath was loud, bouncing off the walls. She felt herself cooling down, but her cloirias-burnt hand was starting to smart and sting again as the effect of the paste Payton had made for her began to wear off. She needed to get Kitt out of the cell. She wasn't going to let the nurses lock her up as they had him. They needed to get as far away from that woman and her machine as possible.

The sight of the burning burgundy liquid was seared

in her memory. Was she angry? She didn't feel angry. Only if she thought about her father, how he had lied, how he was no closer to curing her mother . . . A wave of heat came over her again, sharp and sudden. She longed for it to stop, to feel nothing at all.

She was panting dry sobs by the time she reached the bottom of the stairs and found herself facing an open door and an empty room. Kitt was gone.

'Kitt?' she called.

'Hurry.'

An adult's voice was coming down the stairs after her.

Ani turned and sprinted down the curving corridor. 'Please, please . . .' She didn't know what she was begging for as she removed the grille that blocked the way back through the secret passageway. To escape Jenipher's treatment perhaps (more medicine she didn't want), and days spent in a locked cell like Kitt.

It took all her effort to quiet her ragged breath as she hid in the vent while the nurses stalked past. In the darkness she went over what had happened, trying to make sense of it.

She replayed the moment in her head once more of arriving on stage, blinking at the light and staring faces. Jenipher showing them the gold on her palm, the gold that Kitt had accidentally smeared on her.

What Kitt had said was true: her father had put him

in that cell. He'd kept him captive for Jenipher and her horrible machine. And now Kitt was gone.

Ani sat back and wiped her eyes with her sleeve. She felt faintly sick, but the cool darkness was reassuring. She vowed never to trust her father again. She couldn't trust anybody at King Jude's.

Ani retraced her steps to the Methics Hall, but from there she wasn't sure how to get back home without her father catching her. Their apartment was on the other side of the quad. She hesitated in the doorway and looked at the building next to the hall. It was the Poisons and Explosive Afflictions block. It always smelt of day-old smoke and the occasional waft of sulphur. Ani looked down at her hands; one was thickly bandaged, the other gold, but her fingertips looked normal again, no longer smooth and burning.

A popping sound from the Poisons and Explosive Afflictions block startled her. Then it gave her an idea.

Making sure nobody in the quad was looking in the direction of the Methics Hall, she scuttled into the block and made her way to the main ward. There was only one nurse on duty, and he was busy sweeping up ashes at the far end. Ani walked between the beds. She passed a woman whose arms were covered in burns, her face turned away. Ani walked slower. Was this what Methic Blake thought would happen to her? Is this where the burning fingertips would lead her? The thought made her wrap her pink cardigan around herself tightly.

She stopped at the bed she was looking for. Grayham was a kind old man, but he also had a terrible temper. His rages had built up for many years, unpredictable and furious, until he was admitted to King Jude's. He'd been on the ward for months while the methics tried ice therapy and sedatives to calm him. Many of the other patients were frightened of him, and he didn't get any visitors, so Ani had taken it upon herself to be his friend.

'Gray?'

He looked up from the game of backgammon he was playing against himself.

'Ani! Good timing, I've nearly beaten myself.' He gestured at the board.

'That's good.'

'Is something the matter?'

'No, it's . . .' Ani looked down the ward. The nurse was still busy with another patient. 'I'm sort of in trouble.'

'Some things never change,' he said with a chuckle.

'I know. I was wondering . . . You know when you . . .'

She wanted to ask Grayham about his illness, about the heat and the horror of it. But she knew he didn't like to talk about it, and she felt suddenly shy and worried that he might start asking her too many questions about her own feelings, so she didn't finish her question.

'Ani? What is it?'

'Sorry. Nothing really.'

'This trouble you're in – can I help at all?'

'No. Well, maybe. I need someone to distract the methics and nurses. Just for a moment. Can you start a fire or something?'

'That's not how it works.' His words sounded wet; he was rolling a melting ice cube over his tongue.

Ani was starting to regret coming to the ward at all. She just wanted to get home, so she reached for a lie.

'But I thought you'd be angry today anyway,' she said.

'Why would you think that?' he asked.

'Because of the move.'

'Move?'

'I heard the methics talking. They said that the thing you have . . . What's it called?'

'Spark breath.'

'Yes, that. It's almost as dangerous as fire breath. So they're going to make you swap wards.'

Ani heard a faint popping sound coming from Grayham's bed, like the first sparks of a fire.

'I thought you wouldn't like it . . .' she continued

with her lie. 'I know there aren't any windows. And you'd be next to the Hysteria Ward, which is very loud.'

The popping, cracking sound grew louder. Ani smelt smoke. She felt a little guilty for winding Grayham up, but she knew he'd work out she was telling tales soon enough, and by then she would have the diversion she needed.

'I haven't heard anything about this.' His cheeks went hollow as he sucked harder on the ice.

'I'm sure it will be fine,' she said. 'Pretty boring, though. Because it's so dangerous, you can't listen to the phonograph. Or play games . . .' Her gaze settled on the backgammon board on his lap.

'*What?*'

The dice in his hand glowed like embers and then shot from his grasp, rocketing through the window and exploding in a shower of red sparks over the quad. The ice in Grayham's mouth turned to steam and slipped from his lips as he threw the backgammon board on the floor and began to march up the ward towards the nurse, shouting about his rights to entertainment.

Ani went back to the doorway of the block and saw with satisfaction that the methics were rushing towards the broken window. She slipped across the quad unnoticed, and made her way upstairs, back to the Darkes' apartment.

She burst into her bedroom and then stood, breathing heavily, her hands on her hips. She hadn't thought this far ahead. She didn't know what to take with her, only that she needed to pack and get as far away from King Jude's as possible. The thought of setting foot outside the hospital for the first time made her head spin with fear and excitement.

She sprinkled some water on her moss, then pulled a clean dress from the wardrobe and the green toy bunny from her windowsill and threw them on the bed. Then she put the bunny back, feeling foolish. It was only then she realized how little she had. Her life was in the hospital, not in the apartment.

'What are you doing?'

She jumped. Payton was standing in the doorway watching her. Her eyelids looked heavy.

'What happened to you? You fainted.'

'It was nothing,' Payton said quickly. 'What's the dress for?'

'I'm running away,' Ani declared.

'To where?'

'Anywhere. I don't care. I'm not staying here. Father kept Kitt in that prison so that woman could do tests on him. He lied. I told you. You didn't believe me.'

Payton didn't say anything, so Ani feigned packing, throwing anything she could find on to her bed and wondering if she should wrap her meagre belongings in her cardigan.

'And then he let that woman . . . That stupid machine saying all that stuff . . .' Ani scoffed, but her laugh was nervous; it scraped her throat. 'I'm not angry. I'm definitely not sick – not like that, so that shows what she knows. I can't believe she wants to lock me up! Can you?'

Before Payton could answer, the front door rattled open, and Neel entered. His hesitation back in the operating theatre had been replaced by an anxious, rushing manner, as if he had something unpleasant to do and wanted it over as soon as possible. He stood in the doorway, suddenly larger to Ani than he had ever seemed. He glanced between his two daughters.

'What are you doing?' he asked Ani, taking in the small mound of clothes on her bed. It had been years since Neel had even set foot in their bedroom.

'Getting ready to explode apparently!' Her voice was high-pitched and manic. At the sight of her father, her breath felt hot inside her mouth. She looked from her father to her sister, desperate for one of them to show that they thought it a ridiculous idea. Payton continued to stare at her with tired eyes.

'I must ask you to approach what happened today rationally, Ani.' Neel spread his hands as if trying to calm a cornered animal. 'With a scientific mind.

Jeniipher Blake is the very best methic in Lundain. What happened to you today was a scientific reading, nothing more. It wasn't personal.'

'It wasn't personal?' Ani started to raise her voice. 'It was my *blood*!'

'Plenty of children have had disappointing results in this test. But Jeniipher has a way to make them better,' he said. 'You're so close to a perfect result. There's a special place—'

'What did you do to Kitt?'

'Kitt?'

'The boy you locked up under the operating theatre!'

He scowled. 'You shouldn't have been down there. This is a hospital, not a playground. You could have been seriously hurt!'

'Too late for that!'

Ani spread her hand and held it out to show him her turquoise cloirias burn.

Neel Darke recoiled.

'*You* did that!' Ani insisted. 'Tell me now – what have you done with him?'

'The Midas-fingers patient has been moved for his own protection.'

'You lied before. You said he didn't exist!'

'His presence does not concern you. He is a valuable test subject—'

'Person!'

'Person,' he relented. 'He'll have his blood read and then Jenipher will treat him.'

Ani gaped at her father, then rounded on her sister.

'Don't you have *any*thing to say about this?'

'I—'

'Control your feelings, Ani. It's very important you do what Jenipher and her staff tell you,' said Neel.

'I feel fine!'

But it wasn't true. Her ears were popping, she could hear her own blood rushing through her head. Her palms were sweating again, and her sweat felt hot, as if water from a just-boiled kettle was seeping out of her. She glanced at the window where she'd spat out her medicine the day before. Maybe it had been a mistake. Her father was speaking but it was getting harder to focus on what he was saying.

'I think it was a good thing that you got caught up in all this. We need you to be well. If you would just go with Jenipher—'

'I'm not going! You can't make me. Tell him, Payton!'

'Maybe . . .' Payton's voice was dry, rasping. 'Maybe your blood is setting you up for an accident, Ani. Maybe you wouldn't mean to, but . . . well . . . It's Jenipher Blake.'

'Ani,' her father said sternly. 'You must be treated by Methic Blake.'

The frustration she felt – at Payton, her father, the way they all believed Jenipher – was too much. Ani screamed. Sparks shot from her fingertips and tongue. They singed her mouth. It tasted of acid. But the worst part was how it felt like a relief, getting something out of her that shouldn't have been kept in.

All three of them flinched. Neel and Payton stared at her. Ani looked down at her own hands, the taste of fire fading already from her tongue. Then she realized that she could use their fear. She scrunched up every ounce of fury she felt for them and screamed again. This time, the slither of flame shot off her tongue. Payton and Neel both dived out of its path, and Ani darted for the door. She sprinted down the stairs, back into the fresh air, hellbent on getting as far away from her father as possible.

CHAPTER NINE

'Ani, come back!'

Payton chased after her sister, but Ani had disappeared. It was nearly dusk, and the yellow stone buildings of the quad were patterned by shadows.

'Find her,' Neel ordered, appearing behind her. 'I'll speak to the porter's lodge to make sure she doesn't leave the grounds.'

Payton watched the movement of his blue robes as he marched towards the hospital entrance. She felt shaken from what had happened when she'd touched the blood – and embarrassed. She wasn't afraid of blood. Not even a little bit. She wanted to shout it so that the whole hospital knew. But then she'd have to explain what really happened when she touched blood, she'd have to tell them about the visions, the . . . feelings. No. They would never understand.

She was also shocked at seeing Ani's anger ignite in

what looked like the beginning stages of spark breath. She had grabbed some of Ani's medicine from the kitchen cupboard to take to her, just in case. She couldn't have another member of her family getting sick.

Payton wouldn't admit that she felt guilty about earlier – when Ani had looked at her, begging her to say that the gwaidmesur was nonsense, as if she didn't care what their father or Jenipher thought as long as Payton believed in her. But she couldn't tell her sister what she wanted to hear. Because ever since they'd arrived at King Jude's, Ani had had tantrums and outbursts that only medicine could control. She wasn't well. Payton didn't want to see Ani locked up, but if it was the only way Methic Blake could cure her anger . . .

Payton could hear methics and porters in the quad calling Ani's name, but she could have told them it was no good. Ani knew every inch of the hospital, better than anyone. And there was one place they wouldn't think to look: the ambulans stables.

The drivers were on a break – the brass bell was silent. The youngest of the drivers worked at the top of the ambulans tower and listened for the emergency bells around the city, through rain and sunshine, frost and gales. The stables were always open.

Payton slid the main door open and the smell of hay, manure and animal warmth rushed towards her. The stags looked at her over the tops of their stalls.

White stags had pulled the ambulans carriages at King Jude's for as long as the hospital had existed. Driving ran in families, and it wasn't unusual for a driver to work with a descendant of the stag their great-grandparents had driven. The stag nearest to Payton looked at her and snuffled. Its antlers knocked against the stable.

'Ani?' Payton hissed. She didn't know if one of the drivers had stayed behind to look after the animals, and she knew she wasn't meant to be in there alone. 'Are you in here?'

Sunlight spilt through the door and windows. She walked the length of the stables, keeping to the right, out of reach of the soaring, pointed antlers. The animals watched her with wise, dark eyes and she felt herself soften, and begin to understand why Ani liked it here so much.

'Ani? Are you in here? It's only me.'

'Payton?' A voice came from the other end of the stables. 'Are you on your own?'

'Yes.'

Three ambulans carriages – large wooden carts with leather seats and a covered bay at the back for patients – stood side by side at the end of the room, and Ani's head poked out of one of them. Her eyes were red from crying.

'There you are.' Relief flooded through Payton. She hurried to the cart and pulled Ani into a hug that felt strange from lack of practice.

'Are you feeling all right?' She brought her hand to Ani's forehead. It didn't feel too warm.

Ani squirmed away. 'I'm fine.'

'I brought you some medicine anyway.' She pulled out the vial of milky liquid.

'I spat yesterday's out.'

'I figured.'

'I don't want—'

'Just a little bit. Please. For me?'

Ani glared at her a moment, then relented. She let Payton put one drop on the back of her tongue, like she was a nurse treating a small child. Payton tucked the bottle into the pocket of Ani's cardigan.

'I hope you'll take it now that you've seen what can happen when you don't.'

'I'll take it with me.'

'With you? Where are you going? Oh.' Payton looked around the stables with fresh understanding. 'This is how you're going to run away?'

Ani jutted her chin the way she did when she was ready for a fight. 'It's better than listening to that liar and that woman with the horrible machine.'

'It's called a gwaidmesur.' Payton couldn't help correcting her. 'And you shouldn't call Father a liar,' she added half-heartedly.

'Oh, who cares!'

'Ani, this is serious. What if you really do—' She cut herself short and chose her words carefully. 'You've always had too many feelings. Ever since we got here. Remember when they had to put Mother in the water chamber and you started coughing up all that steam?'

Ani looked away from her.

'Nothing's changed really,' Payton insisted. 'Your feelings still get the better of you. Jenipher will be able to help you. You heard her: it's just one feeling, one adjustment, then you'll have the best blood there is! A perfect score!'

'But they want to lock me up, just like they did with Kitt! Who knows if they'll ever let me out. What if I *am* ill – and I'm not saying I am – but what if I am and they can't make me better? Like . . . like with Mother? Trapped. But you wouldn't care, would you? As long as the methics say it's all right.'

'That's not fair.'

'*You're* not fair. You didn't say anything back there with Father.'

'He wouldn't say you need treatment unless it was for your own good.'

'Yes, he would! He wasn't interested in helping Kitt – he was just going to give him to Jenipher for testing. Anyway, that's not the point. You're my sister;

you're supposed to back me up!'

'Why is everything *my* job?' Payton shouted back at her, then caught herself. She smoothed her hair flat in a gesture she didn't realize she'd learnt from her father. 'Ani, please think about this logically. Where will you go?'

'Out!'

'Out?'

'Into the city – the world! Kitt told me all about it.'

'Ani . . .'

'I'm going far away – I'm never seeing Father ever again.'

'Or me and Mother?'

Ani looked at her, stricken. Payton saw her think, then Ani admitted, 'I wouldn't like that.'

'Exactly. You can't leave King Jude's. It's our home.'

'Not if Father gets that job at Queen Cleo's.'

Payton felt her excitement about moving wane.

'Well, we can't control that. But you'll have *me*. I'll make you my next project. I'll make you and Mother better. Come on.' She held out her hand. 'I'm not going to become a great methic standing around all day smelling deer dung.'

Ani laughed and took her sister's hand.

Then they froze.

'Are those—?'

'The bells!'

'The drivers are coming!' Payton panicked. 'We're not supposed to be in here, we'll get in so much trouble. Ani, come on!'

She tried to pull Ani from the ambulans cart, but she wouldn't budge.

'I'm caught!'

'What?'

Payton lifted herself up to look over the rail and saw that Ani's pink cardigan was snared on a metal hook.

'Yank it off!'

'No! It will rip.'

There was a sound of running feet and raised voices in the yard outside.

'Urgh, Ani! Right, stay still.' Payton hoisted herself up into the ambulans carriage.

The drivers were calling out to each other. They pulled leather harnesses from the wall and opened the stags' stable doors.

Payton's fingers fumbled with the fabric.

'It's really stuck. It has to rip a little.'

'No!'

'Shh!'

The voices of the drivers were all around them. They felt the ambulans jolt as one of the drivers climbed into his seat and shouted to his partner, 'Up towards Carnaby.'

Payton signalled to Ani to stay still. Through a gap

in the canvas cover, they could see the drivers in their bright silk jerseys in King Jude's colours – purple and yellow.

'That's up Queen Cleo's way,' the other driver replied as she fastened the harness and jumped up beside him.

'Collapsed roof in one of the millworker's houses. They can't afford Queen Cleo's fees.'

There was snorting and grunting from the stags; hooves stamped on flagstones and antlers knocked on wood. The stags pawed at the ground, the distant bells making them desperate to race through the city.

'We have to jump,' Payton hissed in Ani's ear.

'But—'

'It's just a cardigan! On three. One . . . Two . . . Thr—'

The cart erupted into motion. The lurch of it flung Ani and Payton back.

It was too late. They were hurtling out of the stables at terrifying speed, racing through the yard. Payton felt Ani shaking beside her. She put out an arm to comfort her, then saw that she wasn't scared at all. She was laughing.

'You're dead,' Payton told her, though she couldn't help but smile just a little. The rush of the ambulans made her feel a twinge of excitement and anxiety. She pushed both feelings down as best she could.

The stags bellowed louder than before as they breathed the dusk air. Bells pealed through the gloom, urging them to go faster, faster, through the open hospital gates and into the streets of Lundain.

CHAPTER TEN

Ani hadn't thought through her plan for escaping King Jude's. She and Payton needed to get out of the ambulans before it stopped and the drivers found that they were on board. But the pace was relentless, even across the bridges and around corners. It was too dangerous to jump out.

'We'll have to wait until they stop,' she said. 'There'll be lots of people and the drivers will be trying to help them. We can slip away then.'

'Are you mad?' Payton replied. 'We're going to stay hidden until we get back to King Jude's and hope no one spots us!'

The street lamps flung bursts of orange light over their faces. One of the stags bellowed. Their breathing was loud and sweat darkened their shaggy fur. They were slowing. Ani craned her head out of the covered cart. It was dusk, and the sky was blue mixed with the glow of the street lights, with only the most stubborn stars looking down on them.

'Look at it all,' she said. 'So many lights!'

Payton joined her and took a look at their alien surroundings. It all blurred and jolted with the movement of the cart. It was difficult to pick out any landmarks.

'The most important thing is to stay hidden when they're loading the patients,' said Payton logically. 'It's the only way we'll make it back without getting caught.'

'Do we have to go back? This might be our only chance to see the city!'

'Yes, we do. This is already bad enough. If Father finds out—'

'But think about what we might see!'

'We have to go—'

'But *why*?'

They'd both raised their voices as they argued; now Payton's voice rang dangerously loud as she said to Ani:

'Because the gwaidmesur is right – you're dangerous!'

'Take that *back*!'

Ani pushed Payton hard in the shoulders, just as the cart turned. Her shriek was drowned out by the calls of the stags and the wheels rumbling over paving stones.

'Payton!' Ani tried to grab her, but her fists closed on empty air.

Payton tumbled out of the cart and rolled on to the cold road.

When Payton finally came to a stop, she lifted her head and saw the ambulans disappear around a corner, with Ani inside it.

It took a moment before she could sit up and methodically test each of her limbs, starting with her neck and back and finishing with her fingers. Nothing felt broken. One of her ankles was painful and she'd banged her knee. She tasted blood on her lip. Her clothes were covered in dirt. She said the alphabet backwards, recalled her name, the date and the name of the hospital where she lived. Then she stood up.

Lundain seemed to tower around her, and everything looked tired and grubby. There was a buzz of noise from a nearby pub, and some coffee houses still had their lights on, their colourful awnings sagging from the rain earlier in the day. People walked quickly, with their heads down and shoulders bunched up, so their coat collars touched their ears. Nobody gave her a second glance.

Payton had never felt so lost.

She looked one way down the street – she saw only a bewildering stream of people and yellow-brown buildings. Then she looked the other way and was taken aback. The street widened before a towering white building, the grandest place she had seen in her life. She had never set eyes on it before, but she had seen enough paintings to recognize it: Queen Cleo's Hospital.

CHAPTER ELEVEN

Ani's heart hammered with panic as the ambulans hurtled onwards.

One of the drivers said something; she caught the word 'Carnaby' again.

The maze of streets all looked the same. Payton would be disoriented, alone somewhere in the tangle of streets behind her, and Ani felt a pang in her stomach. It was all her fault.

The cart juddered to a halt. The stags grunted with relief and hung their heads as the drivers' boots slapped on to the concrete. Ani heard shouts and the groan of a building. Somewhere a baby cried, and a fox barked.

She peered out and took in her surroundings. She could see a house with its roof caved in. It was part of a terrace where watermill workers lived. The beams of the building were exposed. For a moment she was distracted from her own predicament by the destruction, but she couldn't let her mind go too far – she had a choice to make. The drivers were speaking to somebody. This was as good a chance to run as she was going to get. She had to choose between going back to King Jude's or starting a new life.

It was now or never.

She jumped.

'Oi!'

At the shout of the driver, Ani ran even faster across the street, not daring to turn back in case they recognized her.

Her hair streamed out behind her in a dark tangle and her boots kicked up water from puddles. The city smelt of the algae that caked thousands of water-wheels – and the people! Ani had never seen so many of them, all of them moving and restless, so unlike the patients at the hospital. She felt like she'd never run out of the energy that kept her legs moving.

At the end of the street, she paused to look back; there was no sign of the ambulans drivers, or anybody else looking for her.

But as she stood there, just outside the circle of light from a street lamp, she realized that she didn't know where to begin. Kitt had told her a lot about life in Lundain, but she hadn't expected to feel so dwarfed by it. It was as though she was moving in a different, slower world to everyone around her. Payton was somewhere in the maze of streets, but Ani didn't know what direction she should go in to search for her. She had no idea where they were when she'd fallen from the ambulans.

'Excuse me . . .' She stepped into the light to ask a woman for directions, but the stranger barged past without a second glance.

'Miss?' Ani tried a harassed-looking younger woman who was balancing a tray of empty glasses on her hip outside a pub. Her voice didn't sound like her own. It sounded high-pitched, scared.

She tried asking directions from other passers-by, but most ignored her. Even if she grabbed somebody's arm, she was shaken off coldly. All she wanted to know was where she was and where there might be a warm bed for the night. The pub on the corner smelt of stale beer, food, and clothes that needed a wash. Men and women sat at the tables, grey-faced and leaning in towards each other, not saying much. Ani watched the young woman carrying drinks and empty glasses streaked with foam back and forth.

She worked up the courage to ask her again.

'Miss, what part of the city is this?'

Now the woman saw her. She regarded her with a crease between her eyebrows. She looked as if she was going to say something, but then simply pointed over Ani's shoulders and carried on her way, weaving through the tables.

Ani turned around and took a moment to see the signpost the woman had pointed at. Even as she approached it, she felt her heart sink; none of the words meant anything to her. Except one, its white letters pointing east, deeper into the city. *Leadenhall.*

Kitt had lived there.

Leadenhall turned out to be an outdoor market with a wrought-iron and glass covering as magnificent as any hospital in the city. Kit had told her that meat, fish, leather, jewels and mechanical waterwheels were all sold there, and that most days it was busy with a selection of Lundain society, from wealthy merchants to ragged crooks looking to make a deal. Even the financiers from the Guild of Finance would leave their shining, tiled tunnels beneath the city streets to visit Leadenhall from time to time.

But it was night-time when she arrived, the market was closed up and dark, and she was shivering and exhausted. There wasn't much need for security – no merchant was daft enough to leave their wares unattended – so she slipped through the gap in the gates under the slack chain and entered the darkness. It was neither indoors nor outdoors. The ground beneath her was hard concrete, and workshops and merchant offices lined the walls. The roof glittered with different colours of glass. Outside one of the shops, her hands brushed soft fabric – offcuts thrown away to be cut into rags, and she marvelled that anyone could not want them. She wrapped her cardigan tighter around her, curled into the nest of scraps and fell asleep into dreams filled with the ominous hiss of the gwaidmesur.

Ani woke at dawn. The morning cold seemed to rise up out of nowhere, seeping through the gates and the gaps in the roof. Her first thought was of Payton. She hoped she'd made it back to King Jude's. Even now she might be wrapped up in a blanket, indignantly telling their father all about Ani's terrible behaviour.

Her stomach growled and she rummaged in her pockets, even though she knew she had nothing to eat. All she had was her vial of medicine and the gwaid-lamp. She took it out and let the green light swirl into existence. Her fingers still felt smooth and tender from her fiery outburst the day before, her tongue tingled unpleasantly. She wondered: was Payton right? Was she dangerous, on the brink of exploding with flame and fury? The thought made her reach for her medicine. She was about to take some when a scuffling noise made her sit upright.

In the light of the gwaidlamp, she could see that stallholders had left the wares they couldn't sell, like the nest of fabrics she lay on. A set of enormous iron scales hung from the roof beam, swaying slightly. She heard the scuffling sound again. She scrabbled to her feet, imagining rats scurrying about her in the night.

Then she heard a giggle.

'Bring it back!' A child's voice echoed across the empty market.

'It's mine now!'

A boy and a girl, about Kitt's age, ran out of one of the offices.

The girl had dirty, matted yellow hair pulled into a braid, and sharp, changeable features, the sort of face that flitted from elation to upset in a flash. She darted out into the open, holding a floppy fistful of fabric above her head. The boy followed her. He was slower and stocky, with heavy-lidded eyes and long hair.

'Rosa!' he called. 'I found it first, I—'

He saw Ani standing in front of the gate and froze. Then he let out a whelp and ran back towards the office.

Rosa didn't notice at first and continued to taunt him. 'Finders weepers,' she sang. 'Finders weepers, stealers keepers – Oh. Hello.'

She stopped her twirling, dancing run when she saw Ani.

'You're new,' she said. At a glance, Ani didn't look so different to them, with her muddy shoes and knotted hair.

'Yes, I . . .' Ani didn't know how to begin. 'Where is everyone?'

'The market starts soon.'

'What about the others?' Kitt had led her to believe there was a big group of children here. He told tales of roast meat for breakfast and ghost stories at night. Ani had drunk it in. In the gloomy morning light, life in the market looked a lot less fun. For the first time, she realized it couldn't have been easy for Kitt to live there, and it was possible he hadn't told her the full story.

'The other children?' Ani pressed. 'Are there more of you? I need help. I need to find . . .' Her stomach growled. 'Well, lots of things. Like food?'

The lines of sunlight that crept through the gaps in the roof were brightening. Rosa stared at Ani with disconcertingly pale eyes, then gestured for her to follow.

Ani learnt that Rosa and her little brother Fred lived in one of the merchants' offices – as long as the owner never saw them and they ran his errands without a fuss. Ani was taken aback by the office. She'd expected to see fabrics, jewels maybe, riches and indulgences. Instead, it was filled with plants. Many were clustered on cabinets, tables and even the floor, leaves of every colour and pattern overspilling pots and becoming entangled. Trays of seedlings were arranged in a corner under the warmth of a hydrolamp. Carefully labelled packets of seeds covered a dark wooden desk in the middle of the room.

Ani hadn't been so close to this many plants since she'd lived in the Isles. Battersea Meadows was permanently closed, chained shut, and anyway, it was beyond the grounds of the hospital. The methics grew medicinal plants in sterile, clinical conditions in their labs these days. Ani felt sure that most of those she saw now were medicinal plants, rarer and more special than the moss that grew on her window, but she didn't have Payton's encyclopaedic knowledge of medicine. Still, she thought it was unusual to have so many here, far away from any hospital, out of the hands of the methics.

Rosa locked the door and tugged Ani's arm to get her attention. At the brush of her fingers, Ani jumped – Rosa's touch was freezing cold. In fact, Ani could now see that her eyes looked so pale because there were white flakes of snow on her eyelashes. Her lips were almost purple. Despite the warmth of the room, Rosa was freezing. Ani reached out and grabbed her hand, enveloping it in her own warmth. Rosa looked taken aback, but didn't pull away.

'You're frozen!' Ani said.

'I'm fine.'

'You need a methic. The ice . . . It's caused by fear. If you don't make the feeling go away, then you'll—'

Rosa tugged her hand free.

'I'm not going to *them*.'

Ani was going to argue, but then she thought of the greedy gleam in Methic Blake's eyes when she'd read her blood.

'I just don't like the dark,' Rosa explained. A snowflake fell from her eyelash on to her cheek. 'There aren't any lights here at night. It's not a big deal. Come on.'

The three of them sat under the desk, like children playing in their father's study. Fred produced some cream and sweet buns, which they were kind enough to share. Ani followed their lead, dipping the bun into the cream. It was sweet and rich enough to melt on her tongue. The buns were glazed golden, airy in the centre, and only slightly hard from the day before.

The food made her feel the blood rush to her head.

'Do you know Kitt?' she asked them. 'He's your height and has red hair. He used to live here, then he came to King Jude's. That's where I'm from. You know, the hospital?'

Fred chewed his food for too long, so Rosa answered.

'We knew Kitt. But then he got sick. The methics took him.'

Ani nodded, leant towards them, relieved to have someone to share her story with. She started to tell them about Kitt's Midas-fingers, King Jude's, the gwaidmesur, but Rosa and Fred were of a different world, where the only thing that mattered was food, a spare coin from a merchant, knowing where to sleep at night.

'Anyway . . .' Ani soon felt tired again. 'When they were going to lock me up too, I had to run away.' She didn't tell them about her outburst of anger.

'Well. Kitt can't live here any more,' said Rosa.

'When he got sick, it brought a lot of trouble,' Fred blurted, speaking for the first time.

'He's right,' said Rosa. 'Methics, financiers . . . they were always asking questions.'

'Did they not try to make you better?' Ani asked.

'No. They weren't interested. They were just waiting around and hoping we'd get sick with the same thing as Kitt.'

'Why?'

Rosa looked at her like she was stupid. 'He made gold.'

'But—'

'SHH!'

Fred's fingers were pressed to his lips, his wide eyes fixed on Ani to emphasize that he meant her too.

He mouthed something at Rosa. She nodded, then peered slowly around the edge of the desk. Ani couldn't resist looking. There was a figure at the window, hands cupped to the glass to look inside. She ducked back behind the desk.

'Rosa? Freddie? I know you're in there!' It was a boy's voice. 'Mr Augent owes me for the last delivery – if he doesn't pay up, I'm coming in there to get it myself.'

The locked door rattled as he tried the handle. The boy cursed.

'Those seeds aren't free!' he shouted.

Rosa and Fred stayed where they were, perfectly still and silent.

'All right. I shouldn't have shouted. Come on, now. What about some custard tarts from Fenchurch Bakery as a sorry?'

Fred looked like he wanted to move. Rosa gripped his arm and goosebumps formed on his skin at her freezing touch. He stayed where he was.

'Fine, then. Fine! You tell him he's not getting any of my next harvest. Joke's on him, because it would fetch a good price with the methics. Seeds that can heal *anything*. Sure you don't want to warm up, Rosa?'

Nobody spoke until the boy outside had sworn at them one last time, and left.

'Who was that?' Ani asked.

'The Twitcher,' said Rosa. 'Mr Augent said to never let him in. It's one of his rules. The Twitcher will pinch anything. If we don't keep guard, we're not allowed to stay here.'

'The Twitcher?' Ani repeated the strange name.

'Does he live in the market too?'

'No, he lives in Hyde Gardens.'

'Hyde Gardens? Why would someone live there?' Ani knew that all of Lundain's parks were just like Battersea Meadows – locked up and abandoned. The Guild of the Wild had once been responsible for the parks, but it was one of the countless guilds that was disbanded around the time of the Turn.

'Because he's crazy.'

'Crazy, crazy,' Fred repeated.

'He said he has seeds that can heal anything.' Ani felt her mind whirring.

'He says all sorts.' Fred shrugged.

Rosa said something too, but Ani was so lost in thought she barely heard her.

'What?'

'Mr Augent knows lots of methics. He'll help you get home.'

'Oh.' Ani climbed to her feet. 'No. No, no.' She started to feel panicked. Her father might be looking for her, and if this merchant thought he'd get a reward for returning her . . . 'No,' she said again. 'Thank you. But I'm not going back home.'

Rosa scratched a sliver of ice from her skin. 'Then where are you going?'

The question made Ani feel dizzy. Her fingers brushed her vial of medicine in her pocket. She didn't want to take it. But she didn't want to have another explosion either.

'I think . . .Well . . .' A plan started to take shape in her mind. 'Which way is Hyde Gardens?'

The plants inside Hyde Gardens twisted around the black railings. The trees bent into the sky, their knots and curves out of place amongst the neat lines of the city's buildings and roads. They were like the bodies back in the hospital, Ani realized: each one unique. She felt a thrill of excitement. Most people didn't like to speak of the old guilds from before the Turn, but her mother had always made an exception for stories about wilders. Back in the Isles, they were the only bedtime story Ani would listen to. She would fall asleep as her mother told tales of travel and adventure, describing the wondrous plants and places that mattered to the guild. Now she was glad to see their old headquarters.

Rosa's directions had been vague, and at points Ani had had to ask strangers who weren't nearly as kind or keen to talk as the patients at King Jude's had been. Lundain had come to life as she walked – the people were hard-faced, expressionless, hurrying, dodging the doe-drawn carts of the rich and the quick fingers of hungry children.

People hurried past the imprisoned wilderness of Hyde Gardens without a second glance. It stretched for hundreds of acres, a scar of green in the city streets. Ani pressed her face to the black railings, but it was impossible to see through the vegetation.

The railings rose into an arch which read HYDE GARDENS, and then, in smaller letters underneath, UNDER GUARDIANSHIP OF THE GUILD OF THE WILD. Somebody had tried to scratch out some of the words, but they were etched too deep and still showed through.

Ani walked around the fence, but she couldn't see another gate or a gap in the railings. Her feet ached and she began to feel defeated by the city. She cursed herself for following the Twitcher and his strange boast so impulsively. But she couldn't think what else to do. She couldn't risk going back to King Jude's. Did that mean she'd never see her mother or Payton again? *If only Mother would wake up*, she thought. *She'd put a stop to all this.*

She trudged on with her hand skimming the railings as she thought through her limited options. The railings passed rhythmically under her fingers, cool and regular, until she felt something that made her stop. Something was amiss with one of the railings. It felt different. It wasn't warm, exactly, but it was organic, not metal. Wooden.

Ani stopped and looked. The railing looked exactly the same as the others. She wrapped her hands around it and tried to move it. The railing lifted lightly out of place. Her breath caught in her throat.

She quickly ducked through the gap and replaced the fake railing. On the other side of the fence she was immediately overshadowed by trees that were leaning over the railings as if to escape their enclosure. Her heart hammered with excitement at the thought of being inside the abandoned home of the wilders. The moss on her windowsill suddenly seemed like a drop in an ocean compared to all the life around her. She wasn't used to plants this dense and lush and alive – she had always run and played on the paved quads at King Jude's. She started to make her way further into the gardens, picking her way between roots and fallen branches, shivering with trepidation when a fern brushed her arm or a low branch caught in her hair.

In a few steps, the city disappeared. All that existed was the damp, chaotic tangle of vegetation. She couldn't explain why, but it felt like home.

Ani felt a laugh bubble up. Her heart soared. She couldn't help breaking into a half-run.

That was when it happened. A rushing sound like wind in her ears. Ropes appearing from nowhere. And a thickly woven net shooting into the air, trapping Ani inside.

CHAPTER TWELVE

Payton limped towards Queen Cleo's.

Nobody noticed her. With her dirty clothes and her focus on putting one foot in front of another, she looked just like any of the other children who skittered through the shadowy streets. The ambulans with Ani inside was long gone.

The streets and people made her feel dizzy. Lundain wasn't what she'd expected. At street level everything in the city looked tired and dirty, whereas in the hospital everything was clean and orderly. People looked each other in the eye, because they knew each other. But in the city the people were tense, hurried; they ignored each other, keeping their feelings hidden, so Payton kept her eyes on the white building up ahead, with its towers, shining windows and clean-swept courtyard.

There was a line of expensive carriages outside the main gates. The hospital itself was set back from the road, behind railings. Payton wrapped her hands around them, feeling the chill of metal on her palms, and looked inside. Queen Cleo's was nearly as old as King Jude's, built by methics to serve those who lived in the centre of the city. Each hospital had total control over its own borough, and Queen Cleo's had long ago decided to treat the rich merchants of the city. Its extraordinary wealth meant that it had been expanded over the centuries, and each part of the building demonstrated the finest architecture of various periods of history.

Another carriage drew up outside the patients' entrance. Payton saw a woman stooped with age making her way out, with two tall men – so similar-looking they had to be her sons – holding her by the elbow. The woman barked orders and the men dithered, opening doors and fetching scarves, and trying to scoop up a pet fox that scampered around the carriage wheels. Looking the other way, Payton spotted somebody in methic robes going through a different gate. There was the porter's lodge.

Payton trembled, but she wasn't sure if it was tired-ness, nerves, or the frustration and worry about Ani that she kept pressing down inside her. The man in the porter's lodge was dressed in an expensive tunic in the same grey as the nurses who had been helping Methic Blake. He was writing in a ledger and didn't look up when she approached. He was unused to paying attention to anybody who wasn't wearing blue robes. When she cleared her throat, he didn't react. When she leant her forearms on the reception desk, he didn't notice. Then she spotted a tabletop bell – when she tapped it smartly, the resounding ring made the porter jump out of his skin. Ink flicked across his papers.

'My goodness!' He hurried to blot it away. 'Miss, the patients' entrance is over on Bloomsbury Road.'

'I know,' said Payton. 'I'm not a patient. I'm here to see Jenipher Blake.'

'Methic Blake has a very full appointment schedule, and I'm afraid her services come at a price—'

'I said I'm not a patient.'

He wiped his forehead, leaving a smudge of ink just below his receding hairline. Payton found it distracting.

'Then may I ask who you are? Methic Blake is very busy.'

'My name is Payton Darke. My father is Methic Neel Darke. He knows her . . .' But Payton didn't need to finish explaining who her father was or where she'd come from.

The porter immediately opened the little door and ushered her inside.

'Miss Darke, of *course*. I know your father, naturally – he visits so often. Please accept my apologies. Do come in.'

The fact that her father visited Queen Cleo's was news to Payton, but she hid her surprise and stepped into the comforting warmth of the lodge, with its soft lights and tidy stacks of papers and books. She followed the porter through a door on the other side of the room, and they walked down a corridor with gleaming black and white tiles. Payton felt as if her eyes couldn't move fast enough. Everything was bigger, grander, impossibly polished. Where King Jude's had cracked oil paintings of forgotten methics, Queen Cleo's had bright, detailed portraits of almost every famous methic in history. King Jude's echoed with the cries of patients, the laughter of nurses, the hurried footsteps of methics, but this place was silent. Payton pictured herself working here, part of the perfection and order, the building blocks that would make her a methic that no disease could outsmart.

They cut through the corridors until the porter stopped and pulled a fistful of keys from his belt.

'Methic Blake has just returned from her visit to King Jude's. I will see if she is available. Please wait here for a moment, Miss Darke.'

He went through doors veined with a gold pattern and up some stairs. Payton leant on the wall and relished the silence.

It didn't take long for the porter's footsteps to return. When he opened the doors, Jenipher was behind him. She had changed out of her methic's robes, but her Guild Master medallion was still around her neck, its chain visible under the collar of her shirt. Her short hair was messier than before and her feet were bare. She looked much younger than she had on stage only a few hours ago.

'So she is,' she said to the porter at the sight of Payton. 'Thank you, Jarls, I'll look after Miss Darke from here.'

The porter nodded respectfully at Jenipher and left them.

Payton took a deep breath, suddenly shy. She wished she wasn't covered in dirt. She wished she wasn't wearing a dress. She wanted to look like Jenipher, so the great methic would see she was cut from the same cloth.

'Methic Blake?' She drew herself to her full height. 'My name is Payton Darke, my father—'

'I remember you, Payton. Everybody at King Jude's has been very worried about you, running away like that.' Jenipher turned to go back up the stairs. 'You must be hungry and in need of a rest. Come in.'

Jenipher's apartment was a delight to Payton. Large skylights flooded the space with light during the day and allowed for stargazing at night. The shelves were packed with books and leaflets, more than she'd seen in her life. Everything was neat, clean and ordered, perfectly set up for just one person. Payton let her imagination skip ahead to when she would be a grown-up methic living in an apartment that was all her own. Ani would have to knock every time she wanted to see her. Not even her father would be able to tell her what to do. Her hurry to get back to King Jude's started to evaporate.

She walked slowly, trying to keep her curiosity about Jenipher's life to a respectful minimum. She paused at a small oil painting of a beautiful, smiling methic with intricately braided hair and thick glasses.

'Methic Ruth Venner,' Jenipher told her. 'She saved countless lives during the Turn. She was the first to realize that the new diseases were being caused by extreme feelings.'

'I know.'

'Should I expect your sister?' Jenipher asked.

'Ani?'

'Yes. You know, she bit one of my nurses. It was one of the bloodier blood readings I've done.'

'Sorry,' Payton muttered. She turned away from the painting.

'Did you run away together?'

'Sort of. We got separated. I don't know where she is now,' Payton said, trying to be as honest as she could.

'Hmm. And how are you feeling?'

Payton felt herself flush with self-consciousness. She wished Jenipher hadn't seen her faint.

'Much better, thank you.'

'You gave us a scare.'

'It was nothing.'

'What is it? Blood phobia?'

Payton seized the excuse. 'Yes. A bit.'

'Your father mentioned to me that you'd like to be a methic. You can't be a methic if you're scared of blood.' Jenipher was watching her closely.

'Oh . . . well . . .' Payton felt her embarrassment grow. This was not the first impression she wanted to make. 'It's not a phobia really.'

'Then what is it?'

Payton didn't know what to tell her. She thought back to that moment in the operating theatre when she had touched the smudge of blood on Ani's finger. Tunnel vision, a whooshing sound in her ears, and the ground rushing up to meet her as she fell . . . She couldn't tell Jenipher Blake of all people that this wasn't anything new. It happened every time she touched blood. She certainly couldn't tell her what she saw when she closed her eyes . . .

The silence stretched on, and Jenipher seemed to accept that she wasn't going to get an answer. She stopped staring at Payton and went to the stove, poured milk into a saucepan and added crushed herbs and spices.

'What's that?' Payton asked, as Jenipher twisted a star-shaped seed pod to open it.

'Seren spice,' said Jenipher. 'It will help you sleep. It suppresses dreams too. You look exhausted, and it's late. I thought you might like to stay here. Just for tonight.'

'Yes, please.' Payton felt relief and excitement flood through her. She climbed on to one of the stools at the kitchen counter. 'I didn't know there was any seren spice in Prydein. I thought it only grows in far-off, wild places.'

'It does.' Jenipher stirred the steaming milk with a spoon. It started to smell like dry summer grass after rain. Payton's stomach growled. 'But I have my ways of getting these things.'

'At King Jude's we use story therapy for chronic dreamers.'

Jenipher glanced up at her. 'And what do you think of that, as a treatment?'

'Inefficient. You're just supplanting the illness with something similar, only a little less bad.' Payton found medicine an easy subject, and soon felt herself relax, able to forget that it was Jenipher Blake she was speaking to. 'I think methics should be trying to disrupt the dreams entirely. Find out what the sleeping brain is trying to tell the patient.'

'And how would they do that?'

'I read about some old studies that combined talking therapy with sleep deprivation. Also, devil's snare – you have to burn the leaves, crush the ash – it works like a truth serum, only you can tell yourself the truth. It can bring the subconscious to the surface.'

'I know what devil's snare is.'

'Sorry. I'm used to explaining things to my sister. She never remembers anything. Anyway, you can't get devil's snare now. Only the wilders knew where it grew.'

'You sound like you'd make an excellent sleep methic,' said Jenipher, pouring the spice-flecked milk into a cup and passing it to Payton.

'Actually, I want to cure water fever when I'm a methic.'

'Like your father.'

Payton leant over the kitchen counter and wrapped her hands gratefully around the cup. Her eyes took on a hard, set expression under her fringe.

'No,' she said. 'Better than him.'

The next day, Payton woke with sunshine on her face. It poured through the windows and landed in a strip across the sofa, where she had slept a dreamless sleep thanks to the seren spice. For a blissful moment the previous day didn't exist. Neither did her mother, asleep in water on the Inertia Ward, nor Ani, missing in the back of an ambulans. It was as if she had always been here, in Jenipher's apartment, feeling like she'd slept for a year.

She'd been woken by the front door closing. She scrunched up her face against the light and saw Jenipher standing there in her methic robes.

'Did I sleep all morning?' Payton asked, pushing herself upright. Her tumble from the ambulans came back to her through sore muscles and bruises.

'No, it's still early. I like to be the first in the lab. I'll ask for a carriage to take you back to King Jude's.'

'Already?'

Her response made Jenipher smile.

'You didn't want to stay here, did you?'

'I'd stay here!' Payton said. 'Just a little longer. I've never seen a different hospital.'

'Are you hoping your sister will find her way here?'

Payton didn't know what to say. Jenipher sat in one of the armchairs. She didn't relax into the comforting shape of it but sat leaning forward, with her elbows on her knees, looking intensely at Payton.

'People from King Jude's are still looking for her, Payton. She didn't come home last night. We're all very worried. What I saw at the blood reading concerns me hugely. She's a danger to herself and others – she should be in hospital. She needs to be contained. And even though you said you don't know where she is, I think you might, after all.'

'I don't,' she insisted. 'I mean . . .'

'I would hate to see a fine potential methic dishonour herself by lying, Payton.'

Payton hung her head. 'We were in an ambulans.'

'Go on.'

'We were going to Carnaby. But I fell out. I don't know what happened to her. She . . . she wanted to run away. I was trying to persuade her to stay, but the ambulans set off with us in the back . . .'

Jenipher's gaze was steady and scrutinizing. A scientist taking in everything before her, weighing it, assessing it.

'I know it's silly.' Payton didn't want Ani's shameful behaviour to colour Jenipher's impression of herself.

'The gwaidmesur result will have been distressing for her. It's important that we find her.'

'Is it . . .? I mean, do you think . . .?' Payton couldn't meet Jenipher's eyes. She didn't know how to phrase her question, but Jenipher figured it out anyway.

'The gwaidmesur is very accurate, Payton. I have only seen rage like that in one other child. It took a lot of hard work, medicine and time to get it under control.'

'Back at King Jude's, before we ran away, she had this outburst. There were sparks, her eyes looked like coals . . .'

119

'I promise, when we find your sister, I will lead her treatment myself.'

'Maybe she'll come to her senses and make her own way back,' Payton said hopefully.

Jenipher watched her in an awkward silence before changing the subject. 'Wash and eat something,' she said. 'I'll call you down when the carriage is ready.'

In the apartment on her own, Payton had a hurried bath and wolfed down some bread spread with butter. A clean set of clothes was neatly folded on the coffee table in the living room. She saw with delight that it wasn't a dress like she had to wear at home, but women's slacks, which she had to roll up around her ankles, and a shirt. They were the practical sort of clothes that Jenipher wore under her robes. Payton looked at herself in the mirror. Her fringe brushed her eyebrows. She wondered how she'd look if she cut her hair short like Jenipher's.

She didn't want to go home without a chance to see Queen Cleo's properly. Since Ani ruined Jenipher's blood reading demonstration, she thought her father might not get the job at the prestigious hospital after all. This might be her only opportunity to see another hospital until she was old enough for the Trials. She had to look around, she convinced herself. For her studies.

The hallway was busier than it had been the night

before. Efficient nurses went by, as well as the occasional methic in billowing blue fabric. The ground floor seemed to mostly be full of staff, so when she saw some nurses going up a grand marble staircase, she went too. Queen Cleo's didn't have wards the way King Jude's did, with lines of beds, a nurse's station and a methic's desk. All the patients at Queen Cleo's stayed in small, luxurious apartments, which had grand bedrooms, living rooms with frilled lampshades and tightly upholstered sofas, and bathrooms with flowing hot water and deep baths. Glass cases were mounted on the walls outside each room, with gold coins dropped into them – payment for each patient's stay at the hospital. The senior methics emptied them every other day. Payton peered around doors that were ajar and followed nurses as they delivered medicines.

But what Payton really wanted to see was the Feelings Library. Ever since Jenipher had explained how she had used it to make the gwaidmesur, Payton had burnt with curiosity. The closest she'd come to seeing a pure, distilled feeling at King Jude's was the sinister blob she and Ani had found in the old laboratory. An entire library of feelings was like something from her wildest dreams. She had to see it.

She guessed the best place to start was the labs. She found her way there easily enough; the double doors were plain and functional in comparison to the rest of the hospital, and were situated underneath Jenipher's apartment, tucked away.

Payton slipped inside and the first thing that struck her was how everything in the lab shone. Equipment, glass vials and beakers, even the desks were new and gleaming. The workstations stretched on and on; the room was easily double the size of anything at King Jude's. Medicinal plants covered one long wall of the lab – a living medicine cabinet, forming columns of greenery, with each plant growing in its ideal climate. Tiny strip heaters blasted desert plants that sat in bowls of sand, while a fine spray misted water over swamp ferns whose roots swayed in murky water.

A methic was at the front of the room, holding a clear vial of pink liquid in a pair of metal pincers. An audience of junior methics gathered around to listen, except for Jenipher, whom Payton spotted at the back of the room, near the green planted wall. She was leaning back with her hands on a workbench, watching the talk.

'Lovesickness takes many forms,' the methic at the front was saying. 'But this particular strain, which has a very intense dose of longing in it, has been causing a lot of upset amongst our patients. The unique scarring pattern it leaves on the skin makes the name of the patient's object of desire visible for all the world to see, so many of the people we serve here at Queen Cleo's are keen to see us find a cure, more so even than for other, more dangerous or common diseases.'

Payton had seen lovesick patients before. You could smell them before you saw them: their skin let off the cloying, sickly scent of rotting roses. As the illness progressed, patients vomited thick clumps of red petals. Thorns curved out of the surface of their arms and legs. It was painful, embarrassing, impossible to hide. That's why she frowned at the metal pincers holding the vial. The methic was a gangly man. When he spoke, she could see every muscle in his neck moving, and he gestured widely at the end of each sentence. Only Payton noticed the vial slip with each comment.

The liquid swirled inside the glass. It was pure feeling distilled into a vial.

Pure feelings were rare and difficult to get hold of. Most of them had been captured at the beginning of the Turn, as the methics frantically worked to find out what was making people so ill. Payton knew that Queen Cleo's had countless samples.

The liquid moved like it had a life of its own. The tiny droplets went against gravity, climbing the sides of the vial, before slipping back down again. It seemed denser than a liquid, but too fluid to be solid. It glistened and pulsed. It was beautiful. And far too dangerous to be handled without proper respect. Should the pure feeling get out, anybody close to it could get infected. Payton inched further into the room. She didn't notice Jenipher glance towards her without moving her head.

'It is my hope to develop a skin cream that promises to reduce the risk of scarring should the patient contract it. I know a merchant in Leadenhall who is keen to work with us on this.'

Another sweeping gesture. The pink globules wobbled as if hoping for freedom.

'Or perhaps we could offer a bath oil too, as part of a package!'

Most of the methics were making notes, heads down, ignoring the glint of glass.

'Above all, we hope that skin concerns—'

'STOP!'

Payton's shout came too late. The vial slipped from the pincers and smashed.

The methics yelled with alarm, shoved past each other and scrabbled over workbenches to get away from the pink liquid, which began to foam and spit on the floor. The reeking scent of roses filled the room. Payton was the only one who didn't try to run away – she ran towards the spilt feeling, grabbing one of the plants on the wall out of its pot. She ripped off its leaves and fumbled with its small furry pods, desperately trying to split them open.

The escaped feeling began to pop, splatting liquid in

the direction of the methics.

'Get out of the way!' Payton shouted at the methics.

As she got closer, she felt a pulse of warmth in her stomach. For a moment, she thought she could hear music through the walls. A love song.

Her thumbnail found the spines of the pods. Inside was a bitter grey powder, which she flicked out hurriedly. She got as close to the lovesickness as she dared and threw the powder at it. Then she reached over to a workstation, grappling with the tubes on it until she found the red one: the flame hose. She turned the tap and pointed an eruption of flame at the pink liquid.

In an instant, the floor ignited. The contents of the seed pods had soaked up the liquid feeling, and when the flame touched them, they exploded like gunpowder. The space in front of Payton became of wall of pink micro-explosions, popping, fizzing and sparking relentlessly, each reaction leading to a new one. The effect was blinding – heat blasted her face and she was engulfed with smoke.

When the last speck had burnt away, silence descended on the lab.

Payton slowly turned around, framed by smoke, the flame hose limp in her hand.

The methics peered over the edge of the workstation.

'Well, thank goodness Miss Darke knows what to

do in a crisis,' said Jenipher calmly. She flicked a dot of ash off the sleeve of her robes.

'Methic Blake . . .' The man who had been holding the vial stammered and prepared his excuses.

'Clean this up,' she snapped. 'This is the best lab in Lundain and not one of my methics knows what to do when there's an outbreak. If it weren't for Miss Darke – a *child* – you wouldn't be in a fit state to treat any patients.'

She stepped past them, took Payton by the elbow and led her out of the room.

Out in the corridor, Jenipher turned to her with a tight, unreadable expression on her face.

'I told you to wait upstairs. I did not invite you into my lab.'

Payton blinked at the telling off. Just a moment ago she'd felt like a hero.

'I . . . You . . . I'm sorry.' She looked down. She wasn't going to argue with Jenipher.

'But that was clever. Using fen-violet seed powder like that. How did you know to do that?'

'It was the most flammable compound I could see,' said Payton. 'And the powder can hold a lot of liquid, like a sponge. I thought if it soaked up the liquid, the fire could destroy it.'

'None of my methics would have thought of that . . .' Jenipher started to pace and think aloud to herself. 'They're too used to having antidotes at their fingertips. Fancy equipment. It stops them ever thinking on their feet or finding other uses for medicines. You saw how he was handling the vial. They're not afraid of what feelings can do.' She came to a stop and turned to Payton. 'Are you afraid of feelings, Payton?'

Payton thought of her mother and the way water made light ripple across her face, like she was in a dream: unreachable, unreal.

'Yes,' she said.

'If you can learn to follow instructions, you will make a better methic than any of the fools in my lab.'

Payton saw an opportunity and knew she would regret it for ever if she didn't take it. She had failed with her water-fever cure using whatever resources she could find or steal at King Jude's. This place was different. They had pure feelings. If she could experiment on those, she would be able to get closer to the right cure. She just needed to persuade Jenipher to let her stay long enough.

'Teach me,' she said. 'Please. I'll help. I'll be your assistant. I'll do paperwork, fetch things, take your lab notes, run errands.'

Jenipher stared at her.

'I know the blood thing . . . look, it doesn't happen often. I could be a good methic, honestly. We don't have pure feelings to work with at King Jude's. There's so much I can't learn there.' She carried on: 'My father won't let me sit my exams to start my training until I'm sixteen. But I know I'll be ready before then. If I have the right teacher.'

'Payton, you have a blood phobia . . .'

'It's not a blood phobia,' Payton insisted. 'I've got it under control.'

'Hm.' Jenipher gazed off into space, then said, 'I passed my exams when I was fourteen.'

'I know.' Payton braved a small smile. 'I think I can do better.'

Jenipher's face changed when she laughed – a girlish sound that was completely at odds with the cool, collected methic.

'Let's see about that. I'll write to your father and tell him you cannot be spared for the moment. Just for a short while. Queen Cleo's is very different to what you're used to. Let's see if you can keep up.'

CHAPTER THIRTEEN

'Intruder!'

Ani struggled in the net, swaying from a tree branch. She couldn't see who was speaking.

'What?'

The voice tutted and said, 'You think this is hard for you? I'm going to have to sit through another one of Henrich's boring lectures about security.'

All Ani could see were leaves and branches around her.

'Who's Henrich?' she asked.

'It's going to get in the way of my busy day of trying to do nothing.'

Ani's initial fear was fading away. The voice didn't sound threatening, just taunting and rather bored. And almost . . . familiar. She tried to catch a glimpse of the speaker through the branches.

'Can you let me down?' she asked.

'I could. I don't know. It's complicated.' The voice sighed. 'I might just leave you here.'

There was the sound of footsteps moving away.

'No, wait!' Ani cried.

There was no reply. She tried to stand in the net, but its swaying made it difficult and the rough fibres scratched the blue cloirias burn on her hand.

Then something caught her eye. A metal pipe was caught in a tree branch not too far from her. At first glance it looked like it was floating, but then she saw it poked out from under a wooden deck in the treetops. It looked like part of a treehouse. She threaded a hand through a gap in the net and stretched, but she couldn't reach it. She shunted herself along the net, moving to one side of it before flinging herself as best she could in the direction of the pipe. The net began to sway. Slipping and stumbling, she kept going until, at the peak of the swing, the pipe was in reach. She grabbed it. She kicked at the net, trying to climb over its lip while inching nearer the deck.

Her arms and legs were raw from the rub of the rope fibres. With a final terrifying lurch, she crawled out of the net and on to the deck.

She lay there panting, clutching her burnt, turquoise palm to her chest. The restless movement of sunlight through the leaves dazzled her.

'That wasn't very graceful.'

'Argh!' She sat bolt upright at the sound of the voice right next to her.

Instantly, she knew where she'd heard the voice before: in the market with Rosa and Fred.

It was the Twitcher.

He was younger than she had imagined, about Payton's age. He had brown skin, hazel eyes and chaotic, curly hair, and wore a tattered coat that looked too warm to be wearing in spring. He was standing on the deck, looking down at her. As he watched her, his body shuddered, then became still again.

'Twitcher!' She couldn't help the name falling from her mouth, surprised and relieved to have followed him to the right place. 'I found you!'

'It's not polite to call people names.' He said it in a dismissive way and looked away quickly. Ani sensed the name upset him more than he let on.

'Sorry. That's what Rosa and Fred called you. In Leadenhall, this morning.'

'I *knew* they were in there,' he muttered to himself. He stepped to one side and then Ani could see a small wooden house on the deck.

'I like your treehouse.' She winced as she got to her feet and peered over the edge at the leaf-littered ground below.

A metal structure was attached to the house – lots of interconnected pipes and wires winding up a ladder that went up through the treetops as if it was reaching for the sun.

'It's not a treehouse.'

'Oh. It just . . . it looks like a treehouse,' Ani said.

'For your information, this is a highly sophisticated weather station. I wouldn't expect someone as un-educated as you to understand.'

'I was educated by some of the finest methics in the city,' said Ani with a flare of pride.

'Well, they haven't done a very good job. There are woodland creatures who have been sidestepping that trap for years.'

With a swirl of his baggy coat, the Twitcher disappeared into the weather station.

'Wait! Come back!'

Ani scrambled after him.

Inside there was a motley collection of instruments Ani didn't recognize – barometers, thermometers, hygrometers, many of them cracked or falling apart and reassembled lopsidedly with twine – and the smell of damp carpet. A peeling poster about different types of clouds was pinned to the wall. The metal antenna above the little house led to a dark wire that trailed across the floor and ended inside a glass bottle which rested on an old cushion. The Twitcher polished the bottle like it was a prize trophy. As he hunched over it, Ani noticed that his coat was hiding something irregular and bulky on his back. She wondered if he was ill.

'Careful!' he snapped when she walked within a metre of the glass bottle.

'Why do you need to know the weather?' she asked him.

'Because I know everything else already. Now back away. Go and stand over there. *There!* Don't touch anything.'

She backed up until she was in a corner of the treehouse.

The boy settled in a seat at the table and pulled a broken hygrometer towards him. Every few minutes, his entire body would convulse for a second, interrupting his speech and facial expressions.

'Look, I don't want to bother you,' Ani said to his back, 'but I can't go home, and I can't stay in Leadenhall because the methics are looking for me, and I heard you say something about some seeds—'

He turned to her, suddenly interested.

'Do you have money?'

'I . . . well, no . . .'

He turned away from her again.

'Please, it's important! Can they really cure anything?'

He shuddered again. 'None of your business.'

'That's because they can't,' she said, testing him, trying to get a reaction. 'A seed can't do anything.'

'These aren't just any seeds. I have access to some of the rarest plants in the natural world. Things the methics can only dream of.'

'Prove it, then.' When he didn't reply, she said more gently, 'Please. I need help and I can't ask the methics.'

'I run a business, not a charity.'

Ani rummaged in her pockets, then offered up her bottle of medicine.

'What if we trade? The methics made this. It's very effective. It might stop your . . . you know . . .'

He swivelled around to look at her. 'My what?'

It seemed rude to bring up his shuddering, twitching condition, so she reached for another lie.

'It can help with anything.'

'Then what do you want my seeds for?'

He had her there.

'Come back when you have money,' he told her. 'Lots of it.'

With a sinking heart, Ani reached into her pocket once more.

'What about this?' The gwaidlamp flickered green in her palm. 'It's an old wilder tool. Very valuable.'

The Twitcher came over to her and cupped the gwaidlamp in his hands. Ani noticed the gold smudge Kitt had left on its surface with a twinge of sadness and worry. As it warmed to the Twitcher's skin, Ani released it, and was amazed to see that the colour didn't change. His blood also created the colour green, only his was a little darker, richer, with flickers of yellow in it. He laughed with delight.

'I've heard of these, but never seen one.'

Ani grabbed it back quickly.

'Hey, give it!' he said.

'It's a trade, remember?'

He looked like he was going to say something, but he was interrupted by a spasm.

Then he lunged at her, tried to snatch the gwaid-lamp. Ani was quicker. She leapt out of the way, but as she did so, her boot kicked the bottle on the cushion. It began to roll towards the door.

'No!'

The Twitcher dived for the bottle as if his life depended on it, but it was too late. It rolled on to the deck and then over the edge. There was a sound of glass hitting rock and shattering.

'No, no, no, no!'

He crawled forward and looked over the edge. What he saw made him cry out with rage.

'YOU!'

'It was your fault!' said Ani. 'You shouldn't have tried to steal—'

'That was my last one. The *last* one!' His spit flew through the air as he shouted. Ani recoiled from the outburst of emotion and tried to soothe him.

'You'll find another.'

'Really? How? That wasn't some milk bottle you find on every doorstep in the city. It was made from sandglass. Do you know what that is?'

'Sand that was hit by lightning, so it melted into glass and then was reshaped by wilders.'

'It's *sand* that has been *hit* by – Yes. That's what it is.' He seemed caught somewhere between fury and terror.

'I know where you can find one,' said Ani. She disliked the boy, but he was so distressed she thought she should say something to calm him down. He was on the verge of making himself ill. 'I came from King Jude's Hospital. They'll have some there. They have all sorts of old things. That's where I found the gwaidlamp.'

He looked at her with suspicion.

'A hospital. I've never thought of that. I've mostly stolen them from rich people. I suppose I could steal from a hospital . . .'

'You wouldn't have to steal. They're my friends. They'll give you some bottles if I ask.'

'They have more than one?'

'Yes. Loads.'

Ani had no idea if King Jude's was in possession of sandglass bottles. They were rare relics from a time gone by, back when there were countless guilds, including the wilders who made them. She very much doubted that the bottle she had just broken was real sandglass. But the Twitcher's anger had been so explosive, she'd said it to placate him. And for one other reason.

'I'll get lots of sandglass bottles for you. It can be a part of our trade. But first, I want the seeds.'

'And you'll give me the glowing green ball thingy?'

'The gwaidlamp, yes.'

He screwed up his face and stared at her, thinking hard. Ani glared back.

'Urgh. Fine.' He started to climb down the ladder after one of his full-body shudders.

Ani followed him, more curious than ever. 'If you don't like "Twitcher", what should I call you?'

'How about my name?'

'What's that?'

'Estlin.'

'I'm Ani.'

'You're a trap-escaping, sandglass-breaking nuisance is what you are.'

Ani followed Estlin through the ancient woodlands. Eventually the crooked, soaring trees gave way to overgrown grassland that sloped down to a long, silver lake. A few trees stood apart from the others in a riot of white blossom, casting dappled shade on the grass.

'It's so . . .' She couldn't find the words. It was

wild, lush, every inch exploding with life. There was so much to look at, but not like the manic movement of the city. Everything seemed to fit together, just as it should. 'I can see why you'd want to live here,' she admitted.

'Yep. Better than sleeping in that smelly market like your friends, believe me.'

They went back into the woods, heading east under the green canopy. Estlin moved with the confidence of someone who had wandered around the gardens all his life. Ani had never been into anything like woodland before. The flickering light made her blink often, and every few paces smells came to her that were familiar and new at the same time. She wanted to linger and learn what earth smelt like, how fungi, petals and grass seemed to come together into something new. She wanted to investigate every square metre, become acquainted with worms and woodlice, animals that had never been tamed. She wanted to turn over each tobacco-brown log and climb every tree.

But Estlin marched on, his coat flapping around his knees, and she had to hurry to keep up with him. As they walked, the woodland became thicker and wilder, ancient. Finally, they came to a clearing, and they were looking at a line of trees so gnarled and bent with time that they knitted together to form a dark tunnel.

'We're going in there?' Ani asked. She was suddenly

very aware that she was alone with a stranger and nobody knew where she was.

'That's where the seeds grow.'

Ani found it hard to believe that anything could grow in such gloom.

But she held up the gwaidlamp, keeping it safely out of Estlin's reach.

'Let's go, then.'

The ground was dry underfoot, and the air was very still under the trees.

'What is this place?' Ani asked. 'It's like a tree tunnel.'

'It's called a holloway.'

It grew darker the further they walked into the holloway, until Ani realized that it was not completely dark. She dropped the gwaidlamp back into her pocket and saw that there was a strange, silvery light. It was just enough to see by, as if it was night-time and there was a high moon shining through the trees. She looked up and gasped when she saw what was making the ghostly light. Twine nets hung from the branches and were packed with writhing, glowing maggots.

'What are they?' she asked.

'Moonbugs,' said Estlin.

Ani was mesmerized by them. In the mossy gaps between trees were clumps of blue-flowering plants and she noticed how they grew best near the moon-bugs, the tiny flowers drinking in their light.

'They only grow by moonlight,' she realized.

'Real moonlight isn't the most reliable light source. Moonbugs get a better harvest.'

'This is . . .'

'This is it.'

Estlin produced a pair of silver tweezers from his coat pocket. He bent down amongst the flowers and delicately turned the more shrivelled blooms to face him so he could harvest the tiny black seeds inside.

When he had five of them in his palm, he returned to Ani. He held out his other hand.

'Gwaidlamp.'

'Seeds first.'

He rolled his eyes and sprinkled them into Ani's palm. They were easy to spot against the bright blue of her burn. Reluctantly, she handed over the gwaidlamp. Estlin held it close, and it bathed them both in his green light.

'So . . .' Ani nudged the seeds with her fingernail. 'These will cure anything?'

'They sure will.'

'Will they work on spark breath?'

'Yep.'

'What about water fever?'

'Of course.'

'Even sponge skin?'

'Naturally.'

'There's no such thing as sponge skin!'

'If there was, it would cure it.'

'These don't do anything, do they? You're a liar! Give me my gwaidlamp back!'

'No! It's mine!'

'It's *mine!*'

'You traded it.'

'You lied!'

'It's called marketing.'

'Estlin, give it—'

'No—'

'Give – it – BACK!' A flame whooshed from Ani's mouth. Estlin jumped back. It stopped as quickly as it started, leaving Ani feeling shivery and cold. He stared at her.

'You're sick too,' he said. 'What was that?'

'It's nothing. I . . . I'm sorry . . .'

'Estlin? Estlin! What have you done now?'

A man's voice bellowed at them through the trees. Both Ani and Estlin jumped.

'I'm sure there's an explanation,' a woman's voice said gently.

'Open flame, right in the moonflower holloway!'

Two people stepped into the silver light of the moonbugs – a man and a woman, old enough to be her grandparents, Ani guessed, but strong and quick. They were dressed in shabby clothes, but carried themselves with authority, almost like methics. They did a double take at the sight of Ani.

'Oh, Estlin,' the woman said with a note of relief in her voice. 'You have a friend!'

'No, I don't—'

'*Not* his friend.'

Ani and Estlin spoke over each other.

The man held up his hand to silence them and said sternly, 'If she is not your guest, Estlin, then what is she doing in Hyde Gardens?'

'She found her own way here,' Estlin said. 'Got caught in one of the nets. I didn't even help her. She wriggled free like some sort of leggy snake.'

'No one is meant to know the entrance. How did this happen?'

'Like I said, just lots of wriggling, limbs like . . .' Estlin did an impersonation of Ani escaping the net while the man glared at him.

'My name's Tally,' the woman told Ani. 'And this is Henrich. Why don't you tell us what brought you to Hyde Gardens, dear?'

'I'm Ani. I'm sorry to break in, I only did it because Estlin said he had some seeds that could heal anything. I've been feeling a bit . . . well . . .'

'It sounds like you need to see a methic.'

'I can't! I mean, I have, but . . .' Ani swallowed a lump in her throat.

'The fire was you?' Henrich asked. 'Well. Moon-flower seeds won't do a thing for spark breath. They're only good for invisibility blight. And even then, you can't eat them raw. You need a methic to turn them into medicine.'

Ani glared at Estlin. 'So you did lie.'

Henrich pulled the gwaidlamp from Estlin's hands. In his grip it glowed an even deeper, richer green. 'Where did you get this?'

'It's mine,' said Ani. 'He stole it.'

'It was a trade,' Estlin insisted.

Henrich glanced at Ani.

'And what colour does your blood make?' he asked her.

'Green. Like you.'

'Does it now?'

Henrich seemed to hesitate, as if he was considering keeping it, but then he handed it back to Ani.

'A gwaidlamp is a rare thing. I wouldn't trade it for anything if I were you.'

'I won't. Thank you.'

'That's not very nice, Estlin,' said Tally. 'Tricking a poor little market child. They don't know any better.'

'She's not from the market. She fancies herself a methic.'

Tally and Henrich exchanged glances.

'Ani, is that true?'

'I'm not a methic. My father is. I grew up in King Jude's.'

'What are you doing out here?'

'Well . . .'

Tally seemed so kind, and Henrich had been very fair giving the gwaidlamp back to her. Ani didn't want to trust them, but she was exhausted and bewildered, and still scared of how her tongue and gums tingled from the fire. It was the second time it had happened since she'd stopped taking her medicine. She was scared at how quickly it seemed to be escalating.

The moonbugs twisted their luminous bodies in their nets. One of them slipped free and landed with a *puht* on the ground at Estlin's feet. Ani bent down to scoop it up. It snuggled into a crescent moon shape in the warmth of her palm. She closed her fingers gently around the bug and took a deep breath.

'It all started with Methic Blake and this horrible machine she has. No, that's not right. It was my father who started it. With Kitt. He locked him away.' She waved her blue cloirias burn at their confused faces. Ani knew she wasn't making much sense, but it was all spilling out: 'The machine was for Kitt, but they used it on me. They said my blood was nearly perfect but being angry has ruined it and turned it bad. I don't *feel* angry, at least not that often, but they wouldn't listen, they were going to lock me up. So I ran away, and Payton – that's my sister – she was with me, but then we argued, and I lost her. So I went to Leadenhall, like Kitt, and met some of the children, and the Twitcher – sorry, Estlin, I mean – said he had some seeds that can heal anything. And I really need something like that because everyone thinks my blood is bad and so I can't go home, but my mother is there. She has water fever. So I was hoping there was something I could take to make my blood better and maybe my mother too, actually, because it's been a really long time and I need her back.'

Ani was embarrassed when her voice cracked at the mention of her mother.

'It's all right, dear.' Tally patted her arm. 'Take a breath.'

'It doesn't sound all right,' said Estlin. 'If anything, it sounds like you have serious issues. Whoever heard of someone's blood being bad?'

Ani wanted to tell him to shut up, but her throat tightened and all she could do was cough. A shower of sparks came out.

The others stared at her. She glanced down at her palm – the moonbug was curled into a still ball. The luminosity had left its skin.

'I killed it!' It was only a bug, but to Ani it felt like

yet another thing she'd ruined and couldn't fix.

'Now, now.' Tally ran a hand over Ani's hair. 'It's just a bit of spark breath, you didn't mean it.'

'I'm fine by the way,' Estlin said loudly, brushing the faded sparks from his coat.

'Leave her be,' Tally insisted. 'She's been through a lot.'

'I'm getting sick,' Ani said with terror.

'Only because you're pushing the anger down,' said Tally.

'That's what you're supposed to do with feelings!'

'And how has that been working for you? Now listen. I don't know what's been going on at King Jude's to cause all this, but it sounds very upsetting.'

Ani sniffed and nodded.

'Well, just let that be what it is for a moment.'

'What?'

'She's right,' said Henrich. 'Nothing wrong with feeling angry from time to time.'

Ani didn't know what to say. All her life, Payton, her father, all the methics had been reminding her not to get angry or upset. The medicine she took replaced all her feelings with sleepiness. Within an hour of taking it, it became easy not to care about anything. But it had now been two days since she'd last taken any. And these strangers were telling her to just let it all out?

'I—'

Tally raised a hand. 'Just breathe and feel the unfairness.'

'Won't that make me worse?'

'Try it and see.'

At first, Ani didn't know what she meant. She didn't know how to intentionally feel a feeling. She always thought of her stronger, more difficult feelings as an accident she needed to fix. But she tried. She thought of her father and his lies, her mother and her illness, Payton lost in the city.

It *was* all unfair. Ani felt her anger rise, bubble, ignite. There was a whistling sound in her ears and she was sure the steam she could suddenly see was coming from her. She felt scared and glanced at Tally.

'Breathe,' she reminded her. 'Accept it.'

Ani didn't try to rein it in. The anger built and built and then, like a wave cresting, it began to sink again. All that was left was sadness at what had happened to her, and her family.

'Better?' Tally asked.

'Yes,' she said with surprise. 'How did you know to do that?'

'The methics know a lot. But they don't know everything. Not all feelings are bad.'

Ani looked from Tally to Henrich. She had never heard anybody speak about methics in this way. Or feelings.

'Who *are* you?'

They seemed surprised by her question.

'We're wilders.'

Ani gaped at them.

'Not . . . not *real* wilders?' she asked.

'Perfectly real, thank you,' Henrich replied with a slight huff.

'Where are the others?'

'There are no others,' Tally explained.

'So there are only two of you?'

'Three.' Estlin tapped his chest.

'If you're a real wilder, then I'm a moonbug,' said Henrich.

'I'm sorry –' Ani shook her head – 'but you just can't be. There haven't been any wilders in – for ever. You don't have a guild. There are only methics and financiers.'

'It's true; our guild was disbanded not long after the Turn, like so many others. They locked our gardens, burnt our green robes. Lundain used to be a very different city, Ani.' Henrich gazed off into the distance as if he could see it. 'My father remembered it. Green. Calm. But they covered it with concrete and glass, tamed the animals to keep them as pets. They burnt the fields and forests across the country. You have probably never seen wild grass until today.'

'I have, once. I lived in the Isles when I was small.'

148

Henrich's words brought to mind the hazy memories Ani had of living there. Her mother was well and happy. She and Payton were only little, always dressed alike, wandering wind-swept hills and cliffs that overlooked the sea.

'The Isles.' Henrich nodded. 'One of the few places in Prydein where our ways aren't completely forgotten. Tally and I both come from old wilder families. Estlin too, in fact. We stay here to keep our traditions alive and preserve the knowledge of the guild. Just in case our world is ready for the Wild again. We grow and care for our rare plants, take harvests to keep the species alive.' He gestured at the blue flowers. 'Of course, nobody must know we have them. We destroy them so neither of the guilds find out.'

While Henrich was explaining, Estlin had been playing a game, holding a fallen moonbug in each hand, making them dance around and muttering a little play for them, where one was accused of being in love with another moonbug. But when Henrich mentioned the harvest, he quickly said, 'Yes, destroy – we destroy them, all of them, uh huh.'

Ani remembered the stacks of seeds and plants in the merchant's office in Leadenhall and raised an eyebrow at him.

'But I shouldn't be telling you this,' Henrich sighed. 'Not when you're about to go back to King Jude's.'

'No!' Ani insisted. 'I'm not going back.'

'Because of this machine you mentioned?' Tally asked.

'Yes. You give it a drop of your blood and it tells you if you're going to get sick. Jenipher wants to test all the children and make the ill ones better.'

'Jenipher Blake?' said Estlin suddenly. 'The methic?'

'That's her.'

'Estlin, how do you know who she is?' Tally asked.

'I know everything in this city,' said Estlin, bowing with a flourish.

'A blood-reading machine . . .' muttered Henrich. 'This is dark medicine, very dark indeed.'

'You know about it?' Ani asked.

'Of course. They're called gwaidmesurs. Methics have been trying to make them ever since the Turn. They hoped they could find feelings lurking in the blood before they could cause diseases. But blood is complicated stuff. Some things are better left alone.'

'Jenipher is clever. If anyone can make one, she can,' said Tally. Two lines of worry appeared between her eyebrows.

'She has,' said Ani, 'and she's after me.' As she said it, she didn't feel as angry as she had before. She was upset, but there was something else – a frank, strong stubbornness. 'But she won't catch me. I'll stay hidden. Then, when I can, I'm getting my own back.'

'Be careful, Ani,' said Tally. 'Jenipher Blake is not someone you want as an enemy.'

Ani pulled her bottle of medicine from her pocket, unscrewed the lid, and poured the milky liquid on to the ground.

'Neither am I.'

CHAPTER FOURTEEN

Payton soon proved to Jenipher that she could keep up at Queen Cleo's.

Neel had written to say that Payton could stay for as long as she was useful – he also expressed the hope that some time with the methics of Queen Cleo's might inspire some discipline in her. He sent Payton a separate note warning her not to embarrass him or jeopardize his opportunities there. Payton had crumpled it into a ball and thrown it out of the window.

Jenipher kept her so busy that she barely had time to work on her water-fever cure. She shadowed nurses and junior methics. She spent long afternoons in the lab learning how to take meticulous care of the plant wall and the lab equipment. Even on her knees scrubbing the floor under a workbench, Payton felt a satisfaction and purpose she'd never felt before. In the evenings, when Jenipher didn't dine in the Methics

Hall, they ate together in the apartment. Payton listened in rapt silence as she learnt which methics Jenipher admired and which she disapproved of. She started to learn the names of the rich families who came to Queen Cleo's and occupied the plush rooms upstairs, and where tensions and allegiances lay. Jenipher taught her about the delicate economy of the hospital.

'It may seem like gossip,' she said to Payton, sipping wine the colour of sunshine while she cooked them dinner. 'But it's important. Without knowing who can support us financially, we can't keep the hospital going. We wouldn't be able to afford the best medicines or equipment or methics. To take in runaways to be our assistants,' she added with a smile that was becoming more familiar.

Payton had expected to be sent to live with the junior methics, but Jenipher had never mentioned her leaving the apartment, and she didn't dare ask her any questions that would make her think along those lines.

'At King Jude's, we just take everyone,' she said.

'That's why it cannot afford to move forward,' Jenipher explained. 'And medicine must always move forward. Thanks to the wealth of the hospital, I'm expanding my blood-reading programme. If I sat idle while there are so many children I could be helping, I wouldn't be a very good methic, would I?'

Payton nodded, but she was only half listening.

While Jenipher had her ambitions, Payton had her own. Water fever. Every night, even though she was exhausted from working in the labs or with patients, she worked on her research. With each passing day, a solution was becoming clearer to her: she needed something to test her cure on. Methic Gilchrist was right – she couldn't administer a cure to her mother without testing it first. She needed a safe, stable way to do it, where no one could get hurt if it went wrong. The close call with the lovesickness outbreak had given her an idea.

'Jenipher . . . I was wondering. Now I've been here for a while . . . could I see the Feelings Library?'

The Feelings Library – and, she suspected, lots of other interesting things – was somewhere beyond the locked doors in Jenipher's lab. Only the most senior methics were allowed through there. Payton knew she had no right to ask, but she was overwhelmed by curiosity.

'Absolutely not,' Jenipher said. She tipped steaming potato cakes and creamy mushrooms on to their plates. 'The Feelings Library is a very dangerous place. You'd need someone to take you, and none of the senior methics has time.'

'I wouldn't need someone to take me.'

Jenipher shook her head. 'Payton. While you're here, it's my job to look after you. What would your father say if something happened to you while you're meant to be under my watch?'

'*He* wouldn't care.'

'He does seem more focused on his work than his family,' Jenipher admitted. 'I was surprised to find he has children. Anyway, I'm sure your mother would care.'

Payton had been about to shovel a potato cake into her mouth, but at the thought of her mother, her appetite died. Were the nurses changing her breathers correctly? Was anybody still visiting her? Did she know that Payton wasn't there any more and wonder where she had gone? She pictured her mother dream-trapped, heavy with water, worrying that her daughter had given up on her. Tears swelled in Payton's eyes at the thought, and she bent her head over the table.

'Payton,' Jenipher murmured. 'Your feelings.'

Payton sniffed and sat a little straighter. She ate everything on her plate, barely tasting a thing.

Payton adored and respected Jenipher. But she wasn't going to let that get in the way of her water-fever cure. Now that she couldn't visit her mother every day, it was even more important to complete her work quickly.

That night, she forced herself to stay awake long after Jenipher had gone to bed. Jenipher often read late into the night, so it took some time before Payton was sure she could hear the soft, even breath coming from her bedroom and knew that she was asleep. She slid off the sofa and picked up her shoes and a jumper.

A ring of five keys hung on the back of the front door. Payton had spotted Jenipher scooping them up whenever she needed to visit the library. She bunched her woollen jumper in her hands and gently pressed the fabric against the keys. She winced at the scrape of metal against the wooden door, paused, and listened. Still nothing from Jenipher. Muffling the noise with the jumper as best she could, she lifted them from the hook. She didn't let the door click shut behind her – it was too loud; instead she left a large paperback book wedged in the doorway.

She crept down the stairs and stopped in the deserted corridor to put her shoes on. Then she hurried into the lab before anyone could spot her.

The only sound and light in the lab came from the humming heat lamps on the plant wall. The green leaves and mosses were still damp from their evening watering.

'You won't tell anyone, will you?' Payton whispered to them as she passed.

The second key she tried was the correct one. The double doors at the end of the lab swung open, as if to welcome her. She hesitated on the threshold. She never minded breaking her father's rules, but there was no knowing how Jenipher would punish her if she was caught. She would probably send her back to King

Jude's. Payton didn't want to go back one bit, but staying at Queen Cleo's and not working on her cure felt like betraying her mother. She had to do this.

The corridor beyond the doors was disappointingly stark, made from raw stone and earth that had little in common with the gilded halls of Queen Cleo's. Wall-mounted lamps failed to disperse the shadows. There was a door at the far end, and another to the right. The one straight ahead opened easily – the one to the right was locked. Payton decided that it was a sign she was heading in the right direction. She tried more keys, and then was through into another stark corridor.

It was just like a maze, and while she tried to keep her route straight in her head, it seemed to tangle around her. She had no idea if she was getting closer to the library. She could remember the interlocking complexities of the human skeleton without a hitch. If she were a drop of blood in a human vein, she could find her way to the heart with no trouble. But in the windowless corridors, she didn't know which way was which.

She nearly missed the door to the library entirely. Her anxiety had been making her walk quickly. It was a small door, barely higher than her head. The word LIBRARY was carved into a wooden panel in beautiful writing. The rest of the door was reinforced with metal.

Bars crisscrossed it, panels ran up and down it, and there were three different locks.

Payton methodically unlocked each of them, then ducked inside.

She found herself in a vast room filled with endless stacks of oak shelving. There were vials and bottles and boxes and chests of every size and material. The walls and ceilings were painted with faded scenes of methics curing diseases and performing operations. Payton tracked the scenes, and saw one that represented the Turn, the patients fallen and diseased, the methics looking on in despair, falling ill themselves, then concocting medicines that saved people, crowds reaching out to touch the blue robes, thankful, joyous.

Payton knew she had to become one of the people in the blue robes.

She approached the first stack. It was labelled, '0.000–0.099: *Melancholia*. Despair, disappointment, loneliness, guilt and other draining factors.' It was stuffed with see-through boxes that contained distilled, disease-causing emotions. Payton walked slowly amongst them, her footsteps uncomfortably loud. She peered at the feelings – a blue jelly-like substance bobbed in clear liquid, a white string of steam whizzed inside a glass box. As she went past, the blue jelly pressed to the glass as if it was watching her. Payton felt strangely cold and walked quicker. All these feelings, many extracted in the early days of the Turn from patients with the most hopeless conditions, seemed to press threateningly down on her.

She reached the end of the stack and read the next one: '10.00–10.16: *Ire*. Fury, anger, betrayal, hurt, resentment, and other inflammatory causes. Some humiliation.' This one glowed red, and there was the muted sputter of sparks inside the containers.

Queen Cleo's was sitting on an arsenal of toxic emotions. The entire city would go mad, Payton thought, if one of these stacks were to be opened. No wonder Jenipher had warned her it was dangerous.

She lost all sense of time as she explored, torn between fascination and horror. She spent a long time examining a glass tube filled with a gritty, sand-like feeling that was labelled *Greed*. The sand was a bright, sickly green, speckled with gold. She thought about the Midas-fingers boy Ani had talked about and felt a twinge of guilt towards her sister.

She went back to the beginning. Water fever would be somewhere around *Despair*, she reasoned. It took a long time of searching the stacks before she spotted a tiny round orb on a wooden stand. The label – Payton had to squint to read it – said, *Maternal grief*.

'Found you,' Payton whispered.

She plucked the orb from its stand and held it up to the light. All she could see was clear liquid inside. It was almost disappointing, after the strange appearance of the other feelings. She hadn't held it very long when she felt an ache in her arm, then her shoulder. It was as if the tiny orb was too heavy to hold. Even when she brought it down to chest-level, her arm shook with the effort to hold it.

Then, with a gasp, it sank to the ground, still in her hands, which mercifully protected it from breaking open on the stone floor.

How could something so small weigh so much? And how was she going to get it up to the lab if she couldn't even lift it?

She would have to find a way to carry it.

She circled the library once more, looking for an idea, peering into the alcoves and smaller libraries leading off the main room. One held a collection of antique syringes, dating back to when each methic had their own design intricately carved on the metal handles. The next alcove housed test tubes filled with dark blood samples. It made the hairs on the back of her neck stand up. Carved into the stone of the arch were the words: BLOOD LIBRARY. Payton knew that these must be the blood samples that the feelings had been extracted from, before they were condensed into their purest form and stored. Queen Cleo's collection was impressive, dating back years. She wanted to turn away, but she felt herself drawn to it.

On one wall, there was a single test tube set apart from the others. There was a piece of paper wrapped around the tube, with a bright red exclamation mark on it, and some notes. Payton recognized Jenipher's handwriting. She couldn't resist lifting the vial of blood free and unfolding the note.

For M. Blake's research only.
NOT to be extracted. Caution advised.

Payton wondered what was so dangerous about the blood. What did it have to do with Jenipher's research?

She was lost in these thoughts when somewhere, on the other side of the library, she heard it: a door slamming.

She jumped. The glass slipped from her fingers.

She stumbled, lunged to catch it, but missed. The test tube shattered. Blood splattered her hands.

Payton felt the familiar lurching feeling that came with the touch of blood, and collapsed.

Anyone watching would have seen a girl fainting. They would have known nothing of what she saw when she closed her eyes.

For a moment, Payton thought it would be different this time. There was no dream, no visions. All she saw was darkness.

But then her eyes adjusted. She was looking at a

window, only the glass was black, and all she could see was her own reflection.

Then, on the other side, a pale palm pressed against the glass.

'Hello?' Payton whispered. Slowly, she lifted her own hand and pressed it to the one behind the glass. They were the same size.

A girl's face appeared. Payton leapt back. The girl looked as if she was floating in darkness, the glass obscuring the room she was in. There was something spectral and strained about her, as if the effort of keeping her body together was too much. It was difficult to see her face – it was shrouded in dark and dusted with soot. Her eyes glowed scarlet. Burns crusted the edges of her lips.

The girl stared at Payton fiercely.

Before Payton could ask a question – Who was she? Why was she behind glass? – the girl's expression darkened, and a plume of fire, more violent and overwhelming than anything Payton had ever seen, erupted from her mouth.

Payton screamed and jumped back from the glass, but there was no need. The fire hit the glass and slipped away, engulfing the girl in an inferno that seemed to do her no harm.

Payton was still screaming when she woke up on the library floor, with Jenipher standing over her.

CHAPTER FIFTEEN

Ani walked out of the holloway with the wilders, feeling better than she had for months.

'That's not fair,' Estlin complained to Tally, who'd said that Ani could stay in Hyde Gardens for a while. 'She's an intruder. She can't stay.'

'Estlin . . .'

'She broke my sandglass! Besides, we haven't got space for her.'

Ani looked out at the wide open grasslands and sprawling forest.

'You won't know I'm here,' she promised him.

He huffed loudly and marched away, back in the direction of his weather station.

'Don't mind Estlin,' said Tally. 'He's not much of a people person. He and Henrich have that in common.'

'We have nothing in common,' Henrich insisted. 'And if I hadn't known him since birth, I wouldn't believe he was his parents' child.'

'It's not easy for Estlin,' Tally emphasized. Ani got the impression that this was a conversation they'd had many times before.

'So will I stay with you in your house?' Ani asked her.

'Blossom, we're wilders! We don't have houses.'

'Where do you sleep?'

'I'll show you. Come.'

Ani learnt that wilders carried what little they needed with them: a water flask, a canteen for food (although never any cutlery – they ate with their hands), a hammock with a wax cover, and whatever tools that might come in handy for exploring: a compass, a knife, a magnifying glass. They hung their hammocks wherever the end of the day found them. Their hammocks were like wax-scented cocoons that could be hung between tree trunks or by the lake's shore on a starry night.

Tally took Ani to a 'burrow'. They were all over Hyde Gardens – holes dug into the earth and lined with the wax hammock cover to protect whatever was inside.

'Wilders leave them all the time. Not just here. They're all over the country. The world, even.'

'How do you know how to find them?'

'A wilder can always find one. It's how we looked

after each other in the old days. See here? Hammock, canteen, some clothes . . .' Tally tugged each muddy item out of the hole and pushed them into Ani's hands. They were on the edge of the woodland. The burrow was old, just a random patch of mud crisscrossed with twigs and fallen leaves.

'Doesn't the person who hid them here need them any more?'

'No. It's just us now. There you go.' Tally wiped her palms on her legs to brush off the mud.

Ani felt it would be rude to ask what had happened to the burrow's wilder, so she said thank you, and Tally left her to figure out how to use the unearthed items for herself. Ani wrestled with the tangle of the hammock until she gave up and curled up at the roots of a tree, her cardigan wrapped around her. The tree smelt of rain. She breathed it in and felt the knots in her muscles begin to relax. Sleep came for her with a fierceness she couldn't fight.

She didn't feel homesick at all.

In the days that followed, Ani explored every inch of Hyde Gardens. She spent hours watching butterflies in the meadows, flicking grass on to the surface of the lake to tempt the fat golden fish into view, climbing the trees until she could see the brown rooftops of the city. She quickly learnt not to stray too close to the fence.

The only time she revisited the secret entrance, she removed the wooden railing, peeked out on to the street and saw two methics walk by. She watched them stop and question people on the street. One of them held up a hand, as if indicating somebody about her own height, and the woman they were questioning shook her head. Ani could only assume that her father and Jenipher were trying to find her.

But when she was in the gardens, the burden of it all didn't feel as heavy. Without her medicine, she felt calmer. The metallic taste of fire faded from her tongue and her forehead and fingers were cool to the touch. She wondered if Tally and Henrich would let her live there for ever, if she could become a wilder like them, and never have to see a methic again in her life.

The only thing Ani didn't like about Hyde Gardens was Estlin. She began to notice small things: her hammock, which she left folded on the ground, would suddenly get tangled up in the branches of a tall tree, too spindly to climb, and she would spend the afternoon tying sticks together to make a pole long enough to knock it down. Some mornings she went to sip water from her canteen only to find it filled with tiny finger-eels that slept in the earth of the lake's banks. She discovered rude messages written in mud: GO HOME METHIC GIRL. Then her pink cardigan went missing.

She looked all around the places she had slept in recently. She revisited the moonflower holloway, even though she hadn't been there wearing it, and then the weather station. She was standing beneath the weather station, chewing her thumbnail, when Estlin called down to her.

'Lost something?'

'You took it, didn't you?'

'Took what?'

Ani puffed her cheeks with frustration.

'It's not funny, you know.' The cardigan was all she had of her mother, but she didn't expect Estlin would understand. He was a loner who didn't care about anyone.

His head appeared over the edge of the deck. 'Maybe it's not meant to be funny. Maybe it's meant to be a puzzle.'

'What?'

'Yes. You sound puzzled. Maybe you can't handle the *heat*.'

'Estlin—'

'You must be *burning* with curiosity.'

'Can you—?'

'I'm sure an idea will *bloom* soon.'

'Stop speaking in riddles!'

He retreated, and she could hear his giggles drifting down from the weather station. Ani had played pranks on Payton back home, but she wasn't used to being on the receiving end of them. It wasn't fun.

'Estlin, you didn't burn it, did you?'

'No! My friend is wearing it.'

'You don't have any friends.'

'Neither do you.'

'I—' Ani felt the blood rush to her cheeks. She knew Estlin was trying to get a reaction, but he was right: Payton would probably never speak to her again; Kitt had said he wanted to be her friend, but she had no idea where he was. Locked away somewhere to be Jenipher's test subject, most likely.

'Urgh . . . If you're going to cry about it.' Estlin's green eyes peeked over the edge of the platform. 'I'll tell you. Dora has it. By the sunflowers.'

'Sunflowers?'

'North. Over the water towards Buckhill. You'll smell them.'

Ani stomped away without saying thank you. She didn't know who Dora was, but she followed his directions.

She crossed the bridge over the lake. It was another warm day, the first hint that summer lurked a few weeks away, with its yellow grass and lungfuls of pollen. In fact, as she crossed the scrubby grass of Buckhill, she almost felt like she could smell it: warm vegetation and ill-advised bonfires. She walked through a copse of thin saplings and brambles, to find that some woodland had been cleared to farm sunflowers.

The stems grew high above her head in long, neat rows, and at the top of each flowerhead petals of flame blazed around a hot cluster of black seeds. As she drew near, Ani heard them crackle, and occasionally spit a sparking seed on to the earth. At the heart of the clearing, surrounded by the burning flowers, was a scarecrow wearing Ani's pink cardigan.

Dora.

'I knew he didn't really have any friends,' she muttered to herself.

She started towards Dora, keeping her arms pressed close to her body so as not to nudge the plants. The heat seared her face. The burning smell suddenly became sickly and strong, and she realized it was her hair. She ran her hands through it quickly – it was only a strand or two that had burnt, so she pulled them out sharply, then knotted her hair into a tight bun and tucked it under her collar. A few steps further and a seed popped from a flower and landed on her wrist – the same hand as her cloirias burn. She yelped. Then one caught her cheek.

The crackling heat was growing fiercer, and she was only halfway to the cardigan. She thought about leaving it, but that would be letting Estlin win. She wasn't about to let him bully her out of Hyde

Gardens. She could see Dora's sackcloth face, which had a smile drawn clumsily on it, and was scarred with charred holes. The cardigan was starting to get burnt too.

Ani tucked her arms in tighter, screwed up her eyes against the heat and the flying seeds, ran to Dora and yanked the cardigan off her. One of her stuffed arms fell to the ground. Ani kicked it aside and ran back. She was nearly there – she could see green beyond the flaming orange-and-yellow sunflowers – when there was the loudest *pop* she'd heard yet, and suddenly her eye flashed with pain.

She cried out and fell to her knees. Her hands flew to her face, dropping the cardigan. She tried to blink, but her eyelid didn't obey her. It was stuck fast, scrunched with pain. She smelt her hair burning again. She thumped the ground with her fist to stop herself from shouting.

'Ani?'

She heard Estlin calling her, but she couldn't reply. Slowly, her eye started to water, and she did her best to move her face and let the tears work.

'This way. Come on. Up!'

He was at her ear, taking her elbow and pulling her to her feet.

He guided her along a zigzag route through the flames. Occasionally a flower's burning petals or seeds nearly caught them, but Estlin seemed to know exactly where to go to stay just out of their reach.

When they finally stumbled clear of the stems, Ani's eye was streaming and she felt her anger boiling over, hotter than any sunflower.

'What's wrong with you?' she shouted.

'You fell. I was helping you. Here.' Estlin held out the pink cardigan. A brown burn had reshaped the neckline.

Ani snatched it back.

'It's your fault I went in there in the first place!'

'It's just a piece of fabric. You didn't have to go after it.'

Her bad eye was starting to open, revealing a world blurred by tears. She felt anger bubbling up inside her. But it didn't feel poisonous and fiery. It felt right to be allowed to feel it. And it felt even better to throw it in Estlin's face:

'And you don't have to be such an idiot. I *hate* you.'

Pressing her shoulder against her eye, she ran back through the trees.

Ani went looking for the closest thing she had to a friend – Tally, who usually spent her days up by the palace.

The palace had perhaps lived up to its name once, when Lundain was first built on the rich soil of the Tamesas valley, but it had crumbled to ruin before any history book could record it. Hyde Gardens had grown around it, enveloped it. It had been taken over by the Wild.

Ani ran there, her heart pumping anger at Estlin through every vein in her body. Stepping 'inside' the palace meant crossing an invisible threshold, and noticing that the trees weren't trees any more, but pillars and archways covered with ivy, moss, climbing roses, almond-scented clematis and budding wisteria. The knee-high walls seemed like coincidences the first time Ani walked there, but over time she saw they created rooms, corridors and shortcuts, just like at King Jude's, though they had grown rounded, irregular, soft with mushrooms and weeds.

Ani found Tally sitting knitting on the crumbled ruins of a wall. White frills of cow parsley bent under her crossed ankles.

'Estlin tried to blind me,' Ani declared.

'That's not likely, dear,' said Tally. 'Estlin never tries to do anything.'

'Look!'

Tally lifted her eyes from her needles to take in the red, blotchy side of Ani's face.

'He made me go into the sunflowers.'

'Sunflowers can be very dangerous, Ani.'

'I know that now!' She joined Tally on the wall. 'I hate him.'

'He's not the easiest, but be patient with him, dear.'

Ani hesitated. 'It's weird. Even though he really annoyed me – made me *so* angry – it didn't feel like it normally does. It was like . . . It felt right to be angry. But that can't be right. Can it?'

'Only a few days in the gardens and you're on the mend already,' said Tally brightly.

'But how? I stopped taking my medicine.'

'It's the Wild.'

Ani looked at her sceptically. 'The Wild? Am I . . . cured?'

'There's no cure for your feelings, Ani. Only ways of learning to live with them. That's what the Wild does.'

'I don't understand.'

Tally put her knitting needles to one side.

'Sweetpea. You have grown up in a world with only two guilds. There's money and medicine, and if you're not a part of those, then you simply live in fear of them. No wonder it made you unwell. There's a wildness inside of you, and it needs tending from time to time. People aren't supposed to be . . .'

'Locked up?'

'Exactly.'

'That's what they wanted to do to me. It's what they did to my friend Kitt. But it didn't make him any better.'

'There is more than one way to save a life, Ani. It's

true, some people need medicines and nursing. These things are important for healing. But we mustn't forget other important, healing things. Things like diving into cold water, sleeping beneath the stars, eating fruit that's grown warm under the sun. Lying on the grass and thinking of nothing except the shapes of the clouds. That's what the methics have forgotten. But they will remember, one day.' Tally plucked at the singed cardigan on Ani's lap. 'Would you like me to fix this?'

'Yes.' Ani looked out at the trees and grass and flowers with a new sense of wonder. 'Yes, please.'

That night Ani tried to wrestle the wax cover over her hammock. There were bruised, swift clouds rolling over the city. The air felt heavy, the trees so still it was as if they were holding their breath. The rustle of the cover was eerily loud, and its buckles and eyelets and straps confounded her. Ani gave up, threw it on the ground and climbed into her hammock. Her eye was already less sore.

She woke when a fat raindrop smacked her cheek. Sitting up in the hammock, she saw only pitch black – there wasn't even the warmth of the city lights to tinge the sky orange. The trees were alive with the thrumming of leaves in the wind and the creak of branches. She rolled over, only to be smacked by a raindrop again. More followed, and within seconds the wood-land was being hammered, releasing the smell of warm, damp earth. Ani rolled out of her hammock and grabbed its wax cover, wrapping it around her and over her head, with just a gap to peer out of like a rabbit in its burrow. Resigned to not getting any sleep, she sat in the crook of a tree root and watched the water dance silver in the darkness.

A flash of lightning lit up every shadow in the woods, and an explosion of thunder followed seconds later. Ani looked up nervously at the tree and wondered if she would be safer out in the open. It was only a summer storm, she thought. Intense but quick, barely leaving a puddle in the morning.

Lightning hissed between the clouds and then forked down towards the earth. The boom of thunder followed even quicker than before. The woods creaked and moaned, as if they were about to be ripped up by the roots. Another roll of thunder bounced from corner to corner of Hyde Gardens. The rain flew in all directions, drenching everything. Ani decided to head to the lake, clear of the trees, at least until the lightning stopped. She wrapped the cover tighter around herself, got to her feet, and staggered through the trees, slipping in mud, over roots and logs. She blinked constantly to keep the rain from her eyes.

She had no idea how far it was to the edge of the

woods, or if she was heading in the right direction. The trees seemed ghostly, half-concealed by the curtain of rain, but she soon realized she was near the weather station, because she heard Estlin shout between the blasts of wind.

'Estlin?'

She thought he shouldn't be in the weather station in such a storm – the lightning could strike it, or the wind could blow it clean off its platform. She pushed the water out of her eyes and changed direction. The rain had found its way under her wax cover; it flattened her hair and trickled in cold tracks down her neck and chest.

'Estlin!'

The weather station materialized from the darkness so suddenly that she nearly walked into the ladder. She gripped the slippery rungs and craned her neck, yelling Estlin's name. It took another flash of lightning for her to spot him. He was drenched, his coat slick against his body as if it was a second skin, his curls plastered to his forehead and a crazed look in his eyes. One of the roof panels had blown off, leaving the room exposed to the storm. Estlin was using a broom to sweep some of the deluge of rainwater away, along with the mulch that must have been his cloud posters.

Ani started to climb. At one moment it felt like the wind was determined to rip her from the ladder, but the rungs were so wet she couldn't hurry or she'd slip and fall on to the roots below. When she reached the platform, Estlin didn't even acknowledge her. He was grappling with an armful of bottles and jars.

'Estlin, come down,' Ani shouted over the wind. 'It's dangerous up here. Estlin!'

She tried to grab his arm, but he shook her off with a ferocity that made her slip on the planks and land painfully on her elbow.

'You can't stop me!' he screamed at her.

'Stop you? What are you doing?'

'I'm catching the lightning!'

He spoke with feverish excitement; the bottles rattled in his arms.

'You're mad!' Ani left the wax cover on the floor as she got back up. She pushed her sodden hair out of her eyes. 'That's not sandglass. Even if you catch it, it won't hold the lightning.'

'I have to try.'

'Estlin, don't—'

'I don't have a choice—'

He grabbed the metal wire that trailed into the station and began wrapping it around one of the bottles, threading the end of it inside the glass. Ani staggered over and tried to pull the bottle from him. In the struggle, the other bottles slipped from under Estlin's arm and smashed on the floor.

'Get off!'

'You'll get hurt!'

'What do you care?'

The lightning burnt through the sky and twisted itself on to the weather station's antenna. Faster than a heartbeat, it tore through the rainwater. It hissed through the coils of wire – phosphorescent, hotter than any fire – until it landed in the glass bottle.

At that very moment Ani tore the bottle from Estlin's hands and shoved him out on to the deck.

The lightning exploded inside the weather station.

The force of it threw them from the deck on to the wet earth below. Ani landed on her back with a thud.

She lay there, trying to catch her breath.

When she could finally breathe again, she pushed herself up and saw that the weather station was on fire. Broken glass was scattered around her. All of Estlin's measuring equipment, his weather charts and papers, the walls and floor were all burning, crackling and fizzing in the rain, which was already easing off. The antenna hung off the side of the station, bent and broken like a twig hanging from a tree.

She scrambled to her feet and looked around for Estlin.

She spotted a smouldering flame a little way off – the sleeve of Estlin's coat was on fire. He was lying face down in the dirt.

'Estlin!'

She ran to him and rolled him over. He moaned. His face was streaked with mud.

'You're on fire! Take off your coat, quickly.'

She yanked his arms out, threw it on the ground and stamped on it until the sleeve only smoked. Then the crackle of the weather station and the patter of rain were the only sounds. Estlin gazed up at the weather station mournfully. He looked different without his coat. Younger, thinner.

For the first time, it was clear to Ani why Estlin was obsessed with the weather.

'Lightning,' she said. 'You're having lightning treatment, aren't you?' she said.

The rain had made the fabric of his shirt see-through, and she could see Estlin's chest was crisscrossed with thick leather straps. Wires crawled over his shoulders and attached to his chest with electrodes. Strapped to his back, between his shoulder blades, writhing in a sandglass canister sealed with rubber at the top and bottom, was white, roiling lightning.

The weather station, the sandglass, the spasms in Estlin's face and body made sense to her all at once. Ani had never seen lightning treatment at King Jude's – the methics never used it. Only wilders knew how to harness such a huge force of nature. She could only think of one reason why somebody would need such a treatment. A broken heart.

Estlin stood up too quickly. He swayed, never taking his eyes off his burning weather station. The fire was already beginning to die down, subsiding inside what was left of the walls.

'Here's your coat.' Ani picked it up and brushed the leaves and mud from it, suddenly awkward.

'That was the last of the spring storms.' His voice was low and hoarse. 'There might not be any more until the autumn. Weeks. Months.'

'We'll get you some sandglass before then,' she said.

'This is the last one I have,' he snapped, jabbing his thumb over his shoulder at the flickering canister. 'If it runs out, I won't be alive to collect it!'

'Oh.'

What she had done by breaking his last sandglass bottle suddenly hit Ani.

'I'm sorry. I didn't know.'

He looked at her, shivering in the ember light of the weather station.

'No, you . . . You shouldn't be sorry. You saved my life,' he said.

'You saved mine in the sunflowers.'

'I'm sorry about that.'

She smiled. 'I forgive you.'

'Come on.'

'Where are we going?'

'The one place around here that's always warm.'

By the time they reached the sunflowers, the clouds were clearing, and the stars peeked through to check on them. Steam came off them as their clothes dried in the warmth. Ani and Estlin slept back-to-back, a safe distance from the spitting seeds. Ani took longer to drift off. She was painfully aware of Estlin's lightning, that she was sleeping next to an element that, if it ever escaped, was strong enough to kill them both in an instant.

CHAPTER SIXTEEN

The stone floor of the library stuck to Payton's cheek. Something smelt metallic and cloying. At first she thought it was the broken vial of blood, then discovered it was her own blood, where she'd bitten the inside of her cheek.

She pushed herself upright quickly. The head rush made the vials on the shelves appear to lurch. She twisted around to find Jenipher watching her.

'J-Jenipher . . .'

Speaking made her feel nauseous. Some part of her felt that she was still with the fire-breathing girl. Her heart was pounding with terror. Was the inferno she'd just seen what Ani could turn into? She felt the over-whelming urge to find her sister and hold her close.

'It's Methic Blake,' Jenipher corrected her. 'I told you that you were not allowed in here.' She had changed into the unreadable, stern methic.

'I'm s-sorry. I know I shouldn't have, I just wanted to find . . . for my mother . . .'

'I know. I realized what you were trying to do when I found my grief sample rolling around on the floor. Do you have any idea what could happen if something like that was released?'

'I know.'

'It's incredibly dangerous. I was beginning to see you as a potential methic, not a reckless child, like that feral sister of yours.'

'I know it was wrong,' she said. 'But I'm desperate. My mother—'

'Payton, you are not the first person to have a loved one suffer from a disease,' Jenipher snapped. She then closed her eyes and touched her Guild Master medallion. Payton recognized an experienced methic pushing down her feelings.

Opening her eyes again, Jenipher observed her thoughtfully, then looked at the spilt blood smeared across the floor. 'You fainted again.'

'Yes.'

'But you said it's not a blood phobia.'

'It's not. I was just tired. Lightheaded. I didn't eat enough.'

'Look at me.'

Payton didn't know why she struggled to do this. It was as if the methic could read her thoughts and see the strange visions for herself. Jenipher stepped forward and the glass from the shattered vial crunched underfoot. The sound made Payton wince.

'There's something you're not telling me.' She fixed Payton with her penetrating gaze. 'I need to know the truth.'

'I told you.'

'Yes. But I need to *know*.'

Jenipher reached into the pocket of her methic's robes and brought out a pill box. She opened it and held out a tiny white pill to Payton.

'Take this.'

'What is it?'

'You can have it as a pill or as an injection,' Jenipher said sharply.

Payton hesitantly placed the pill on the back of her tongue. Just before she swallowed it, she breathed in the smell of burning leaves.

'Devil's snare!' Payton recognized the truth compound she and Jenipher had spoken about when she'd first arrived at Queen Cleo's. 'But you can't get devil's snare any more.'

'There's a black market for anything. I'd lie back down if I were you.'

Almost immediately Payton felt the Blood Library spin around her. She slumped back and Jenipher came to crouch down next to her.

Payton's tongue felt heavy and loose, and her vision blurred so that all the vials of blood around her appeared to blend into one shining red wall. A taste of bitter herbs filled her mouth.

'Jenipher?' She couldn't stand the whimper of fear in her voice.

When Jenipher replied, her voice sounded closer than it really was, almost as if it was coming from within Payton's own head.

'Stay calm. This is very simple. I will ask you questions. You will tell the truth.'

Jenipher's voice warped and echoed, until it didn't really sound like Jenipher at all. It sounded like Payton's conscience was speaking to her, stating simple facts to soothe her. She couldn't imagine lying to the voice; it would have been like lying to herself.

'Your name is Payton Darke,' the voice said.

'Yes.'

'Your father is Methic Neel Darke, of King Jude's Hospital.'

'Yes.'

'Your mother has water fever.'

'Yes.'

The voice paused. Payton was starting to relax. Listening to the voice was like floating on a still body of water. It made her feel weightless, careless.

'You wish to be a methic.'

'Yes.'

'You wish to cure your mother.'

'Yes.'

'Because you believe your father will fail your mother.'

A twinge in her stomach – an anger that felt very far away from her in that moment. 'Yes.'

'Mmm,' said the voice thoughtfully. 'Parents can disappoint us, just like anybody else. But it stings so much worse.'

Payton whispered, 'Yes.' After a pause she asked, 'Who are you?'

Straightaway, a wave of nausea came over her. She groaned and the voice warned, 'It is better if you do not ask questions. Questions are not the truth.'

'I understand.'

'You know where your sister is.'

'No.'

The nausea left as suddenly as it had arrived.

'You are in the Blood Library.'

'Yes.'

'You handled a blood sample.'

'Yes.'

'You know who this blood belongs to.'

'No.'

'You broke the vial.'

'Yes.'

'On purpose?'

'It was an accident.'

'And then you fainted.'

'I didn't mean to,' she said. 'I never mean to.'

The voice didn't reply, and Payton felt certain it was because it was listening to her. And waiting. Because somehow the voice knew. It knew the secret she kept locked carefully away. It knew what happened whenever she touched blood. She had never been tempted to tell anybody about it before, but with the voice she felt safe. She felt like the voice would understand.

'It's always an accident,' she continued. 'I can't control it.'

'Tell me what happens.'

'Everybody says it's fainting, but it's not really. When I touch the blood, I have these dreams – visions – I don't know why. I'm not squeamish. That's why I hate it when people say I'm scared of blood. I'm not. I'll make a good methic, I think. But I can't tell them what really happens.' Her tongue was feeling less heavy. Her vision began to sharpen again.

'What really happens?'

'The blood . . . it takes me somewhere.'

The voice was changing. It no longer felt like Payton was speaking to herself. She felt her heart beating faster as she became more aware of the room around her.

'Somewhere else? Where? Where does it take you?'

'Jenipher?'

The devil's snare was wearing off. The taste of herbs was gone. Payton sat up and found Jenipher staring intently at her, her face impossible to read. Even though Payton knew the voice she'd heard had been Jenipher's, she couldn't shake the feeling the devil's snare had created: that she'd been speaking to the most trusted version of herself.

'Where exactly?' Jenipher asked.

'It's stopped working.'

'Answer me anyway. Answer me because you want to.'

'I . . . I don't know where to begin.'

'At the beginning.' Jenipher crossed her legs. She and Payton were sitting facing each other on the floor of the Blood Library, like they were equals. 'I'm listening.'

Jenipher wanted a methic's explanation. One that was detailed, ordered and left nothing out, in case it proved important later. Payton explained as much as she could. She talked and talked, and Jenipher listened with her chin in her hands and her elbows on her knees. A hard, keen energy tensed her features.

Payton explained that her memories of the first dreams were hazy. As a little girl, she didn't have them at all. As she got older, they were more of a strange lurching feeling, like falling into another place for a moment before falling back. She had told her mother, who had told her not to worry. They were just special dreams. But she made her swear never to tell anyone, not even her father, because some people were jealous of the dreams. Payton had made the promise willingly. It hardly seemed to matter – she rarely touched another person's blood anyway. But the visions grew more vivid as she got older, then her mother became ill, and the one person she could speak to about them was taken away from her. They moved from the Isles to King Jude's and the dreams became full-blown visions she couldn't escape from, full of strange places and currents that she couldn't fight. Only the vision could release her – she could never find her own way out.

'At the blood reading,' Jenipher said, 'you touched your sister's blood . . . It happened then, didn't it?'

'Yes.' It felt a relief to finally admit it to someone.

'I knew something wasn't right. You looked asleep, but focused. Then when you woke you looked . . . frightened. When you asked to stay here, I'll admit I wanted to see if it would happen again.'

'You did?'

'Such a promising young methic. You had no problem dealing with our patients. You didn't mind looking at blood. Why would the touch of it have such an effect on you?'

Jenipher leant forward and took Payton's cold hands in her own. Jenipher's hands were dry and strong. A healer's hands. Payton felt like she would trust them with anything. The weight of her secret was lifting already.

'Do you believe in fate, Payton?'

'No.'

'Neither do I. But I believe that, with enough time and enough chaos, some of us get to experience something like it.' She squeezed Payton's hands and then released them. 'I think you can read.'

'Of course I can read.'

'No, you misunderstand me. I mean: read blood.'

'No. There aren't measures or feelings or anything like the gwaidmesur,' Payton explained. 'I told you, it's like a dream. There's nothing logical about it.'

'But there is. It's a logic you cannot see yet. Now. These visions. Is it like you have access to two worlds and you can't hold both of them in front of you?'

'Yes!' Payton leant forward. She had never heard the feeling, which she'd always thought was specific to herself and her visions, explained so clearly by somebody else. 'Do you get them too?'

'No.'

'Oh.' She couldn't hide her disappointment.

'But I've waited all my life to meet somebody who does.'

'Really?'

'A human gwaidmesur is very unusual. I've never met one. They used to have their own guild, you know. It was very small, because the natural ability to read blood is so rare. But people were suspicious of them. Blood reading was declared unethical. The guild was disbanded and its members were . . . well, persecuted. Such a special gift,' Jenipher said sadly, 'yet they were thrown away as if they were no better than any of those other useless guilds.' Payton was trying to concentrate on what she was being told, but she was distracted by the expression on Jenipher's face. It was only there for a flash, but in that instant she looked at Payton as if she were the most precious thing on the earth.

Payton didn't like how it made her feel: warmed, protected. She didn't trust the feeling.

'I don't see what dreams have to do with blood reading,' she mumbled.

'Our blood . . .' Jenipher became the methodical methic explaining the science of the world again. She rubbed her fingers against her palms and looked down at her own flesh. 'Our blood holds everything that we are. Every feeling we have, even the ones we aren't aware of. The machine we have matches the blood to the pure, distilled feelings I have loaded into it. Then it measures them. But a human blood-reader is far more sophisticated . . . It's like . . .' Jenipher paused as she tried to explain the phenomenon in a way the girl could understand. 'A blood-reader can instinctively use those feelings to create an entire world. Like the most detailed painting. What the machine does is only a pencil sketch in comparison.'

'So, when I touched Ani's blood,' Payton said slowly, 'I was looking into some sort of world made out of . . . her?'

'In a way, yes. And you can do it with anyone.'

'That blood I touched earlier, from the vial. It was horrible. There was this girl, and fire—'

'Forget about that. That girl is long gone. Payton.' Jenipher spoke like a parent pleading with their child. 'This is a rare and powerful gift. And you've brought it to *me*. Just as I'm trying to get the blood-reading programme running. I'm trying to save a whole generation from the wretched burden of feelings! You can help me. I'll teach you. There's nothing about medicine that can't be learnt here at Queen Cleo's. I'll help you harness this gift, and you can be a part of the programme.'

'I can still be your assistant?'

'More than that. When I'm gone, you can continue my work. You will be my legacy, along with all these children I'll save. Children like your poor sister. Doesn't she deserve to live safe from her darkest feelings?'

Payton remembered how it felt when the inferno hit

the glass between her and the fire girl in the blood vision. She certainly didn't want that for Ani. And yet . . .

'I don't think I can.' The flash of disappointment on Jenipher's face was almost more than Payton could bear. 'You don't understand. My mother needs help. I have to become a methic for *her*. If I leave her treatment down to my father, she'll never wake up. The other methics will find and help Ani.'

'Your father is closer to a water-fever cure than you think.'

'No, he isn't. He's not even working on it. He's doing the blood-reading programme with you.'

'Payton, you don't understand,' Jenipher insisted. 'With this gift, you'll be more than just a methic. You will be the most powerful methic in over a hundred years. You won't rot away in a hospital with a reputation like King Jude's. That sample of maternal grief alone isn't enough to help your mother – if it was, I would have given it to your father. Making cures isn't as simple as that. You need resources to cure a disease like water fever, and I can give you them. Do this, and one day you'll have anything you want. Queen Cleo's labs. The best methics. Botanicals from the black market. Access to everything in our Feelings Library.'

Payton felt a knot in her stomach grow, but it was different to the fear she felt when she'd taken the devil's snare.

Hope.

Wonder.

She dared to picture it: a future where she not only cured water fever, but where every methic in the city respected and marvelled at her. She'd be like the methics in the paintings in the Feelings Library, when they started to treat patients after the Turn. Her father and Ani and Gilchrist would regret doubting her, holding her back. Her mother would beam with gratitude and stroke her hair when she woke up.

'A powerful methic?' she asked.

'The *most* powerful methic.'

CHAPTER SEVENTEEN

After the storm, Estlin and Ani barely left each other's side.

Ani was Estlin's very first friend, and he began to see what all the fuss was about. He had somebody to help him fix the weather station and play pranks on Henrich. When he went to the market, it was nice knowing that somebody would be waiting for him when he got home, and Ani was always keen to hear about what he had seen and done. She longed to join him, but Estlin had seen too many methics walking through the city, stopping people to ask if they'd seen a small dark-haired girl.

Estlin had admitted to Ani that he didn't know of anything in Hyde Gardens that could help with spark breath or water fever. Ani confessed that she had no idea if there was sandglass at King Jude's – and she couldn't risk going back there to check for him. Ani was happy in Hyde Gardens, but, as the weeks passed, she began to feel trapped. For as long as her father and Jenipher had people looking for her, she couldn't leave. She began to worry that she'd never see her mother or Payton ever again. When these thoughts made her sad or angry, she went to the lake and threw stones into the water; she watched the ripples until they flattened into nothing, and she felt better for it.

Ani and Estlin spent most of their time at the weather station. Its tree had been gouged in half by the lightning strike, its bark stripped in places to expose the pale, vulnerable wood beneath. Burnt leaves littered the ground around it, smelling smoky and autumnal. They picked up shards of glass and laid new planks for the deck. Ani shared stories of King Jude's, and Estlin started to tell jokes just to hear her laugh.

Having nothing else to do, Ani helped Estlin with his secret harvests of valuable plants, flowers and seeds to sell to the merchants. She learnt which ones were the rarest specimens, tended by the wilders to protect them for future generations. She also learnt which ones were nothing more than common weeds, which Estlin 'marketed' as something different.

'You shouldn't do that,' Ani was telling him one day as they whacked new nails into the blackened ladder for the weather station.

'Why not?'

'It's lying. What if someone really needs what you've promised, like I did when I first met you?'

'You mean like you did with the sandglass?'

'I was just trying to make you feel better.'

'That's what I'm doing here. What other people believe is their problem. Making money is mine. The financiers taught me that.'

'You know financiers?' Ani was impressed. She had seen the gold-robed men and women visit King Jude's once in a while, but she'd never spoken to them.

'Yep.'

'Why would financiers talk to you?'

'Because I'm fascinating.'

'Seriously!'

Estlin shook his head as if he was trying to decide if he could trust her with a secret.

Ani scoffed. 'You're full of it. You don't know any financiers.'

'Fine. I'll show you. But you can't tell anyone, all right? Especially not Tally and Henrich.'

'I won't.'

'Promise?'

'Yes!'

'Swear it. Swear on the gwaidlamp.'

Ani pulled the gwaidlamp from her pocket. Estlin put his hand on it, so the shades of green light swirled together.

'I swear.'

'Great.' Estlin shuddered as a pulse of lightning coursed through him. 'We have to go to see my dad.'

Ani blinked with surprise, thinking she'd misheard him. 'Sorry – did you say your "dad"?'

Estlin didn't reply. He was already disappearing into the trees. She had to run to catch up with him.

Estlin headed south until the trees thinned out into a wide, sun-filled clearing. It was a part of the gardens Ani hadn't explored yet. The trees stood apart from each other, and only the leaves of the oldest, tallest ones could touch overhead. The light was buttery and slow-moving from the lack of breeze.

'What kind of trees are these?' Ani asked, wobbling as she leant right back to look at them.

'Sgerbod trees.'

'We're not really meeting your father, are we?' Ani had always assumed Estlin didn't have any parents. Only Tally and Henrich. He'd never mentioned any family.

She followed him through the clearing. The bark on the sgerbod trees was strangely smooth and knuckled, like bones locking together.

At the far end of the clearing, Estlin approached a particular tree and walked around it. Ani followed, and gasped when she looked at the tree trunk.

'It's horrible!' she blurted, without thinking.

The bark did indeed look like bones. Because it *was* bones. The trees grew on exposed roots, with dark, mossy caves visible beneath them. While most of the roots plunged into the ground, others had pulled something up out of the earth. A body. The tree had scooped someone from their grave and cradled their remains, its bark growing over the skeleton. Ani could see the shape of a ribcage, even an outstretched hand.

'It's not horrible,' said Estlin, with a hint of hurt in his voice.

'No, it's . . . I didn't mean . . . I was just surprised, that's all. So that's your father?'

'Yes.'

The shape of the skeleton showed a body that was lying back, as if pulled up by its chest, its arms and legs hanging down in surrender. Estlin reached out and placed a hand over the outline of fingers, knuckles and carpal bones.

'Did the tree . . . kill him?' Ani looked up at the leaves, innocent and bright above her.

'Yes, Ani. These are mad killer trees. Don't tug their leaves, they hate that.'

'Um—'

'Obviously not! Look, wilders are buried like this when they die. The sgerbod tree brings you up, out of the earth and into nature again. For ever. Most of my family are here. Except on my mother's side; they're in Battersea Meadows.'

Ani had never imagined that there were living graves in the tangle of trees she saw from her window back at King Jude's.

'Is your mother there?'

'No.'

'Where is she?'

'I don't know. She left.'

She waited for Estlin to say more, but when he didn't, she simply said, 'Oh,' and reached her hand out tentatively to touch the tree's bark. She was almost surprised to find that it felt just like any other tree. Her fingers were close to the outline of Estlin's father's hand, but she couldn't bring herself to touch it.

'How did he die?'

'Invisibility. After my mum . . . you know. Whatever.'

'I'm sorry.'

Estlin turned around and leant against his father's tree. His face relaxed and his shoulders lowered, the way a person does when they are hugged.

'At least he's here,' he said. 'He was really passionate about preserving the ways of the wilders. He wanted to get more people to join in secret, to save the other parks, teach people about the ways of the Wild again. I know there aren't any real wilders any more, but he'd have wanted to be buried like one. It was the only good part about him dying, actually. No feelings means no disease: he became fully visible again, so I got to see him one last time.'

'Is that when your heart broke?'

'Yeah . . . Henrich didn't want to take me to the methics. He's never trusted them. So he found some sandglass, tracked the storms and made me this.' He jerked a thumb over his shoulder.

Ani asked him something she'd always wanted to know, but it had never felt like the right time.

'Does it hurt? The lightning?'

'Yes.'

Ani looked at the other human shapes in the trees around them – the graceful curve of vertebrae, the haunting smile of a skull. She was starting to see what Estlin meant. It was beautiful. Better than a dark, cloying grave under the earth.

'When we die, will we turn into one of these?' she asked.

'I don't know.' Estlin came to stand beside her, his hands deep in the pockets of his singed coat. Ani felt him twitch at a release of lightning. 'Sgerbod trees are only for proper wilders. That's not me.'

'Methics let other methics study their bodies. They have their anatomy modelled in wax or sketched by artists, and then they're displayed around the hospital. Methic Gilchrist's grandfather's bronchioles are in the

Small Dining Room – they did it by filling the airways of the lungs with resin then letting the tissue around it dissolve.'

'That's disgusting,' Estlin said matter-of-factly.

Ani turned to him. 'But bones and lungs and things aren't the important bits, are they? Your feelings are what makes you who you are.'

'I never believed that.'

'Really?'

'Feelings mostly come and go. I'm still me. That never changes.'

'I definitely feel better since being here. Tally's right – sometimes wild things can fix you just fine. I wonder what the gwaidmesur would say if it measured my blood now.'

'Who cares? No one really knows what's inside another person. Especially not a machine.'

Ani was glad to hear that that was what Estlin thought about the gwaidmesur. Even if everyone back at King Jude's thought she was bad and dangerous, he never would. She felt a rush of affection for him as he leant against his father's tree.

'I promise not to tell anyone your father is here.'

'Oh! No, *he's* not the secret.'

'Then what is?'

'This.'

He gestured at the ground.

A weed grew enthusiastically beneath their feet in the shade of the sgerbod tree, choking out any grass. It was dotted with black flowers no bigger than a fingernail.

'What is it?' Ani asked as she crouched down.

'WAIT! Don't touch it!' Estlin shouted so suddenly that she almost fell. 'It's called anghofio,' he told her. He rummaged in his coat pocket and unrolled the strip of leather that contained his tools, plucking out a pair of scissors and some pincers with long handles. Carefully, he pinched a single flower stem and cut it. He dropped it into an open vial and sealed it tightly before he let Ani hold it.

'It only grows under sgerbod trees,' he explained. 'It's very rare. But if you see it, you should never touch it.'

'What's so dangerous about it?'

'Anghofio. In the Old Language, it means "forgetting".'

'What does it make you forget?'

'Everything. That's why they grow under sgerbod trees. My dad told me that wilders first planted them there in case, when visiting someone you love, your grief became too much. You could touch the flowers and forget whose grave you were looking at. You'd forget ever loving them. You'd forget how to feel anything at all.' He looked up at his father's tree. 'But I don't really know why anyone would want to do that.'

Ani thought of her mother in her water chamber.

Thinking of her there made her sad, but she certainly didn't want to forget her. Not even for a second.

'I don't either.'

She admired the minuscule flower in the vial. Its petals were so dark they seemed to absorb light. It was hard to imagine something so small could have such a strong effect.

'So why do you grow it if you don't want to use it?'

'If I tell you, you can't tell *anyone* what I've done.'

'I already promised I wouldn't. You can trust me.'

'All right, then. It all started a few weeks ago. Before you arrived. The financiers asked for a meeting with Henrich and Tally. I wasn't meant to go, but I sneaked along because I wanted to see inside their guild. They asked Henrich and Tally to harvest the flowers and sell them to the Guild of Finance. Ani, you wouldn't believe how much money they were offering.'

'Just for these?' Ani held up the flower in the vial.

'Yep. But Henrich and Tally said no. The financier they were speaking to didn't like that. But then he offered them something else. He said, if they gave him the flowers, he'd reinstate the guild. He'd let us be wilders again.'

Ani's eyes widened. 'That's amazing!'

'But Henrich and Tally still said no.'

'What?'

'When they got back to Hyde Gardens, they had a

huge argument; Tally wanted to burn all the anghofio to stop anybody getting it, ever.'

'Why didn't she?'

'Because it's sacred. It would be like cutting down a sgerbod tree – you can't do something like that and call yourself a wilder. Henrich wouldn't let her. And he's right. You can't destroy it. But harvesting is different. Don't you think?'

Ani narrowed her eyes. 'Estlin. What have you done?'

He took a deep breath, then his confession came out so quickly it sounded like one word: 'I've-been-harvesting-the-flowers-on-the-sly-and-selling-them-to-the-financiers.' He wiped his forehead. 'Phew. I actually feel better for telling you.'

'You've been selling them? Even though Tally and Henrich clearly think it's a bad idea?'

'You can't tell them! You promised.'

Ani shook her head. 'I won't, but . . . why do the financiers want the flowers so badly?'

Estlin shrugged. 'Apparently they sell it to that methic you don't like. Now listen – there's lots here. And I'll need some help harvesting them all. Henrich and Tally still argue about it from time to time, and I'm worried Tally might do something stupid and destroy it. I can offer you two per cent of the profits . . . All right, five. No, three!'

Ani couldn't think about maths. She was too fixated on what Estlin had just said.

'The methic I don't like? Do you mean Jenipher Blake?'

'The woman with the short hair. Works at Queen Cleo's.'

'That's her . . .'

'Three and a half. Final offer.'

'Why would Jenipher suddenly want to buy loads of forgetting flowers?'

'Who cares! I'm making you the offer of a lifetime!'

'Oh.' Ani felt a chill zip straight up her spine and back down again as a thought entered her head. 'Oh, no.'

'What?'

'It makes you numb. Like, feelingless?'

'If you touch lots of it.'

'She was talking about a treatment programme. My father was too. He wanted her to heal me. Estlin – this is how she's going to do it!'

'It's for medicine?'

'The gwaidmesur tells Jenipher if you have bad feelings . . . but how does Jenipher then get rid of those feelings? With *this*. This is why she's buying it. She's going make anyone like me . . . well, numb.'

She and Estlin looked at the anghofio flower while this theory sank in.

'You can't sell it to her,' Ani said finally.

'I don't sell it to her, I sell it to the financiers,' said Estlin defensively. 'Besides, it's too late.'

'What?'

'This is the second spring harvest. They already have lots of it. I don't get paid until I hand over all of it, but when I do, I'm going to build a weather station like you've never seen.'

'This is more important than your stupid weather station!'

The look of hurt on Estlin's face made Ani feel terrible as soon as she'd said it.

'Sorry. I'm sorry – of course we'll work on catching more lightning. That's important too. It's just . . . If I go back home, they'll give me whatever horrible treatment she's made from these flowers. What if I forget everything? Even my mother? I can't ever go home . . .' The full horror of this idea began to descend on her. 'I can't go home. And it's not just me. My father was finding test subjects for Jenipher Blake. She'll do it to anyone without balanced blood, like—' She clapped her hands to her mouth, but a cry escaped her lips anyway. 'Kitt!'

'Who?'

'He was my friend.'

'She's mad.' Estlin shook his head. 'Though I suppose that's methics for you.'

'We have to stop her!'

'We?'

'Yes! If we stop her using these flowers, she can't make any medicine.'

'We?'

'Then I'll be able to go back to King Jude's. I'll show them that the Wild healed me. They won't be able to lock me up if there's nothing wrong with me!'

'I really want to talk about this "we".'

'Who else is going to do it? The financiers just want to get paid. The methics are all scared of her. It has to be us!' Ani tossed the vial with the harvested flower on the ground. 'Let's show them what the Wild can do! What do you say?'

Estlin took a deep breath, pushed his hands deep into his trouser pockets and looked thoughtfully at the sgerbod grove, which was solemn with the silence of his ancestors. For a moment, Ani saw him as he could be: prince-like, heroic. Then he took a pie out of his pocket.

'Nope.' He bit into it deeply.

'Estlin!'

'Ani, this is guild stuff!' Crumbs sprayed on to her face. 'Let's just leave it alone and get rich. We'll be much happier here. We'll catch some lightning, swim in the lake, go star-gazing. Leave all that nonsense to the grown-ups.'

'How can you say that?'

'Look at it this way. If you're trapped here, then I get to see you all the time.' He spread his hands and beamed. 'I'm just being a good friend.'

'That's not how to be a good friend!'

'Isn't it?'

'A good friend puts their friend first.'

He cocked his head to one side as he thought about this. 'Are you sure? That doesn't sound much fun. Friends should be fun.'

Ani knocked the pie out of his hands. It rolled into a cluster of anghofio flowers.

'Hey!'

'Estlin. We're going to speak to the financiers. And we're going to make sure that Jenipher can't use these flowers on *anyone*.'

When he didn't say anything, she added, 'I wouldn't go back to King Jude's all the time, you know. I'd be here lots too.'

'Promise?'

'I'll swear on the gwaidlamp. If you promise to help me.'

She held out the gwaidlamp. The bark-covered bones of Estlin's father were bathed in the green light.

'What will it be?' she asked him. 'Money or friendship?'

CHAPTER EIGHTEEN

'Estlin!'

He swung round, the sack of flowers over his shoulder.

'What?'

'What if it doesn't work?'

'It will work. You'll have me there. Besides, I know all the escape routes. I never trust a financier.'

'Are you sure you can't see any methics?'

He looked up and down the road.

'None. Let's go. Quick.'

It wasn't a perfect plan, Ani thought, but it was the best they had. There was no way she could storm into Queen Cleo's Hospital and turn the place upside down looking for the anghofio flowers without Jenipher capturing her. She needed to know more about what Jenipher was up to, and she needed to be sneaky about it. A few clues from the financiers was her best hope.

She and Estlin had filled the sack with moon-flowers, then, they had carefully harvested just a few of the anghofio flowers and scattered them on top. When they took the sack to the financiers to sell, as long as they only peeked inside, they would be none the wiser. And she and Estlin would seize their chance to find out where Jenipher was keeping the rest of the anghofio so they could destroy it.

But when she was finally about to creep out of Hyde Gardens for the first time, Ani began to doubt herself.

The sun had just set, and the city's street lights sputtered. After replacing the wooden railing at the secret entrance, Ani and Estlin kept to the shadows as much as they could. They were heading towards a corner where the gardens ended and the city became busier. There, illuminated over a dark stairwell, was the sign of the financiers – a gold circle.

They stood at the top of the stairs, looking down. Nobody came or went. It was silent.

'Do we just walk in?' Ani asked nervously.

'Yep. We find someone and ask for Darian. He's the one who wants the anghofio.'

The walls of the stairwell were smooth, polished brick. When they reached the bottom, there was a door. Something glinted on the threshold. Estlin knocked.

It opened a crack.

'We're here to see Darian Montagu.'

He held up the sack of flowers, and the door swung open.

The Guild of Finance was a complex warren of passageways, offices and apartments that ran underneath most of the city. The entrances to the guild, with their illuminated gold signs, were a common sight in most parts of the city, although nobody outside of the guild knew how they were all linked. Ani didn't know what she'd expected, but she found herself staring down a long corridor, lined with cream tiles and glittering gold bricks. Chandeliers dazzled overhead, low enough that some adults would have to stoop.

'The Guild of Finance,' Estlin whispered to her dramatically.

A woman in gold robes had opened the door. She looked younger than many of the junior methics, Ani thought. She didn't speak to them – only crinkled her nose at their dirty clothes – and began to lead the way through the labyrinthine corridors.

Ani and Estlin walked side by side, running their hands over the gold bricks, trying to pick up flecks of jewels they spotted on the floor when they were sure the woman leading them wasn't looking.

'Just think how much gold must be down here,' Ani whispered. 'They probably have whole rooms of it.

Mountains of it!'

'I saw a room full of rubies once when I walked past. They were in all these little glass boxes that lined the walls. They were guarded by badgers, though.'

Ani glanced at him. 'I can't tell if you're joking.'

'Believe what you want. I'll probably never find it again – they take me a different way every time.'

They reached a corridor that was longer and wider than any other. There were bejewelled doors at regular intervals. One door was less glittering and majestic than the others. It was plain wood, with thin lines of gold decorating it in an intricate knot pattern. A simple blue crystal was embedded in the centre of the pattern.

The woman knocked on the door, then turned to Estlin and tried to take the bag of flowers from his hands. He clutched it tightly.

'No. I deliver them myself.'

She looked as if she might argue, but at that moment he shuddered from a lightning release. She cried out at the jolt of electricity and quickly let go. Then the door opened.

'Estlin. And . . .?'

'A friend. I have your order.'

'Then you are welcome.'

A gold medallion hung around Darian Montagu's neck. Ani had only seen one once before, on Jenipher

Blake. It meant that Darian was the Guild Master.

He ushered them into the office, closing the door on the gold-robed woman without even a thank you. Ani suddenly felt very small in the presence of the most powerful person in Lundain; she couldn't help looking at him with a mixture of awe, curiosity and shyness. The anghofio flowers must be incredibly valuable if the Master of the Guild of Finance was interested in them.

Darian was dressed all in black, his gold robes draped over the chair behind his desk. He invited Ani and Estlin to sit opposite him. Ani perched on the edge of the chair, then found herself sitting back and sinking into it. It was deliciously comfortable.

'We are not acquainted,' he said to Ani, his voice smooth as honey. She couldn't pin an age on him. His skin was unlined and his hair was fair and shining. All of his features were fair, she noticed. His eyes were a cold blue, and his eyebrows and lashes were so pale it was like they weren't there at all until they caught the light. It made his gaze all the more penetrating.

'I'm –' Ani hesitated only for a beat – 'I'm Rosa.'

Estlin glanced at her. 'I needed help with the harvest.'

'I can see that.'

Darian slipped on a pair of leather gloves and held out a hand for the bag. Estlin reluctantly handed it over. It took all of Ani's self-control not to look at him as Darian pulled a set of brass scales close and balanced the bag on it. He checked the weight, then opened the bag only a fraction to look inside. He nodded approvingly. Ani let out her breath slowly.

In one swift movement, Darian was up again. He pushed at the corner of his office wall and it swung inward, revealing a walk-in safe. Ani craned her neck to look inside, but anything of interest was kept inside iron chests.

When she heard a growl from under her feet, she nearly jumped out of her skin. A badger waddled out from under Darian's desk and looked at them with beady, angry eyes.

'Told you,' Estlin mouthed at Ani.

Darian shut the bag inside the safe, returned to his desk and began to count out gold coins. He pushed a small stack of them towards Estlin.

'Thank you, Estlin,' he said. 'Until next time.'

'Yes.'

When neither Estlin nor Ani moved, Darian asked, 'Is there something the matter with the payment?'

'No! No, thank you, it's just . . .'

'We were wondering what you do with the harvest?' Ani asked.

'We sell it to an interested party.'

'Right. I know. It's just . . .' She didn't know how to begin the conversation with him. 'They're quite dangerous, the flowers, and—'

'My buyer understands what it is they're purchasing,' Darian assured her. 'Now, if you'll excuse me. I have a busy day.'

The badger began snuffling at Ani's feet. She longed to nudge it away, but she didn't dare.

'We found something in Hyde Gardens when we were harvesting,' Ani told him. 'We thought it might be valuable.'

Darian made a steeple from his fingers and rested his chin on them. 'Really?'

'Yeah.'

Ani placed the gwaidlamp on the table with a *thunk*. She didn't miss Darian's eyes widening just a fraction.

'What an interesting trinket,' he said with a mild smile.

'I know what it is. I know how rare they are.'

The smile vanished and he became sharper, more business-like. Ani preferred him that way.

'How much?' He reached forward and wrapped his fingers around the gwaidlamp, without lifting it from the desk. Ani saw gold light flicker in the gaps between his fingers.

'We don't need money. We'll trade it for information. As long as you don't tell anyone we were asking for it.'

Darian released the gwaidlamp and looked at Ani. He really looked at her, she noticed, as if seeing her for the first time.

'Who are you?'

'We know Methic Blake is buying the anghofio flowers.'

Darian's gaze became particularly still and cold.

'I couldn't possibly comment.'

'Where does she take it?'

'Why would you want to know that?'

'Because she's going to do something bad with it.'

'Then take it up with the Guild of Medicine.'

'She *is* the Guild of Medicine. Look, just tell us where she keeps it. Which hospital – Queen Cleo's? King Jude's?'

When Darian didn't answer, Ani stood up and took the gwaidlamp off the desk.

'Thank you for your time,' she said with a coldness to match his.

She headed to the door, the badger at her heels. Estlin pulled the coins for the anghofio flowers towards him, then hesitated, standing between Ani and Darian, unsure if she really meant to leave.

'Very well.'

Darian's words made Ani stop, her hand on the door handle. He came towards them. Estlin backed away until he was pressed against the door with Ani. Darian scooped up the growling badger, tucked it into the crook of his arm and stroked its bristling grey fur.

'The place you are looking for is not one of the

hospitals. It is called the Observatory. Although, I'm afraid this is a rather foolish trade on your part – it is not a place you are able to visit.' He held out his hand.

Not only was she trapped, but Ani also believed in keeping her word when it came to a trade. She placed the gwaidlamp in Darian's palm.

'Thank you,' she said. The three of them watched the filaments glow yellow. The badger sniffed it curiously, its nose pressed against the glass. Ani felt a pang at the thought of never seeing her own green light again.

'My pleasure.' He rubbed his thumb over the smudge of gold that Kitt had left on it.

She opened the door and she and Estlin were nearly over the threshold when Darian gently took hold of her hand. Startled, she didn't resist. He peeled her fingers open to reveal the blue scar on her palm.

'Miss Darke.'

Ani froze.

'How strange,' he mused. 'The methics are looking for you, yet here you are asking questions about the methics.' The gwaidlamp in his hand glowed brighter and brighter. Darian's eyes looked almost violet as they reflected the colour. 'I don't concern myself with the politics of those quacks, with their potions and grubby hospitals. But rumour has it that your father is saying that your return to King Jude's would fetch a good . . . *price.*'

'NO!'

Ani yanked her wrist free and pushed the financier as hard as she could. He staggered – and dropped the gwaidlamp. There was a terrible smash and its filaments scattered across the floor. The startled badger wriggled free and landed on its paws, snapping at the air.

'Run!' Estlin yelled.

He grabbed Ani, and together they pelted down the corridor.

The badger's screaming bark followed them.

They bolted around the corner, up flights of stairs, but the badger was close behind. In between its barks they heard Darian shouting, ordering the financiers to stop the children.

'Down, boy! Down. Bad badger!' Estlin tried kicking it, but he tripped and fell. The badger latched on to the hem of his coat.

Ani rushed back to help him.

'Just take it off!' She yanked the coat off his shoulders and threw it at the badger. It became a furious, snarling bundle of fabric.

'Let it go.'

'I need it!'

'You don't!'

She helped Estlin up.

The guild was busier the further they went, and they barged past groups of shocked, gold-robed financiers.

One of them dropped a purse of coins that clattered and rolled all over the floor, but Ani and Estlin were gone before they could even shout at them.

'Which way?'

'Here!' Estlin tugged Ani up more stairs and down a golden corridor. The shouts behind them were getting louder. One final staircase – Ani felt her lungs burning – and they were at a door like the one they came in through. They yanked it open, and ran up the stairwell.

It led to an ordinary Lundain street. The air felt fresh after the underground guild.

'Come on.' Estlin pulled her down first one side street, then another. Ani couldn't keep up with the twists and turns, but when they were far away from the guild entrance, she jerked them into a stop.

'The Guild Master!' she pressed her turquoise palm to her forehead in horror. 'I shoved the *financiers'* Guild Master.'

'And I couldn't . . . be prouder of you.' Estlin gasped as he drew breath. 'Stupid badger. That coat will never look as good on him as it did me.'

They were in a narrow alley. The only light came from the lightning on Estlin's back. Ani wished they had the steady green light of the gwaidlamp to illumi-nate the way. They were quiet for a while, catching their breath, until Ani asked, 'The Observatory . . . what is that?'

'Hmm. I've only ever heard stories about it. To be honest, I didn't know it was real.'

'What do you mean?'

'Well, for one thing, when the other kids in the market mention it, they say it's haunted.'

Ani scoffed. 'That's ridiculous.'

'Either way, it makes sense as a hiding place. If the rumours are right, it's somewhere in Greenwich.'

'How long will it take us to get there?'

'Us?'

'Yes. Us! You and me.'

'I said I'd take you to the financiers . . .'

'You mean you won't come with me?'

'And do what?'

'Destroy the anghofio flowers! Stop Jenipher from using them so I can go home!'

Neither of them risked raising their voices. The argument was hissed through their teeth.

'But I don't want you to go home! Why can't you just stay in Hyde Gardens with me? We could turn back, get home before the financiers and methics find us. We can just hide and catch lightning and stay in the Wild. None of this has anything to do with us.'

'I can't hide for ever. I need a plan to get back. My mother . . . I can't just leave her. Listen. You don't have to come,' she said. 'But you can't say this has nothing to do with you. You went behind Tally and Henrich's back and sold the anghofio. Whatever Jenipher does with it, that's on you. You're already involved.'

Estlin hung his head.

'I'm going to find the Observatory,' Ani told him. 'I'm going to destroy the anghofio flowers. And if I see the gwaidmesur, I'm going to smash that into little pieces too.'

CHAPTER NINETEEN

At Queen Cleo's, Payton read blood. Sample after sample was brought up from the Blood Library for her to practise on. With every touch, she descended into the dreamworld of another soul.

She saw:

A grey sea whipped by the ferocious wind. Her skin longed for salt and waves.

A bakery – the smell of yeast, icing sugar weightless in the air. It felt blissfully like home.

A townhouse – cold, empty, eerie. Something had happened in the attic there. Something terrible.

Payton learnt to hold her place in these dreamworlds and explore them. Each one was full of feelings and memories, which gave the worlds a strange current that pushed or pulled at her. Sometimes it was as if the blood was holding secrets and didn't want her to see them. But Jenipher said it was important to follow the currents: truth could only be found by going along with them.

Payton worked in Jenipher's apartment so the other methics didn't know what they were doing. After each reading, Jenipher listed the feelings the gwaidmesur could measure and made Payton map her own findings on to a graph. It was difficult. The visions were so much subtler than the machine allowed for. Feelings could take any form in the vision – people, places, weather, objects, even strange urges and fears that she felt within her own body. Payton explored countless forms of anger, envy, loss and misery, and struggled to identify them as they shifted and hid within the visions, the blood not wanting to surrender its secrets. It took weeks of practice.

At first Payton was only allowed to work on samples from the Blood Library. But soon Jenipher wanted her to practise on real patients. Payton was disappointed when she found out she wouldn't get to visit the patients herself.

'We can't have you doing readings in person until you know exactly what you're doing,' Jenipher told her. 'But I have a whole collection of patients that have been read by the machine already. I want to see how you compare.'

Each evening, one of Jenipher's methics would knock on the door, a tray of blood samples in their hands. Payton saw how they always craned to look over Jenipher's shoulder into the apartment, desperate to know what the samples were for.

'We have some fascinating cases here,' Jenipher murmured as she sorted the samples. 'They all have feelings that need treating one way or another. You must practise finding them.'

Every day, Jenipher extracted tiny drops and smeared them on glass slides for Payton to press her index finger into. Her fingertip was permanently stained the colour of rust. She lost count of how many worlds she had fallen into. But the more she read, the more she realized that Jenipher had been right: there was a logic to the worlds inside the blood.

In one reading, Payton was in a ramshackle house somewhere in the city. She had the strong sensation that her parents were nearby; she had to remind herself that they were simply the parents of the blood's owner, not her own. She wandered from room to room, taking in the mounds of laundry, a beloved toy fox, dirty curtains.

'Focus on the present,' she heard Jenipher's voice from far away. 'You're drifting into the patient's past.'

Payton stopped walking. Jenipher was right: there was a feeling of longing within the house. It was like a memory and a wish at the same time.

'Be mindful of your body. When you stop concentrating, that's when you faint.'

She did as she was advised, and took a moment to focus on her fingers, her toes, the feeling of her tongue against her teeth. It was a dangerous thing, entering another person's blood. It was difficult not to take on their feelings as her own and become overwhelmed.

She felt a gentle pull coming from the kitchen. She walked into its current.

The kitchen was empty except for a clock that didn't have any hands. She stood at the kitchen table – an invisible hand squeezed her shoulder. She let out a long breath. The hand felt comforting, an incredible relief. But when she turned to see whose hand it was, there was no one there. The shock of it made her lose her grip on the vision.

She woke up on the sofa, back in the apartment.

'What happened?' Jenipher wanted to know.

'I was doing fine. Then I thought there was . . . nothing.' She rubbed her eyes, which were still seeing pulsing purple-and-yellow shapes when she blinked. 'Can I have a break?'

'No, you need to write down your findings. What's the feeling in this one that needs to be treated?'

'I don't know.'

'Well. What do you know about the patient?'

'A young girl . . . she's from the city. Something happened to her parents. She was alone for a long time.

She wonders what happened to them . . . She misses them.'

Jenipher was matching what Payton was saying with the patient's notes that accompanied the blood sample.

'Yes, yes, that's right. So, in this case, we're treating . . .?'

Jenipher had the worn expression of somebody who had lived in their work for weeks and weeks. Her forehead and chin were shiny, and purple curved under her eyes.

Payton sipped some water, only realizing then that she'd been clenching her teeth.

'Can I take a break?' she asked again.

'You don't need a break, you need to *focus*,' Jenipher insisted. 'The patient's feelings. Would you say they were excessive? What needs treating?'

'It's . . . not like that. It's not that simple.'

'Yes, it is. The gwaidmesur tells us it is.' Jenipher sighed with disappointment. 'The feeling that needs treating for this one is loneliness. There's also some yearning in there we should take care of.'

'No.'

'I'm sorry?'

Payton hadn't realized she disagreed with Jenipher so strongly until she'd blurted the word out.

'Sorry—' She caught herself. 'I just meant . . . those aren't the feelings I saw there. A little bit of those things, maybe, but mostly . . . love. The loneliness and yearning were caused by love. To get rid of them, you'd have to get rid of the love and—'

'A gwaidmesur doesn't measure love,' Jenipher said irritably.

'Maybe it should.'

'It doesn't matter what is causing the bad feelings. And if she cannot control them, then she will become unwell. She needs treatment. You need more practice. I'll put the kettle on. In a few days you'll do a demonstration in front of the methics here. After that, we'll go straight to the Observatory. You'll be able to meet some of those patients in person. I've been able to delay the programme for our work, but we must continue soon. I want all of the patients there retested by you.'

Jenipher stood up and went into the kitchen. Payton stayed where she was, huddled on the sofa. She held the glass slide with the blood sample between her thumb and forefinger. She hoped the girl found her parents soon.

The morning of her demonstration in the lecture theatre of Queen Cleo's, Payton woke to find a bundle of cloth on the chair where Jenipher usually sat. She clambered off the sofa and picked it up; it was a set of robes. They were a deep purple.

Jenipher walked in while Payton was still admiring them.

'A bit of drama always helps to get things over the

line,' she said. 'They're for you.'

'Me? But only people in a guild wear robes.'

'In the old days, gwaidmesurs had their own guild. I'm not suggesting we bring it back – there wouldn't be much point in a guild of one – but I hope the robes will remind the methics of the important tradition that has re-emerged through you. Put them on.'

Payton pushed her arms through the sleeves and pulled the robes around her.

'Excellent. You're tall, which helps,' said Jenipher. 'It's better if you don't look too young. Come and look.'

Jenipher didn't have a mirror in her apartment but she placed Payton in front of a framed diagram of Venner's Wheel, the chart that mapped all feelings against the diseases they caused. Payton admired her dark outline. She looked like a grown-up.

'The readings used to be ceremonial,' Jenipher explained. 'Rumour has it, to become a Guild Master you had to have your blood read by a gwaidmesur, so they could see that your intentions were pure and honourable.'

'Why don't they do that now?'

'Some people thought it gave the gwaidmesurs too much power. They thought nobody should be trusted with such gifts.'

'Will people think that about me?'

Payton's worried eyes met Jenipher's in the glass's reflection.

'No. Because you have me. I'll always protect you and guide you to use your powers for the right thing.' Jenipher gently turned Payton to face her and looked at her in the robes. 'Perfect. You just need the finishing touch . . .'

Jenipher presented her with a mask. It was nothing like the ones Payton and Ani had worn in the old laboratory; it was made of a soft, dark fabric. It was a strange mauve colour with gauze sewn over the eyes. Payton turned it and realized she could see through it, but nobody would be able to read her expression.

'A gwaidmesur's job is to read, not be read,' Jenipher explained. 'Feelings are to be—'

'Observed. Treated. Never felt,' Payton supplied. 'I know. I can do it.'

Jenipher smiled.

'Then let's go and show them.'

Under the glaring stage lights of Queen Cleo's theatre, Payton felt as strong and emotionless as a statue. Through her mask she saw looks of wonder and fear while Jenipher placed drop after drop on her finger. The whole room leant towards her for her readings:

'A house by the sea. Needs treating for . . . fear.'

'A celebration in a field, midsummer. Needs treating for . . . jealousy.'

'A stable. Needs treating for . . . anxiety.'

With each drop, it became easier. Everything she had learnt with Jenipher helped her navigate the blood visions and find the feelings in them. Soon she realized she could find bad feelings in anybody if she looked hard enough.

When they reached the end of the demonstration, she felt a trickle of sweat run from her hairline down the side of her face, but she didn't dare remove her mask. The methics rose in rapturous applause, while Jenipher bowed in front of them.

Payton didn't bow. She decided that gwaidmesurs did not bow for methics.

She didn't remove her mask until she was in the carriage with Jenipher, and the braying does were taking them south towards the Observatory.

'Did you see their faces?' The colour was high in Jenipher's cheeks as she turned to watch Queen Cleo's shrink behind them. 'They couldn't believe it. And this is only the beginning.'

She squeezed Payton's arm. Payton felt the tremble of her grasp through the purple fabric of her robes.

'It is,' she agreed. 'But . . . what happens now?'

'Finding the feelings is just the first step.' Jenipher spoke quickly, not looking at her, as though she was lost in thought. 'When we find the feelings, we then obliterate them.' She turned to Payton, her eyes shining with tears of hope. 'It's nearly over, Payton. All of the illnesses we've lived with ever since the Turn. All the ill people. We're going to save them all.'

'How?'

'I have a way. You'll see.'

Payton sat back and let hope wash over her. As she'd read drop after drop of the samples, she had felt her own thrill grow. She felt a part of something bigger than herself. Feelings were awful, but Jenipher would cure every sick child in the city. Payton couldn't help but admire her. Jenipher was determined, brilliant, relentless. Everything her own father wasn't.

And if the treatment worked on the children, Payton thought, maybe grown-ups would be next . . .

Payton closed her eyes and clasped her hands, imagining that one hand was her mother's.

CHAPTER TWENTY

Ani and Estlin slept for a few short hours in a side alley on a quiet street. Estlin had shaken her awake and they had walked through the grey and sleeping city. They reached the River Tamesas at dawn.

'The river will be the quickest way,' Estlin insisted. 'We just need to find someone we can trust. The longer we stay on the streets, the sooner we'll get caught. Especially in daylight. The guilds have lots of friends in the city who don't wear robes.'

The idea of a boat journey thrilled Ani. She had often watched the distant waters of the Tamesas from her window at King Jude's. But she had never seen Strand Bridge, the nine-arch granite bridge that connected the two halves of the city. Even in the early hours of the day, it was a hub of activity: waterwheel engineers, sacks and crates of merchants' wares, fishing folk, people steering boats large and small.

'It smells like salt,' she said.

'What did you expect? Oi! Keef!'

Estlin called out to a fisherman at the end of the dock. His boat was one of the smallest. He was unloading nets of shining black mussels.

Keef looked up and saw Estlin. His face fell.

'Whatever you're after, Estlin, I want no part of it.'

'I'm just saying hello.'

'Hello, then.'

Keef heaved another sack on to the dock. Estlin had to leap to one side to stop it from landing on his toes. Ani became aware of people beginning to glance at them – they might have been mistaken for two market children, but the flashes coming from the lightning underneath Estlin's shirt were much more noticeable without his coat.

'While I'm here – saying hello – I was wondering, are you heading downriver to the docks?'

A group of men were watching them more closely now. Ani stood behind Estlin to shield him from view.

'If I was, it's none of your business. You still owe me for smuggling those seeds a few weeks back. Your "lost wallet" act might work on the merchants—'

'I'm glad you brought that up, because . . .' Estlin pulled out the fistful of coins Darian had given him. He gave two to Keef. 'That should square us up, shouldn't it?'

Keef stared at the coins, then sniffed and pocketed them quickly.

'Just about . . .'

Ani pinched another coin from Estlin and gave it to Keef.

'This is for the late payment.'

'Much appreciated, miss.' He nodded to her.

'So . . .'

Ani was running out of patience with Estlin's haggling. She wrestled the rest of the coins from his fist.

'And this is for a lift downriver, to Greenwich.' She pushed another coin into Keef's hand.

'What do you want to go to Greenwich for?'

She handed him more coins. 'This is for no more questions.'

'I don't want any trouble . . .'

'And this is for us to go right away. Before there's any trouble.'

She handed over the last of the coins. Estlin scowled at her. Keef looked at the two children, then glanced at the dock behind them.

He hauled the final net of mussels on to the dock, then gestured for them to climb aboard.

They sped downriver, the breeze blowing their hair from their eyes, their shoes and ankles getting wet as they tried to balance in the stern of Keef's boat.

A few times he glanced at Ani curiously.

'Don't let him drag you into any troubles, miss,' he said, jerking his head at Estlin.

'I won't,' Ani promised.

'Trust me, it's not that way round,' said Estlin.

'I'm not asking questions –' Keef held up a hand, steering the boat expertly out of the way of a larger one – 'but you got family in Greenwich?'

'No.'

'You a nurse?'

Ani was surprised by the question.

'No. Why?'

'Too young to be a nurse, I suppose. That's all you get going to Greenwich these days. A few nurses.'

'Where do they go?'

'One of them told me there's a children's hospital there. Just a mile inland. But between you and me, miss, I never heard of a place like that.'

Ani elbowed Estlin in the ribs and he nodded. It had to be the Observatory.

As the river curved, Ani saw the masts of the Lundain docks on the north bank. On the south there was only a narrow strip of stony beach.

Keef took them as close as his boat would allow.

'Which way do the nurses go when they come here?' Ani asked him.

He seemed reluctant to tell her, but then he admitted, 'I don't know where they go exactly. But rumour has it, they walk straight into Greenwich Forest.'

'Why would a nurse go to an abandoned wilder forest?' Estlin asked as he and Ani jumped into the water.

'It's not for me to ask questions of the methics. Take care, miss,' he said to Ani kindly.

Ani's shouted thanks were lost to the sounds of the river. Her face felt grimy with salt. Her feet and the bottom of her dress were cold and wet.

She turned to Estlin. 'Which way from here?'

'I don't know exactly. But we should get off the riverbank and out of sight. Greenwich Forest was the biggest of all the wilders' places. I don't think we'll miss it.'

They shook the water from themselves as best they could and began to walk. Near the bank there were abandoned, rusting boats, a line of empty buildings with broken windows, and a quiet, disused road. Behind the buildings was a line of trees.

'Is that it?' Ani asked.

'I guess so.'

'Don't you know?'

'Hyde Gardens is the only wilder place I've been! It's hard enough looking after that place without getting caught.'

Skirting around the buildings, they found the woodland was hemmed in by a brick wall. It was old and crumbling in places, but still far taller than them.

'We'll have to climb,' said Estlin. 'I'll go first. You don't know what's on the other side.'

'Neither do you.'

The dilapidated brickwork offered the perfect foothold as Ani ignored Estlin's offer and started to scramble up. At the top, she reached down to help Estlin, but he ignored her outstretched hand and hauled himself up alongside her.

They jumped down on to a mulch of pine needles and bark. The trees soared above them.

'Wow . . .'

Estlin and Ani walked side by side, awed by the towering trunks and the warm scent of decay. 'These woods must be ancient. Even older than Hyde Gardens.'

'I can't believe the guilds just locked all this away,' said Ani.

'Henrich and Tally wouldn't believe this.'

For a moment it became easy to forget about finding the Observatory and the anghofio flowers. The forest was wondrous. Ani imagined herself and Estlin living there, growing older, making their home there. She was lost in the fantasy of it, until she heard Estlin, who was a few paces up ahead, cry out.

'What?'

She ran towards him, stumbling over roots.

The forest had stopped suddenly, like a breath cut short. Ahead of them was scarred scrubland, dotted with tree stumps. The earth was raw, exposed, packed flat. Nothing grew. And in the middle of the wasteland was a round tower.

Ani didn't need anybody to tell her that this was the Observatory.

It was vast, bigger than most of the buildings at King Jude's. Ani counted six storeys in total. It was built from new Lundain brick and freshly hewn wooden beams in a smooth, precise circle. Countless windows made dark gaps in the curving walls, as if the tower had many eyes, staring at the deadened forest around it. Ani shivered.

'The forest . . . What have they done?' Estlin whispered.

She looked sideways at him and then looked away quickly. Estlin's eyes were shining, and she sensed he wouldn't want her to notice.

'I guess it's the only place in the city you can build something like this and keep it a secret,' she said.

'These trees are as old as the earth. They can't just . . . I mean, how could they . . .?'

'There weren't any wilders to protect them, Estlin.'

'Well, not any longer. We're here now,' he said.

The only time Ani had seen him so angry was when she'd broken his sandglass bottle. A grey mist ringed the building, even though the sun was up and there hadn't been any fog overnight. It meant that any entrance was concealed. There wasn't a soul in sight.

'Do you think it's guarded?' Estlin wondered.

'I don't know.'

'Do you really think it's a hospital?'

'It can't be. There are seven hospitals in Lundain. This isn't one of them.'

'It looks new. Maybe Jenipher built it. The guild's eighth hospital.'

Ani didn't want to think about Jenipher. She wanted to run all the way back to Hyde Gardens and never venture out again.

'Let's get a closer look,' said Estlin.

'Shouldn't there be methics and nurses?' Estlin muttered.

'What if there's no one here at all?' Ani wondered hopefully.

'Only one way to find out,' he said. The lightning made Estlin's shoulders jerk up and down, but his face was set and determined. They set off. Ani glanced back nervously at the trees. When she looked ahead again, she had the distinct feeling that the fog was nearer, as if it was coming forward to greet them.

'Er . . . Estlin?'

The fog had reached him. He froze. Then he began to tremble and look at the ground.

'Estlin?'

Ani started to run towards him. He didn't move – not even a twitch from his lightning treatment.

Now she was in the fog too. It swirled and pressed in on her, as if it was drawn to her. It was unnatural.

'What the—?'

She didn't see Estlin until she tripped over him. He was a leaden, curled shape on the ground. Her foot caught his leg and sent her rolling.

She cried out in shock and gasped in some of the tasteless white plumes of fog. She felt her blood turn to ice.

'Estlin!' She crawled back to his still form. She rolled him over and saw that all the colour had left his face, his expression frozen at some terror she couldn't yet see. She tried shaking him, but it was as if he couldn't see her.

Something slithered over her wrist.

She looked down. The earth was moving. Something black, slimy and writhing was emerging from the mud, and then another and another. A stench filled the air. An eel-like creature squirmed out of the grass and crawled over Estlin.

'No! Get off him!' Ani shouted. She tried to grab it,

but it slithered away, and then another one was there, trying to slip up Estlin's shirtsleeve.

'Leave him alone!' Goosebumps shuddered over every inch of Ani's skin at the sight of them. Her diaphragm kept tensing as if she was about to vomit. Every fibre of her wanted to avoid touching the revolting creatures, but she couldn't stand how they were slithering over Estlin. Every time she tried to pull one off him, it slipped away. It happened again and again, until she realized: she couldn't touch them.

'They're not real!' she said to herself. 'They're like a dream. It *is* a dream. It's nightmare vapour!'

Back at King Jude's she had seen methics treat patients with 'dream vapour' – distilled dreams turned into a gas that they stored in metal tanks so that distressed patients could breathe it through masks to give them gentler dreams. The fog was suspiciously like that dream vapour, only whoever had made it had clearly chosen the worst dream they could find.

'Estlin!' she shouted, even though she knew he couldn't hear her. She needed to tell herself: 'It's not real. Not real, not real, not real.'

She took his icy hands in hers and started to drag him. The eels roiled and writhed and tried to tug him back. It felt as if the entire world was made out of them. It was difficult to remember a time before the eels. Why were they going to the Observatory, Ani wondered? She put one foot in front of the other. Why was she clinging to Estlin? Shouldn't she leave him? This thought took hold of her mind, but her hands seemed to remember a time before the creatures and knew not to let go of him. Her feet knew to go forward.

She didn't know where she was going.

She barely knew her own name.

'Not real,' she whispered to herself over and over, only she didn't know why. Did she mean the person whose hands she was holding? Should she let go?

Then the hands squeezed hers, and the only thing she knew for certain was that she shouldn't let go.

'Not letting you go,' she said to the damp, strong hands in hers. 'Never letting go.'

The slippery earth creatures were winding around her ankles. Every step was slow and heavy.

Every few moments the hands she was holding seemed to pulse, squeezing hers, and each time she held on even tighter.

'Not real – not letting go – not real – not – letting—'

Her mind and body were so at war with each other, she wasn't looking where she was going. The moment she felt air beneath her foot instead of earth came as a shock, and she toppled headfirst into a ditch, dragging Estlin after her.

It was like waking from a dream. The eels disappeared

into the vapour. What had seemed so real and horrifying moments ago lost its edge, and all that was left was her hammering heart and distrusting mind. Ani sat up and looked around.

She was in a tangle of grass, dead leaves and loamy water that had collected at the bottom of a ditch.

Estlin was already up, leaning against the bank, his face drawn and his arms wrapped around himself.

'What were those . . . things?' he whispered. 'I've never seen . . . I've heard wilder stories, but never heard of something so . . . like a nightmare.'

'I think it *was* a nightmare,' said Ani. 'It's the fog.'

The fog flowed over the top of the ditch – it didn't sink and join them. The air smelt of mould but there wasn't anything to suggest that moments earlier the world had been filled with squirming, glistening creatures.

'How is that possible?'

'Methics.'

Ani found the twitch of Estlin's face reassuring, a sign that he was returning to normal.

'Well, one thing is obvious. There must be something going on here the methics don't want people to know about,' he said. 'Otherwise they wouldn't do something like that to keep people out.'

'Unless it's to stop people leaving,' Ani suggested with a shiver.

'Do you still want to go in?' he asked.

'I'm not sure . . .'

'Oh, thank goodness.' He slumped against the slope of the ditch. 'Because, no offence, but this is the stupidest idea anybody has ever had.'

Dirty water soaked Ani's knees. Estlin was right, she thought. It was madness. She should turn around, go back to Hyde Gardens with him, and hide from the methics and financiers for however long it took for them to forget about her. Even if it was years . . . But it wasn't that simple. Jenipher would still be testing children with her gwaidmesur. Kitt was still missing somewhere in the city. Payton was no doubt back home at King Jude's, worrying about her . . .

Ani crawled up the bank as far as she dared without risking breathing in the nightmare vapour. The grass was cold and damp on her front. Through the waves of the vapour, she could see the entrance: double oak doors crisscrossed with metal. They were curved, just like the building.

She sighed. 'OK,' she said reluctantly. 'Let's go back.'

They would have to walk back through the vapour, so she took a deep breath and held it. But when she stood up, Estlin grabbed her hand and pulled her back into the ditch.

'Wait! Do you hear that?'

She was quiet a moment, listening: it was the sound

of a carriage. Before long, a doe-drawn carriage emerged from a path through the trees. It wasn't an ambulans, but it carried the colours of Queen Cleo's Hospital. The carriage was enclosed, with only a small gap for the reins to slip through, so it could be driven through the fog as if it was as harmless as mist. Ani and Estlin inched up the ditch and watched closely.

The carriage stopped outside the front doors. Two figures stepped out. Ani gasped and gripped Estlin's arm – he shushed her sharply.

One of them was Jenipher.

The other wore unusual purple robes, and a mask that hid their face.

Jenipher tied the reins to a metal hoop on the wall. She paused to say something to her companion, then opened the front door. There didn't appear to be a lock or security of any kind. She simply stepped inside, the hooded figure close on her heels, and the door slammed shut behind her.

Ani and Estlin both exhaled loudly.

'It's her!' she cried.

'I know.'

'I wonder who the other person was? It didn't look like a methic, but they wore robes like they were in a guild.'

'I never heard of a guild wearing purple.'

'Me neither. What do you think it means?'

'No idea. So many mysteries in the world. Oh, well – let's go.' Estlin turned to crawl up the ditch back towards the trees, but Ani tugged his shirt and pulled him back.

'No. I'm going in there.'

Estlin grabbed at his hair. 'Ani, no! You just said—'

'I have to! We've just seen Jenipher. This is where she's doing her "treatments". Estlin, what if Kitt's in there? With the anghofio flowers? I was so worried about what would happen to me that I didn't think about . . .' She looked up at the curving walls. Suddenly she realized that no child in the city would be truly safe from Jenipher.

'I'm going,' she said firmly.

She began to crawl awkwardly along the ditch, slipping on the grass, keeping a wary eye on the irregular gusts of fog. Estlin groaned and followed her.

'We just need to get through the fog,' Ani said. 'It doesn't go all the way up to the walls. We'll hold our breath and run.'

'Easier said than done.'

'It's not far.'

'Not far for you. Have you ever tried holding your breath through an electric shock?'

'You can't hold your breath?'

'Not very well.' Estlin peered worriedly at the white fog.

'Just stay close to me. I'll get you out of it before the nightmare sets in.'

'Maybe . . . Maybe you should go on ahead.'

Ani rounded on him. 'Are you really going to let me go in there on my own?'

He sighed. 'No.'

Before she could say something reassuring, he'd pulled himself up and over the top of the ditch and was running for the doors. Ani took a hurried gulp of air, pinched her nose, and followed him. Estlin's form was just ahead of her in the gloom – she saw the flicker of his lightning, his shoulders twitched – he stumbled.

She caught him under the arm to stop him from falling, and in a few paces they were out of the fog. Estlin coughed and hacked, running his hands over his arms and legs and hair to rid himself of the last sensation of the eels. Ani took a deep breath and placed a hand on the wall of the Observatory.

'It's all right,' she reassured Estlin. 'It was just a bad dream. It's gone now.'

'Oh, yes,' he replied. 'It's all easy from here, isn't it?'

They stood side by side in front of the double doors.

'No wonder this place doesn't need any locks,' said Estlin.

They stepped inside.

When their eyes adjusted to the gloom, they saw they were in a grand cloakroom, which was mercifully empty. It had smart black and white tiles on the floor, and rows of grey tunics hanging on the wall. Estlin plucked one of the tunics from the hooks.

'These are for children,' he said, holding one up to his shoulders. 'Here.' He pulled another one down and tossed it to Ani.

'What's this for?'

'If we're lucky, a disguise.'

Ani pulled the scratchy fabric over her dress. Estlin struggled with the tunic, and beneath his shirt Ani again saw the network of wires and leather straps that kept his heart beating.

'That won't work,' she said, going over to him. 'Look.' She pressed the fabric on his back. 'The lightning shines through. You'll have to wear two.'

'But they smell!'

'I don't care. We've got to be careful. If that horrible fog is on the outside, who knows what's inside?'

'Good point. Give me that.' He grabbed the second tunic. Ani had to help him yank it over his lightning bottle.

There were two doors on the far side of the cloakroom. They stood in front of them, adjusting their grey tunics. The one on the right was labelled MAIN WARD. The other: POST-TREATMENT.

'Where would they keep the anghofio flowers?' asked Ani.

'I don't know,' he replied. 'But "Main Ward" sounds busier, doesn't it?'

'It does, but also . . .' Ani had been listening at the other door. 'Smell that.' Up close, there was a floral scent so light she could have been imagining it.

'Anghofio.' Estlin nodded.

Ani opened the Post-Treatment door a crack and peered through. She saw a curved, dark corridor.

'All clear,' she whispered.

They shut the door carefully behind them. The corridor was wide and lined with bare, empty beds. There were two levels: the top row folded down from the walls above the others like bunk beds. Ladders leant between the beds. It was one large, deserted dormitory. It made Ani feel uneasy.

'What's our plan?' Estlin whispered as they peered at the empty beds. 'Look in every room in this place until we find the flowers?'

'Pretty much.'

'That's a terrible plan.' A lightning pulse made him hiccup – it echoed horribly.

'Keep quiet!'

'I can't help it.'

'You can help speaking!'

'What was that?'

'What? Aargh!'

One of the beds further down the corridor moved – a white sheet rising from a mattress. Ani and Estlin grabbed each other and cowered back against the door.

'A haunted hospital has to be the worst sort of hospital,' Estlin whimpered.

'It's not a ghost.' In the gloom, Ani saw a braid of hair hanging down the sheet. 'It's a girl!'

She let go of Estlin, no longer afraid. The girl was just a patient, no different to somebody she'd meet back at home at King Jude's. As she went to get a better look, Ani stopped in her tracks.

'Rosa!'

The girl slowly turned her blank gaze towards Ani.

'It's not just her,' Estlin said. 'Look.'

When they looked more carefully, they saw that many of the beds on the upper level were occupied by still forms under crumpled sheets.

'Estlin, it's Rosa! From Leadenhall.'

'The girl from Mr Augent's office?' Estlin drew closer and saw that Ani was right.

Rosa could see and hear them. She watched Ani waving her hand, but she didn't speak, or smile, or frown. Up close, she smelt intoxicatingly of flowers – like honey and pollen and sunshine and fruit all at once.

'Rosa? Are you all right?' Ani touched the girl's

wrist. It felt warm – she remembered how icy cold her skin had been back in the market. Ani felt a twinge of hope. Perhaps Rosa was better. 'Rosa? Hello?'

'Hello,' Rosa whispered mildly.

'Rosa, it's me, Ani. And Estlin. You know, the Twitcher?'

'Do you have to call me that? I'm right here.'

'Sorry.'

Rosa stared at them both. There was no trace of recognition in her face. The flakes of snow that had been caught in her eyelashes were gone. She looked just like any other girl.

'We met in Leadenhall,' Ani explained. 'I'm the girl from King Jude's.'

'What's Leadenhall?'

'The market.' Ani felt panic rising in her belly. 'Leadenhall Market. Your home!' She looked up and down the ward. 'Where's Fred?'

Rosa's glassy eyes squinted for a second, as if there was a memory vying for her attention, but then her face relaxed again: serene, unfeeling.

'Who's Fred?'

Ani chewed her lip. Some instinct made her reach out and smooth the girl's braid.

'She doesn't know her own brother,' she whispered to Estlin.

'Only anghofio flowers can do this,' he replied.

'You mean she . . .?'

'She doesn't feel anything for her old life. She can't remember it.'

Ani squeezed Rosa's wrist once more. She looked with concern at her thin face and shiny, unresponsive eyes.

'How do we make her better?'

'I don't know,' said Estlin. They looked up at the rows of beds. 'There are so many . . .'

Back in the cloakroom, Ani and Estlin tried to calm themselves down.

'My father was going to send me here,' Ani told him. 'My own father. Do you think he knew about the anghofio flowers? He couldn't have, could he?'

'It's all my fault.' Estlin's voice cracked as he admitted it. 'If I hadn't sold the harvest in the first place . . .'

'Don't say that.'

'It's true! Ani, what have I done?'

'Something we're going to fix. Look at me!'

He pulled his gaze from the floor and saw Ani's fierce yet frightened face.

'Maybe we should tell the other methics what's happening here. But what if they know too? What if they're all in on it?' She exhaled slowly. 'I wish Payton was here. She'd know what to do.'

'It's down to us.'

'I know. Let's see what else we can find.'

The door marked MAIN WARD opened on to a similar, curving red-brick corridor. They followed it wordlessly.

They heard the children before they saw them.

As the corridor opened up, Ani stopped in her tracks so suddenly that Estlin nearly bumped into her. The entire Observatory was spread before them.

'I guess that's why they don't need guards or anything,' Estlin said.

The round building spiralled high above their heads – all six floors lined with doorless cells. In each, there sat a child wearing a grey tunic. Their chatter, laughter and games bounced off the round walls as they called to each other in their cells.

In the middle of the room, rising as high as the highest floor, there was a wooden plinth, with a round room at the top and a spiral staircase leading up it. It was made of wood and stone, with many windows all around it. Long tables were arranged like a star around it on the ground floor. From the top of the plinth it was possible to see into every single cell. Just one person would be able to oversee the entire Observatory. Ani squinted up at it.

'Well. At least we tried.' Estlin shrugged.

A red bell lashed to the side of the plinth began to ring and the children all began to emerge from their cells. Some of them were only a few paces ahead of Ani and Estlin, but they all turned left and followed the spiralling floor down to the tables on the ground floor, not even glancing at the two intruders. There was chatter and jostling and giggles – completely different to the disturbing quiet of the Post-Treatment Ward.

'Come on.' Ani hurried to join the children, falling into line with them. She heard Estlin swear under his breath and his shuffling steps keeping up with her.

A nurse was moving among the tables and spooning a beige sludge into the bowls laid out. The children started taking seats, targeting the ones that already had food in front of them. The rhythm of footsteps as they came down from the upper floors was hypnotic. Children were filling the ground floor from all sides. Ani felt her palms sweating. They needed to blend in, but they didn't understand the rules of this place.

Then: a glint across the room.

She grabbed Estlin's sleeve, not trusting that what she'd seen was real.

A flash of red hair.

A glimmer of gold.

'Kitt! There's Kitt!'

'Keep it down!' Estlin warned.

She started walking quicker, weaving through the crowd, hurrying and nudging people subtly out of the way. Estlin struggled to keep up with her. The crowd thinned as more children sat down and then Kitt was standing in front of her as clear as day.

He had grown a surprising amount. His cheeks were hollower than she remembered, and he had fewer freckles from being out of the sun for so long. But he still had the glimmer of gold on his lips and in his dark eyes. He'd been given an ungainly pair of woollen gloves to wear to keep his Midas-fingers from spreading.

Before she could contain herself, Ani had rushed up to him and thrown her arms around his neck.

'I thought I'd never see you again!'

'Ani, what are you doing here?'

'It's a long story—'

'When those nurses took you—'

'Are you all right?'

'It should have been me—'

'It doesn't matter now.'

Questions tumbled out faster than they could answer, until Ani realized that people were staring at them. She let Kitt go and stepped back, trying to look more casual.

'When did they bring you here?' said Kitt.

'They didn't. We broke in. Kitt, you can't stay here.'

'I know it looks strange, but it's not so bad. Lots of food and people to talk to. Half the kids I used to play with at the market are here. It's like a new hospital for children. Much more fun than King Jude's.'

'Kitt, you don't understand—'

'Let's sit down,' Estlin muttered in Ani's ear. 'They're looking at us.'

Ani took Kitt's mitt and led the way to seats as far away from the plinth as possible, leaving a few empty chairs between them and the next group. Their bowls were still empty; the nurse hadn't reached them yet.

'Kitt, this place is dangerous.'

'Who's this?'

'This is Estlin. I met him in Hyde Gardens. He's a wilder.'

'Not a real one,' Estlin said quickly.

'Yes,' said Ani proudly. 'A real one.'

Kitt looked at both of them. 'You've been to Hyde Gardens?'

'I'm surprised they're keeping you here and haven't sold you to the financiers,' Estlin said. 'You'd fetch a fortune with that . . . condition.'

Kitt's expression hardened. 'I'm going to get treated soon. Methic Blake says she'll make me better as soon as she knows how to distil my feelings.'

'You've spoken to Jenipher?' Ani asked.

'Distil feelings?' Estlin repeated. 'What does that mean?'

'It means I won't be sick any more.'

'Kitt! Jenipher Blake – she's your methic?'

'Yes. She's mostly in the Eye when she's here. That's what we call up there.' He nodded at the room at the top of the plinth. 'There's always a methic or nurse up there. They watch over us. That's why none of the rooms need doors.'

'It's a prison,' said Ani.

'That locked room in King Jude's was a prison,' Kitt told her. 'Here there are no locks or doors. I can sit and breathe the fresh air and look at the trees from my window. Did you see the trees? They're wonderful.' He sighed.

'The ones they didn't kill,' Estlin muttered.

They fell silent as the nurse dolloping out the questionable porridge reached their table. Kitt started wolfing his down as soon as it hit his bowl. Ani wrinkled her nose at hers. Then she realized that the nurse was looking at her and Estlin closely.

'You the new arrivals?' she asked.

'Yes.'

'Were you cold?' She pointed at the two tunics Estlin was wearing.

'Yes,' Ani lied quickly. 'The nurse who brought us said it was fine.'

For a moment it looked as though this nurse was going to say something, but then she continued on her way.

'And they just . . . keep you here?' Estlin asked Kitt.

'They look after us until we're ready to be treated. When you arrive, they take you up to the Eye and . . .'

He paused dramatically. 'They read your blood. They can see your feelings.'

'I know,' said Ani. 'Listen—'

'It turns out this –' Kitt waved his mittens to show he meant his Midas-fingers – 'is caused by greed. But the methic said that wasn't necessarily a bad thing. So I haven't had my treatment yet.'

'No, you mustn't let them give you any treatment! That's sort of why we're here. Kitt, we're looking for some flowers. Little black flowers. Have you seen any?'

'No.'

'Not anywhere?'

'When I had my blood read in the Eye, that smelt like flowers. But yesterday one of the nurses told us . . .' Kitt leant in as if to share a secret. Ani saw the gold glimmer on his tongue. 'They're bringing in a human blood-reader.'

'A *human* blood-reader?' Ani repeated. 'You mean a person does it? How?'

Kitt shrugged. Ani glanced beyond him and saw the nurse talking to two children. The nurse turned and looked straight at her and Estlin. Then she started walking between the tables towards them.

'They've noticed us. We have to go,' she interrupted Kitt. 'Quick.'

Estlin was already getting to his feet.

'Kitt, come on.' Ani gestured furiously for him to get up.

'What?'

'I'm not leaving you here! We have to get out.'

'But I like it here—'

'We know a way. Trust us!'

Estlin led the way, with Ani trailing, half-dragging Kitt. They tried to walk as quickly as possible without running, but most of the children were sitting and eating; it was difficult to be inconspicuous.

'Children,' the nurse called.

'Ignore her,' said Ani.

'Children!'

'Do you think she knows?' Estlin hissed.

'Don't look back!' Ani told him.

'Children, stop right there!'

'GO!'

'Ani, wait!' Kitt tried to hold Ani back, but she and Estlin sprinted towards the entrance.

They just needed to reach the cloakroom so they could get back outside. Ani felt sick at the thought of facing the fog again.

They were nearly there, the door was finally in sight – with another nurse standing on the threshold.

They skidded to a halt, trapped.

CHAPTER TWENTY-ONE

Payton had never felt more powerful; she had never felt more alone.

The carriage cut through the city so fast that when people in the streets saw the poised, regal figure in purple robes through the window, they shook their heads – it must have been an ordinary methic, the colour a trick of the light.

As they travelled, Jenipher explained about the Observatory to Payton. How she'd borrowed money from the financiers to build it deep in Greenwich Forest, far from the meddling eyes of the rest of the guild.

'What do the financiers want with any of this?' Payton asked.

'We have something that could be of value to them.'

'But they have all the money in the world.'

'Not money. Not exactly.' Jenipher reached out and

adjusted Payton's mask as she spoke. 'We found a patient with Midas-fingers.'

'Midas-fingers!' Payton remembered the argument between Ani and her father back at King Jude's. 'Kitt . . .'

'I'm sorry?'

'Nothing.'

'The financiers are keen that we find a way to stabilize and . . . *enhance* his condition.'

'Enhance it?' A sense of unease crept over Payton. 'I don't understand.'

'All the financiers have asked – in exchange for the supplies and money we need to run the programme – is that we help to make the way the boy produces gold more consistent.'

'You're not going to cure him?'

'Now, Payton—'

'You're a methic! You take an oath! Now you're making a patient worse *on purpose*? That goes against everything the guild stands for.'

'Sometimes individuals must play a role in helping medicine's wider cause.'

'You won't be able to control his condition. You can't control another person's feelings.'

'I assure you –' Jenipher whipped the reins to drive the does faster – 'that is exactly what I will be able to do.'

'Methic Gilchrist says—'

'Gilchrist and his kind won't understand,' snapped Jenipher. 'Not yet. They will once they see our results. As will you, Payton. Unless you do not trust me? Perhaps this step as gwaidmesur is too much for you, maybe it's too soon.'

'No!' Payton said quickly. 'I . . . I do understand. It's just surprising, that's all. So many new ideas.'

This seemed to please Jenipher.

'It is an exciting time in medicine,' she acknowledged. 'A lot for a young mind to take in.'

Payton did trust Jenipher, who was brilliant and brave and willing to do anything to undo the devastation of the Turn, but she couldn't shake the doubt gnawing at her stomach. She stared out of the window, and they didn't speak again until they reached Greenwich.

Payton was awed by the trees they sped through once they reached the forest. It brought the Isles to mind with a pang. In that moment, all she wanted to do was show the trees to Ani. It was like Battersea Meadows, but even bigger, older, wilder – until suddenly it wasn't. The woods opened up into a wide clearing, where the green had been stripped from the earth to be replaced by the most extraordinary building she had ever seen.

'I designed it myself,' Jenipher said proudly as their carriage passed through a band of mist and pulled up at the front door. Payton stepped out and looked up at the towering walls and endless windows.

In the Main Ward, the chatter of the children hushed as they saw Jenipher – now a familiar sight to them – followed by the masked figure in purple robes. Payton admired the design of the Observatory and how it kept each child in their room without the need for doors and locks. She felt the weight of their eyes on her.

'This way.' Jenipher's hand on her shoulder guided her to the central plinth. They climbed the spiral staircase. The sound of children's voices grew again as they began to gossip excitedly.

Payton stepped into the room at the top of the plinth and relaxed when she saw that it was a laboratory, the sort of place where she felt at home. The lab was sparse and functional, without any plants growing on the walls or other methics going about their work. There was a large glass fume chamber at one end, with a shiny new control panel. For liquid or gas treatments, it was an efficient way to administer medicine to a patient without exposing anybody else to the substance. Payton had seen plenty of similar chambers at King Jude's. For a moment she thought of the one in the old laboratory, and remembered running away from whatever was inside it, laughing with Ani until her stomach hurt. She pushed the thought away. There was no other equipment in the lab other than the gwaidmesur machine, an old, ornate medicine cabinet and a hospital bed.

A boy sat on the bed, wrapped in a grubby towel, and a grey-uniformed nurse stood by the fume chamber's control panel.

'Just in time,' said Jenipher. 'Is this our latest patient?'

'He's just been treated,' the nurse informed them. 'We'll move him to the Post-Treatment Ward in a moment.'

Jenipher went over to the medicine cabinet, but Payton was more interested in the boy. He wasn't much younger than her, but he was shorter and skinnier. He was looking at her with calm, trusting eyes.

'How do you feel?' she asked him.

He didn't reply.

'What's his name?' Payton asked.

'Not my job to know names,' said the nurse.

'What's your name?' she asked the boy gently.

His wide eyes were on hers. Something in his gaze made him seem even younger.

'Can you tell me?' Payton asked. Ani would know how to get him talking, she thought. She persisted: 'What are you called? Where did you come from?'

'I don't know,' the boy whispered back. His face creased with concentration and a flash of frustration, then it cleared, leaving his expression blank. 'Nothing. Nowhere.'

His hair was dark, and his skin was dirty – he needed a bath, Payton thought, even though there was a strange, floral scent coming from him.

There was something about the smell that made her shudder. She took a step back.

'Payton.'

Jenipher called her attention to the wooden medicine cabinet. Payton saw that it was ornately carved with flowers. Inside, on every shelf and lining both doors, were vials and vials of black liquid. It was dark like the space between stars in the night sky. Darker, even. Darker than ink, than onyx, than pupils straining to see in shadow. Each vial was a tiny abyss. Jenipher was holding one between her thumb and forefinger.

'A Blood Library?' Payton asked, even though she knew there was no way the black liquid was blood.

'The treatment.'

Payton drew closer and took the vial from Jenipher. The floral smell was coming from the medicine cupboard too.

'What's in it?' She held it up to the light, but nothing shone through. She couldn't think of a plant that could produce such a colour.

'It's made from anghofio flowers.'

Jenipher said it with reverence, as if it was the most

precious thing in the world. She opened a drawer in the cabinet and brought out a wooden chest carved with the same ornate flowers.

'Look.' She lifted the lid and Payton saw it was full of hundreds of tiny black flowers. Their smell was almost overwhelming.

She reached out to touch them, but Jenipher snapped the chest shut.

'Careful,' she warned.

Payton searched her encyclopaedic knowledge of plants before asking, 'Why have I never heard of it?'

'They are . . . difficult to acquire. But I have a way. They are very powerful. I have found a way to turn them into this solution –' she touched the black vials – 'which is the perfect strength.'

'The perfect strength to do what?'

'To remove a person's feelings.'

Payton glanced back at the boy. She saw now that it wasn't dirt in his hair, on his skin or the towel; it was the remains of the treatment. He'd been sprayed with the anghofio flower solution in the fume chamber.

'What else does it remove?'

'Nothing,' Jenipher insisted quickly.

Payton looked at the black liquid again.

'Is this why he can't remember his name or how he got here?'

'Unfortunately, memories are a source of feelings,'

Jenipher said. 'But he will go out into the world and make new memories, without feelings attached to them.'

'But every memory has a feeling.'

'Not with anghofio. No child should have to feel such pain or sorrow or anger that they become sick. And now, thanks to this medicine, they won't have to ever again.'

A worrying thought had entered Payton's mind, and it clearly showed on her face, because Jenipher asked, 'What's the matter?'

'My . . . my sister was going to come here.'

'And she will, as soon as we find her. Don't worry.' Jenipher squeezed her arm.

Payton didn't explain that now she had seen the boy on the bed, she was glad that nobody could find Ani. In fact, she hoped she'd stay missing for a long, long time.

'Methic Blake!'

Another nurse burst into the lab.

'What is it?' Jenipher disliked being interrupted.

'Two children . . .' The nurse had clearly run up the stairs – she was struggling to catch her breath. 'Broken—'

'They've broken out?'

'No, methic. Broken *in*. I let them all out for lunch and then—'

'Where are they now?'

'Downstairs.'

'Bring them here.'

The nurse left and Jenipher pulled Payton's mask back up.

'Your first patients,' she said tenderly. 'The start of an exciting new dawn.'

Payton waited patiently. Jenipher went to the door to speak to the nurse and the two children that were being brought to her. When she returned, Payton couldn't help but notice that she was suppressing a smile.

'I must warn you, it will be one of the most difficult readings you've done,' Jenipher told her.

'Why?'

'Because you will have to set aside your feelings. Like I've taught you. Like a methic.'

Payton stood a little straighter. 'I always do.'

'I know,' Jenipher whispered. 'I believe in you.'

These words made Payton feel invincible.

But all her training could not have prepared her for the moment when the two children were brought, kicking and yelling, into the Eye.

One of them was Ani.

Payton swallowed a gasp.

Her little sister was as filthy as any child living on the streets, and the twitching boy next to her wasn't much better. The nurse had them kneel on the laboratory floor. Their hands were tied behind their backs. How long had it been since Payton had watched her sister be carried away by the ambulans bouncing through the streets of Lundain? Weeks. All because Ani had refused to go to the Observatory. Now she was here after all. Payton felt sick. She tried to hold on to what Jenipher had said. She could do it. She could set aside her feelings for her sister.

She was standing in the corner: tall, masked and still. Ani didn't notice her at first – all her venom was directed at Jenipher.

'Let us go!'

'Ani Darke,' Jenipher said. 'I'm so pleased you found your way to us after all. Clever girl – knowing where you belong. And who do we have here?'

Estlin lifted his head and said evenly: 'Estlin Glas.'

Jenipher did a double take at the name. 'The financiers' wilder boy?'

'That's right,' Ani snarled. 'We know what you're doing here with the anghofio flowers. It shouldn't be allowed.'

'I am the Guild Master,' Jenipher replied. 'Nobody decides what I'm "allowed" to do except me. Now, I know you were read by our gwaidmesur, our machine, back at King Jude's. If I recall . . . anger, wasn't it? Spark breath. Well, I must say you look better than I would have expected. But you will be read again. Our human gwaidmesur is even more accurate.' She gestured to Payton.

Ani's furious and fearful gaze turned to the figure in purple robes. Even wearing her mask, Payton was expecting Ani to recognize her, but she didn't. Her face showed only defiance, and a hint of fear. Payton breathed deeply and tried to see not Ani but just individual features: brown eyes, tangled dark hair, a raised chin. She pushed away the images of what she looked like when she was a baby, or sleeping, or angry with their father, or worried about their mother, or laughing uncontrollably because she could never get her feelings under control.

Jenipher stepped forward to take the blood samples. Without untying Ani's hands, she held her thumb in a vice-like grip. Ani struggled and tried to fight back, twisting and spitting. Payton wanted to ask Jenipher not to hurt her, but she pushed the urge away immediately. Ani yelped when the needle found her thumb, and Jenipher turned back to Payton triumphant.

Payton didn't hold out her hand.

She didn't move at all. Jenipher had to grab her left hand and hold it flat.

When the blood touched Payton's skin, it took her to King Jude's. Ani's King Jude's. The perfect version of it that was conjured when she touched her blood.

The sight of it was so comforting it nearly made her cry with relief. The sun shone and plants grew all around – ivy coated the brick walls, trees cast dappled shade, the paving stones were replaced with grass. The hospital's waterways trickled, the sound soothing and peaceful.

Payton stood still, feeling the sun on her face. Ani's blood was a peaceful place. How could that be? Shouldn't there be anger, fire? A current in the air caught her attention. She followed it, as Jenipher had taught her to.

It pulled her across the quad and into the Inertia Ward – which was soft with moss, twisted roots and mud – down into the cellar where, in the real world, her mother slept. In the vision, Ani was there.

The room was filled with water chambers, where algae and water lilies grew. Ani started to walk the length of the ward. Payton followed carefully. In the first water chamber was a boy with red hair and gold speckled across his skin. In the next was Estlin, the boy who was kneeling next to Ani in the Eye. The Ani in the vision ran a hand absent-mindedly over the lid of his chamber. Payton felt a deep feeling of protection, safety and affection.

This was where Ani kept the people she loved, Payton realized. She looked at the chambers in the next row and saw staff and patients from King Jude's lying there, peaceful and submerged.

Her heart lurched at the sight of her own face, smiling and serene in her own chamber. She rested her fingertips on the lid.

She hadn't expected to find herself there. She was touched that Ani kept her down here, whether she knew it or not. On the surface of things, they argued and criticized and judged each other, but here, in Ani's blood, in the very essence of her, was proof that she loved her sister.

Payton felt tears gathering behind her eyes.

She shook her head, trying to rid herself of the feelings: tenderness, frustration, longing. But they were building like waves, threatening to take over.

She needed to stop the vision. She was about to leave when she felt one more push of the current. This one was stronger than any she'd felt.

Ani was at the end of the ward, bending over a final chamber. Their mother's chamber. Biting back the guilt she felt, Payton went to join her.

Ani started to slide the lid off the chamber.

'Don't!' Payton wasn't meant to communicate with the vision, but she couldn't help it. It was like watching Ani jeopardize their mother in real life. Without the water chamber, she would die.

But Ani ignored her. When the lid was pushed back, Ani dipped her hand into the water. Blood started to seep into the water. It was coming from Ani, but there were no cuts on her hand.

Payton watched the scarlet patterns swirl, brushing against her mother's skin, touching her lips.

'What are you doing?' she asked the vision. 'What does this mean? What does blood have to do with it?'

Her mother's eyes opened. They were bright and ocean-blue.

The shock of it made Payton cry out.

She couldn't bear the joy and hope.

She lost her grip of the vision. She was swept from the flooded ward, out of King Jude's. She woke up on her knees on the floor of the Eye, where she tore the mask from her face and finally allowed herself to weep.

CHAPTER TWENTY-TWO

'Payton!'

Ani saw her sister's face appear from behind the mask – flushed, tired, crying for the first time in the longest while. She rushed to her side.

'Your sister?' Estlin asked in disbelief.

'*You're* the gwaidmesur? How?' Ani wanted to embrace Payton, but she couldn't with her hands still tied. 'What did you do to her?' she shrieked at Jenipher.

Payton wiped her eyes on her purple sleeves.

'I'm s-sorry.'

Jenipher rushed to her too, pushing Ani out of the way.

'Are you hurt?' she asked urgently.

'No—'

'You weren't ready. I knew you weren't.' Jenipher was there, adjusting Payton's robes and smoothing her hair. 'Manage your feelings, Payton – let them go.'

'Ani . . .' Payton struggled to gather her breath. She was weak, trembling. All her strength had left her when she'd lost control of the vision.

'You need more practice,' Jenipher insisted. 'In time even *she* won't be able to derail you with her emotions.' She glared at Ani and pulled Payton, still shaking, to her feet.

Ani didn't know what to think. Payton had always fainted at the touch of blood, but not this time.

'Never mind,' Jenipher went on. 'You've already been read by the machine. We know what to do with you.'

She seized Ani, her fingers pinching her skin through her tunic, and dragged her towards the fume chamber.

'No!' Estlin shouted.

'Payton!' Ani yelled.

She tried to twist free, but Jenipher was stronger. The door of the fume chamber opened. With her hands tied, all Ani could do was try to dig her heels in, wedge her feet in the door frame, but a sharp kick in the ankle sent her stumbling in. The door slammed behind her. She was trapped in the glass box.

'Estlin, help!'

He didn't need telling. He was on his feet, ready to rush Jenipher, but she was too quick. She snared him in a vice-like grip and pushed him to his knees. He struggled, watching Ani through the glass – she saw the apology and despair written across his face.

Jenipher gripped a fistful of his hair and yanked his head back so that he was looking her in the eye.

'The financiers have told me all about you. *Twitcher.*'

Estlin winced. Jenipher reached down the back of his shirt and prised his lightning bottle free. Ani noticed Payton stare at it wide-eyed. Jenipher held it for a moment, watching the chaos of the electricity, before placing the bottle in Estlin's bound hands. 'Do you have any idea how easy it would be for me to detach this and let your heart do the rest? Do not tempt me.'

She drew herself back up. Estlin stayed where he was, his head hanging over his lightning treatment. Ani wanted to bang on the glass, to scream, to threaten and curse Jenipher, but she didn't dare. Not when Jenipher could kill Estlin just by removing the pads from his chest.

'We'll treat you now,' Jenipher said to Ani. 'Your father says he wants you back – once your blood is perfect.'

She went to the medicine cabinet and pulled out a vial of black liquid. Ani had no doubt what was in that vial. Estlin saw it too – he looked from the vial to Ani, horror descending on him as he realized what Jenipher was going to do.

Panic made Ani's heart beat so hard she was certain it would break. Would it hurt? Would she still know Estlin's face afterwards? Or Payton's? Her mother's?

She wiped her forehead on her sleeve. She would cling to her feelings, she decided. She wouldn't let the anghofio flowers do their work. If she focused on something hard enough, it couldn't be torn away from her. She squeezed her eyes closed. She thought of Hyde Gardens – the weather station, the green of the trees, Estlin's jokes. She tried to let the joy of it fill her up.

But as Jenipher slotted the vial into the slot in the fume chamber controls, Payton stepped forward.

'Wait.'

Ani opened her eyes. Jenipher turned to Payton.

'What is it?'

'Just . . . don't do it.'

'It will make her better, Payton. She won't feel a thing.'

'But I haven't told you what I saw in the reading.' The weakness Payton had felt after the reading was beginning to leave her. The colour was returning to her face and her hands shook less.

'She's been read by the machine – we know enough.' But Jenipher's hand hesitated over the controls. Payton recognized the curiosity of a good methic.

'She's not sick,' she said firmly. 'Her blood . . . I don't know how to explain it, but it was completely different this time. Everything was . . . gentle. At peace. Even the difficult things. I saw King Jude's, but beautiful and green, and we were all in water chambers, all the people she loves. And you were there.' Payton turned to Estlin. He looked at her apprehensively. 'There was peace and love and happiness.'

'Only a medicine like this can balance the girl's blood,' said Jenipher. 'That's what I'm doing here. It's what your father wants for her.'

'How do you know? He's not here.'

'It was part of our agreement to let you stay with me at Queen Cleo's. I get you; he gets a girl with perfectly balanced blood as soon as we find her. And now we have.'

Ani couldn't believe what she was hearing. Her father wasn't close to either her or Payton, but she was certain that if he could have only one of them, it wouldn't have been her.

Payton pulled Jenipher's hand away from the controls. She snatched the vial of anghofio flower solution from its slot.

'No!'

'Payton, I've had enough of this.'

'The machine isn't like me. It can only read bad feelings – anger, sadness, fear, greed—'

'Because those are the feelings that cause illness!'

'But there are other feelings! What about joy and love and hope? You've been teaching me wrong, making me be like the machine, so I can only find what's bad. But there's good in there too. I can feel it in the blood. In Ani's blood!'

Ani was only half following the science of feelings that Payton was trying to explain, because behind her and Jenipher, Estlin was inching forward. Ani saw why. Jenipher had dropped the needle she'd used to draw Ani's blood on the floor. Everybody was looking at Payton. Ani hoped that it would stay that way.

Jenipher had her hands on Payton's shoulders, speaking slowly, a teacher explaining to her student, 'Even the good feelings aren't enough. What happens when love ends? When we're robbed of happiness? When we lose all hope? The good feelings open the door to the bad. It's better not to have them at all. That's how the anghofio works.'

'You'd get rid of love just because it hurts sometimes? You're wrong. All of this is wrong!'

Ani glanced back at Estlin. He was bent forward awkwardly, and she saw that he was trying to twist his hands free from the ropes.

'No feelings means that nobody has to be ill ever again, Payton,' Jenipher reminded her. 'How can you wish to be a methic and not want that? I thought better of you.'

'No. I thought better of *you*,' Payton retorted. 'I thought you were a great methic. But you're not. Feelings make some people ill, but they can heal others. They just need balance.'

'Don't discredit yourself with such a ridiculous hypothesis, child.'

There was a flurry of movement behind them; Estlin's hands were free.

'Jenipher, you have to trust me—' Payton pleaded.

'Let her go!' Estlin's voice rang out clear and bold. He was standing with his lightning bottle grasped in both hands. 'Now.'

Jenipher hesitated. She looked from the lightning to the boy, to Ani.

'You wouldn't dare,' she sneered. 'It would kill you.'

'Not just me.'

'Estlin,' Ani warned through the glass. 'Don't . . .'

Payton backed away from him. But Jenipher wasn't afraid. Her delicate features were calm, composed, barely betraying a hint of disgust. She stepped away from the control panel and approached him.

'Hand it over,' she ordered.

'Let her go,' Estlin repeated. 'I'll do anything. I can get you more anghofio flowers. Just don't use them on her.'

A lightning release made him twitch – even Jenipher flinched.

'If you don't let her leave with me right now, I will destroy this place,' he insisted.

'I don't do deals with wilders.'

Jenipher turned back to the fume chamber.

Estlin's eyes met Ani's. She saw the desperation on his face. It scared her more than anghofio flowers ever could.

'Estlin . . .' She shook her head. 'You mustn't.'

He swallowed. The bottle shook in his trembling grip.

'Please,' Ani begged.

Another twitch sent a tear running from his eye.

'Plant me as a sgerbod tree,' he said to her. 'Like a wilder.'

'ESTLIN!'

He closed his eyes and twisted the cap.

Lightning erupted out of the sandglass.

CHAPTER TWENTY-THREE

Ani screamed.

Instinct made her curl up and close her eyes as the fume chamber around her imploded. She felt a shard of glass shoot past and slice her cheek.

When she opened her eyes, she saw that the fume chamber had shattered, and one half of the Eye's circular wall wasn't there any more. There was only a dizzying drop. The rest of the room was rubble, glass, dust and broken furniture.

'Ani!'

She didn't see Payton until she was right in front of her, pressing the sleeve of her fine robes to her cut. She was dimly aware of Payton untying her hands. She rubbed her old cloirias burn with relief.

'Estlin . . .'

Ani lurched over the bricks and glass and wood. Even with her blurry eyes, it didn't take long to find him – the lightning had blasted away anything that had been near him, so he lay alone at the edge of the Eye. As the ringing in her ears eased, Ani heard the confused and frightened shouts of children echoing across the Observatory.

Estlin's hair was thick with dust. His hands were burnt, his eyes closed. The wires and pads were still attached to his chest. Ani pressed her hands over them – his skin was hot to the touch, but he lay still.

His heart wasn't beating.

'Payton!' Ani turned to her, hacking and coughing. 'Do something! He's not breathing.'

'Move.' Payton pushed her aside and bent her ear to Estlin's mouth, her hand over his heart. 'He is. But only just. He needs more lightning.'

'That was his last bottle.'

'I know where we can get more. What happened to Jenipher?'

'Who cares? Just help him!'

At that moment, there was a movement amongst the rubble. Ani and Payton froze and watched in terror as Jenipher's outline rose from the ruins – she staggered to her feet, then fell to her knees again.

'She's hurt,' said Payton.

'Just leave her!' Ani yelled as Payton rushed to Jenipher's side.

Jenipher's usual composed expression was gone. She

looked dazed, anxious and, above all else, angry as she surveyed the decimated laboratory.

'No . . .' Jenipher exclaimed wretchedly. Payton followed her gaze: the medicine cabinet had been destroyed by the blast. The vials were cracked and leaking – black liquid was dripping from the shelves and forming puddles on the floor.

Jenipher tried to stagger towards it, but Payton held her back.

'No, don't touch it!'

Jenipher clearly knew she was right, but she still shook her hand from her sleeve angrily. She fell to her knees and howled with rage.

'Jenipher . . .'

The methic turned to look at her and Payton took a step back in shock. Sweat was beading on Jenipher's forehead. Her eyes were turning a strange colour.

Payton came towards her – she wanted to check her for a fever. The destruction of the lab and the anghofio flowers had brought all her feelings to the surface; there was a risk that it was too much for her. Payton placed her hand on Jenipher's forehead, not seeing the drip of blood that had appeared in her hairline. It touched her skin.

Jenipher wasn't a patient. Payton knew she had no business reading her blood. But when she felt the now familiar force tugging her into another world, she couldn't resist.

Jenipher's blood took Payton to a place she had been just once before.

She was standing in front of a pane of black glass. Fire-proof glass. She was visiting the fire girl revealed by the blood sample back in the Blood Library at Queen Cleo's. The sample hadn't had a name on it. With dawning dread, Payton realized why.

The fire girl was there, in shadow. But this time she stepped into the light.

It was Jenipher. Younger, more fragile and frightened than she was in the present day, but there was no mistaking her.

Payton felt a surge of anger and loss run through her, but it wasn't her own. It was within Jenipher's blood.

Steam was coming out of Jenipher's nose, ears and mouth.

Her skin was starting to burn and blister.

Her eyes glowed red.

Jenipher opened her mouth and a scream of flame poured out, an anger that had been pushed down for countless years.

Payton cried out and held her arms up to the heat, then all at once she came back to the Eye, and realized that the heat had not disappeared.

Jenipher, the methic who controlled her feelings

better than anyone, couldn't supress her rage any longer.

'We need to get out of here.'

Payton hurried over to Ani and Estlin.

'We'll have to carry him. Take his other arm.'

'What's happening?'

Looking anxiously at Jenipher, Ani hoisted Estlin up, pulling his arm across her shoulder. His skin was growing cold.

'She's sick. I just saw it in her blood,' Payton said. 'An incendiary disease like I've never seen before. She's been supressing huge amounts of anger all this time, so it's built and built, and now if it gets out . . .'

'I think it already has.'

A crackling, spitting noise of kindling catching was coming from Jenipher's body. Red welts rose on the surface of her skin. The tips of her fingers were smoking.

As the anger seeped out, she seemed to find her strength. Her red eyes locked on to the girls.

'Payton . . .' She coughed and a flame shot from her mouth, red, orange and blue. It struck a fallen wooden beam that erupted in a blaze. 'You must . . . finish what we've started.'

'I can't!'

'Look at me!'

Jenipher walked towards them slowly. Ani was trying to drag Estlin towards the spiral staircase.

'This is what feelings do.'

All at once, Payton understood Jenipher. All of her great inventions – the gwaidmesur, the Observatory, the anghofio flower treatment – were to save children from the terrible feelings she'd had her entire life.

'I'm sorry,' Payton told her, 'but I won't do this for you.'

'Payton!' Jenipher screamed.

Payton ran after Ani and Estlin. They went away from the drop and towards the half of the room that was still intact. They were nearly at the door when Jenipher lunged and grabbed Payton's sleeve. There was the foul smell of her robes burning. Payton tore them off so she was just in her trousers and shirt, and pushed Ani and Estlin through the door. She then pulled it shut behind them, with Jenipher on the other side, burning.

'Now what?' Ani cried.

Below them, the Observatory was in chaos. The children had watched half of the Eye explode and then burn.

Jenipher pulled at the door handle. 'Payton! Open this door! Open it NOW!'

When she didn't open it, she hammered and shouted and screamed.

'We have to get Estlin to King Jude's,' said Payton.

'We can't let Jenipher out, she'll burn the entire Observatory down!'

'Ani!'

A voice called to her from below. Ani looked down and saw Kitt halfway up the spiral stairs, his mitts gripping the bannister.

'I saw it explode, I knew you were in there—'

'Kitt, get up here, we need you!' Ani turned to Payton. 'Hold on, I have an idea.'

'Whatever it is, do it quickly.'

Payton was sweating with the effort of keeping the door closed as Jenipher pushed. Soon it wouldn't be much use. The door was wooden. It was beginning to catch fire.

Kitt joined them. He paled at the sight of Estlin, unconscious and slumped against the bannister.

'Kitt.' Ani pulled him towards her. She started trying to remove his mitts. 'We need you to lock her in.'

'What?'

'Gold doesn't burn. Right, Payton?'

Payton looked at Ani's friend for a moment. 'Midas-fingers!' she exclaimed when the first mitt came off. 'I'm sorry I didn't believe you when you told me,' she said to Ani.

'Never mind about that now,' she insisted.

The heat was building behind the door. They scrunched their faces against it. The flames were rising. Jenipher rattled the handle. It was coming loose.

'There!' Ani peeled the second mitt off Kitt's hand.

His fingers and palms were stiff, coated in thick layers of gold.

'I don't know how. I can't control it!'

Payton pulled him to her side.

'It comes from greed,' she said. 'Give in to your feelings. Think of all the things you want – all the things you don't have yet.'

She pushed his hands towards the handle. Her shoulder hurt from leaning against the door. The bottom of it was burning in earnest.

'Really picture it.'

Kitt frowned. At first nothing happened. But, as he concentrated, the gold began to grow. It built and built and soon was coming out in a rush. The door handle began to shine – it became thick and misshapen with gold until it was so stuck Jenipher couldn't even make it rattle.

She hammered on the door.

Kitt pressed his palms to the wood. It turned to gold under his touch, and the flames slowed where they met the metal and died back.

'You did it!' Ani cried.

At that moment, there was a blast of fire from

within the Eye as Jenipher's fury was fully unleashed.

'That should hold,' said Payton grimly, wiping the soot from her face. 'But Estlin's heart won't – and we can't get to King Jude's quick enough.'

'King Jude's?'

'They have lightning there. We have to go home.'

CHAPTER TWENTY-FOUR

Ani drove, with Kitt shouting directions in her ear while Payton crouched on the plush carriage seat and monitored Estlin. He was fading quickly, each breath shallower than the last. His lips were darkening to a bruised, purple colour.

'Quicker!' she called.

'I'm trying!' Ani shouted back.

Even in her panic, she found delight at being able to drive a carriage. The does understood every twitch of her reins as they careered down the streets, weaving dangerously close to other carriages and people.

'Are you sure there's bottled lightning at King Jude's?'

'Methic Tumnal has some,' Payton said with certainty. 'He collects old medicines from the early days of the Turn.'

'Why didn't I know that?'

'Well, if you'd just taken your studies a bit more seriously—'

'There's Battersea Meadows!' said Kitt. 'Ani, left here. Left!'

They took the corner too tightly, and all four of them slammed across the carriage.

'Take the ambulans entrance,' Payton advised calmly.

'That's what I'm doing.' Ani couldn't bear the sight of Estlin unconscious, with his head in Payton's lap.

'Look. We're home.'

Payton leant forward between Ani and Kitt, and for a moment nothing existed except the towering, honey-coloured brick walls, the glinting windows, the buttresses and arches that they hadn't seen since they ran away, the day of Ani's blood reading.

The ambulans yard was exactly as they'd left it. It was like they had never been away.

But there wasn't time to celebrate. They clambered down, helping Payton lift Estlin.

'What's happening to him?' Ani asked, draping his limp, cold arm around her neck to hold him up.

'His heart's slowing right down. It needs a big shock.'

The quad was brown-blue in the twilight, and lights were starting to come on in the wards. It was supper time, the girls realized. Most of the methics were in the

Methics Hall or the Small Dining Room. Nobody seemed to have any idea that only a few miles away, the Guild Master was trapped in an inferno made from her own feelings.

They were halfway across the quad when Ani stumbled. She was exhausted, and Estlin, with one arm over her shoulders and the other over Kitt, was a dead weight.

'Sorry – I can't—' She needed to put him down, and she paused to get her breath.

'This is taking too long,' said Payton. 'Wait here.'

She sprinted into the building ahead of them, and Ani lay Estlin down on the ground. She squeezed his hand – it was freezing cold. She couldn't bear it any longer. She was shaken by great wracking sobs that seemed to come from deep within her ribcage. Was this how people get heartbroken, she wondered? She thought of Hyde Gardens. She would plant him as a sgerbod tree, just as he'd asked. Then she'd be able to visit him. The thought of it made it a little easier to breathe.

'He'll be all right,' said Kitt, but she could only nod in response.

'I hoped his heart would heal,' Ani told Kitt, wiping her face. 'After everything . . .' She knew it was selfish, but they'd been happy in Hyde Gardens for a while. Deep down, she'd hoped that their friendship would be enough to heal his heartbreak.

'Some things go too deep to heal,' Kitt told her. 'You just have to live with it.'

Their arrival was starting to draw attention. There were shouts by the ambulans entrance when the drivers discovered the Queen Cleo's carriage blocking the way. Nurses looked out of the windows.

'Ani?' Nurse Wheeldon appeared in the doorway of the Department of Dreams, Delusions and Disturbed Thoughts. 'Is that you?'

'My friend's sick.' Ani's voice cracked as she said it. Something about being home made her feel small. She wanted the methics and nurses to scoop her up and make everything better. 'Payton—'

'Payton's here?'

Nurse Wheeldon almost ran across the quad and pulled Ani up into a tight, rough embrace. Then she pushed her back and held her at arm's length.

'What on *earth* were you thinking, running away like that? And where have you been? You're filthy.'

More nurses appeared in doorways and windows. Methics gathered in the doorway of the Methics Hall and crossed the quad to join them. Cries of surprise and relief mingled in the commotion.

'I was in Hyde Gardens. It made me better, but then I had to go to this place, the Observatory . . . Jenipher – I mean, Methic Blake – she was doing this experiment. She was using anghofio flowers on children.'

'Impossible!' said one of the methics.

'I saw it,' Ani replied.

A younger methic bent down to examine Estlin.

'Payton's going to heal him,' Ani said weakly.

'Heartbreak,' said the methic to a friend who had joined him and was nodding knowledgeably. 'You're too late.'

'We *know* it's heartbreak,' said Kitt.

'Give him space.' Ani tried to tug them away.

More of them were crowding round, crouching over Estlin, plucking at his wires and pads, marvelling at Ani's return and at the boy in clumsy, gold-encrusted gloves. Ani tried to convince them to leave Estlin.

'Payton's helping him. She's going to treat him. Leave him—'

'Move!'

The crowd sprang back as Payton strode up, clutching three sandglass bottles of lightning, which she placed down carefully on the ground next to Estlin.

'Help me,' she said to Ani, pulling off his shirt. Once she could get at the straps that had held the lightning bottle in place, she then slapped Ani's hands away. 'Let me!'

The three bottles were caked in dust and cobwebs. Ani guessed most of the methics didn't even know the hospital had them. She picked one up, and for a moment felt the exhilarating thrill of clutching a natural power far greater than anything she'd touched before. The flickering, forking light was mesmerizing.

The methics watched Payton work, growing in number and curiosity. One person made a comment about the outdated treatment, but one withering look from Payton was enough to shut him up.

'This should work.' Payton glanced at Estlin's purpling lips. She kept her nerves pushed down – nobody around her guessed she felt trepidation – but she was dealing with a highly dangerous substance, and she didn't want Ani to know how slim Estlin's chances were.

She found the leather cap for the bottle. One twist and the lightning would be released into the wires.

'Right. This is it,' she said.

Ani put her hand over Estlin's. Payton shook her head and pried Ani's hand away.

'Better not risk it,' she said.

'Payton,' said Nurse Wheeldon, 'I really think you should let one of the methics—'

Payton twisted the cap.

She heard the electricity zing through the wire. Blue sparks spat at the ends of the wires. Estlin's entire body convulsed.

Once.

Twice.

Then he gasped.

Ani laughed with relief and threw her arms around him. Kitt started to clap, and soon all the methics followed his lead, applauding Payton while she tried to get at Estlin to check his heartbeat.

The blood rushed back to his face. Bewildered, he took in the crowd of blue robes around him.

'Did . . . did it work?'

'It did. We got out. You're an utter idiot,' Ani told him, 'and you should never have done it.' She placed the newly connected lightning bottle in his hands. 'Open this one, and I'll give you a broken arm to go with your heart.'

Estlin fell back on the ground, the lightning clasped to his chest like it was his dearest friend.

'Nurse Wheeldon, can you take him to the Heart-break Ward?' Payton asked.

'Certainly. And I think the Elemental Disruption Ward needs to take a look at you, young man,' she said to Kitt, placing her fists on her hips like she did when she was telling Ani off.

'Do I have to?' Kitt asked fearfully.

'Don't worry,' said Payton. 'It's a normal ward. No one will lock you in this time. Ani can take you. Can't you, Ani?'

Ani was still crouched next to Estlin, but she wasn't listening. She was as still as a fox, unblinking, fixated on a gap in the crowd. Payton followed her gaze.

It was their father.

He looked sleep-deprived and fatter, and, instead of relief or joy at their return, his face was etched with an apprehension that was ripening into fear.

Ani was gripping one of the spare bottles of lightning. Her glare was pure acid.

'Ani,' Payton said carefully. 'Don't . . .'

But when Neel Darke saw the look of rage on his daughter's face, he turned on his heel and walked back towards the laboratories. Ani sprang up and pelted after him. Payton followed her, chasing the flashes of lightning into the building.

Ani followed her father down the deserted corridors. She wanted to cry. She wanted to make him cry. She wanted to unleash the lightning and blow a hole in King Jude's.

The moment Jenipher had read her blood played over and over in her mind. The awful diagnosis and the threat of being locked up. The mention of the treatment, which she now knew was anghofio flowers. Her father standing, barely raising his hand. Her father, silent during the blood reading. Her father, in their apartment after the reading, suggesting that she go with Jenipher to have the treatment . . .

She half expected the fury to splutter out of her mouth, flaming her breath like it once threatened to, but her body didn't work like that any more. Ever since Hyde Gardens, she had been able to feel anger without losing control.

'Ani!' Payton called to her, but neither of them stopped.

The workbenches in Neel's laboratory were clear and empty. Payton found him with his back to a fume chamber. Ani stood before him, holding the lightning aloft like a sword.

'Ani, put it down,' she ordered.

'Don't tell me what to do. You weren't the one he was going to send to the Observatory.' Ani faced her father. 'Did you know what the treatment was? Did you know she was going to use anghofio flowers on me?'

He tried to step back, but there was nowhere to go.

'Control your feelings, Ani,' he implored.

'I am in control. Did you know? Did you know what the side effects of it are?'

'Payton, get your sister to—'

'Answer her,' Payton interrupted. 'Did you know?'

'Ani, sweetheart . . .' Coming from her father, the endearment felt wrong. It was like a stranger calling out to her. 'This is all very complicated. And I think there have been some misunderstandings. You ran away before I could explain—'

'Did you KNOW?' Ani screamed so loudly her voice echoed through the lab.

Neel looked helplessly from one daughter to another. Then, 'Well . . . Yes.'

The worry that had gnawed at her insides broke. Ani felt the earth wobble for a moment. As if the natural order of things – that her father was somebody she should be able to trust – had been broken beyond repair.

She took a step closer. Neel was sweating, never taking his eyes off the bottled lightning.

'Estlin needs that,' Payton reminded her.

'I've had people out looking for you all over the city. Every day, every night.' The words spilt out of him without his usual control. He was scared, Payton realized. He was panicking.

Ani narrowed her eyes with suspicion.

'I noticed. Why?'

'To bring you home.'

'Or to give me anghofio flowers? Why would you want me to have that?'

'I was thinking only of our family. Ani, my darling, it's because you're so special. You're my . . . my . . .'

'Cure.' Payton finished his sentence. They both stared at her. 'A supply of balanced blood.'

'What?' Ani was confused, looking from her sister to her father.

Payton muttered to herself like a methic untangling a particularly difficult problem. 'It all started with the blood reading, didn't it? Jenipher showed us all that Ani has perfectly balanced blood. Except for the anger. You wanted her to take the anger away.'

'Of course I did. What father wouldn't to cure—'

'No. Not a cure for her anger. You know what I'm talking about.'

'Listen, girls . . .'

'It's why you helped Jenipher with the blood-reading programme in the first place, isn't it? You wanted to know when she found a patient with perfectly balanced blood. You just didn't expect it to be Ani.'

'I—'

'Back in the Observatory,' Payton continued, her voice gaining confidence as all the pieces of the puzzle began to make sense, 'Jenipher said you wanted Ani back, but only when her blood was balanced. But why? Ani was taking medicine, she was fine. Anghofio flowers are so extreme. You wanted her anger gone so badly, but not because you were worried about her health. You wanted her blood.'

'I don't understand!' Ani cried, more bewildered than ever. 'Payton, what's going on? A cure for what?'

'For water fever.'

Ani stared at Payton in disbelief, the lightning flickering and forgotten in her grasp. Neel's expression darkened.

The idea was intoxicating. Ani didn't know as much

about medicine as Payton or her father – she had no idea that blood could be such a powerful ingredient. *Her* blood.

She could free her mother from the glass chamber she slept in.

'I'm right, aren't I?' said Payton. 'Jenipher once told me that you were closer to a cure than I knew. This is what she meant.'

'It hardly matters now.' When Neel looked at Ani, he didn't conceal the disappointment he felt. 'She isn't better. She hasn't had the anghofio-flower treatment. Once I get you back to Jenipher—'

'Jenipher won't be treating anybody,' Payton told him. 'And Ani *is* better. I saw it when I read her blood.'

'You don't know how to use a gwaidmesur.'

Payton's lips curled into a grim smile.

'I *am* a gwaidmesur.'

Neel narrowed his eyes. 'Liar. Human gwaidmesurs no longer exist.'

'Yes they do. I read Ani's blood. In the vision . . . I didn't know what it meant at the time . . .' Payton was thinking of the richly planted Inertia Ward, how Ani had placed her hand in their mother's water chamber, the blood floating through the water . . .

'If I can cure Mother, what are we even arguing about?' Ani cried. 'Let's go! Now! We have to help her. Use my blood.'

'We can't,' said Payton, still staring at Neel.

'We could,' he replied.

Payton strode forward and took the lightning from Ani's hand. Neel stumbled in fear and ran into the fume chamber in the vain hope that a sheet of glass could protect him from his daughters' wrath. Payton walked calmly up to the control panel and pressed the button to lock the door.

'Payton, what's going on?' Ani asked. 'If I'm a cure for water fever—'

'There's no *if*.' Payton couldn't bear to turn and look at her sister. 'You *are*. But we can't use your blood. I've studied every way of making a cure – including this one. A lot. To cure Mother, we would need all of your blood. It would kill you.'

'Then how can we use it?'

'We can't. To wake her up, we'd lose you.'

Neel's palms pressed white against the glass. 'Payton. Try to understand. I hadn't made a decision.'

'That's the problem.'

The meaning of the conversation finally dawned on Ani, and she was glad Payton had taken the lightning from her. Her hands trembled uncontrollably.

'You were going to kill me to make the cure?'

'Methics have to make terrible choices. This would be a career-making cure. Not to mention the fact that I love her—'

'So do we!' Payton shouted. She took a deep breath and regained control of herself. 'You have to swear to give this up,' she said. 'It's not just you. If other methics know, they will hunt Ani.'

'That's why it's best that I take control—'

'It's why you have to keep it a secret! Destroy your research, never tell a soul. All families have secrets, don't they? This can be ours.'

Payton willed her father to agree with her. He was quiet for a moment, but when he spoke again, she knew she would never feel more disappointed in anyone or anything.

'If Ani has the anghofio treatment,' he said, 'and things go wrong in the blood extraction, she won't feel it anyway.'

'How *could* you?'

'If – if it will . . .' Ani stumbled over her words. 'I mean . . . I can try . . .'

'No!' Payton's voice cracked. 'It's not your choice. This isn't how methics work.'

'Payton,' Neel pleaded. 'You have the mind of a methic. If Ani's willing, we can try.'

'It will kill her! Who else knows about this?' she demanded. 'Who else has seen your research since the blood reading?'

'Nobody.'

'Good.'

Payton bent her head over the control panel. She was now certain that for as long as her father knew what Ani's blood could do, her little sister would never be safe. She pushed her feelings down as best she could. She was determined to make her choice like a good methic. Calm, logical, for the good of others. She tuned out her father's pleading from the behind the glass.

'Payton. Payton. My clever girl, always such a clever girl,' Neel appealed to her. 'I know you see it too. I know how others would see it, but *you* understand. You know these things are never black and white. Wouldn't you have done the same? Wouldn't you go to the ends of the earth to be the best methic you could? Think of the lives saved, the pain over. Ever since the Turn, it's all that matters. You understand. My little methic. You would have done the same, wouldn't you?'

Payton was clear-eyed as she looked up from the control panel. She had made her decision. The only one that could keep Ani safe.

The vial of anghofio she'd taken from the Eye when she'd stopped Jenipher shone jet-black in the fume chamber's medicine slot.

'No.'

She pushed a lever. Darkness rained down on Methic Neel Darke.

CHAPTER TWENTY-FIVE

Payton stood alone on the threshold of the Methics Hall.

She had been back at King Jude's for a few days, but she hadn't gone back to wearing the dresses Nurse Wheeldon insisted on. She wore a loose shirt and trousers as she had at Queen Cleo's with Jenipher. She had cut her hair short so it fell to her jaw and, as she waited to be summoned, she felt the evening breeze cool her neck. When she heard the clock strike nine, she opened the door. The guild wanted to speak to her.

The hall had been cleared of its dining tables. There were seven chairs in a semicircle, one for every hospital in Lundain. Only six of them were filled – Jenipher's, in the middle, the rightful place for the Guild Master, was empty.

Payton stood before them, feeling like a little girl once more, not the competent young woman who had returned from the Observatory.

'Miss Darke,' a middle-aged woman with tight grey curls addressed her first. 'How is your father?'

'He was moved on to the new ward for the anghofio-flower patients today,' she replied. 'He is calm.'

'Such a tragic accident. All the hospitals of Lundain will be united in finding a way to care for patients like him,' said a man with a bald head and an enormous red beard.

'Thank you,' she murmured. She hadn't told anybody that she had given her father the treatment to protect Ani. Everybody at King Jude's believed that Neel Darke had accidentally touched the liquid when the vial Payton had brought back from the Observatory had broken.

'We have many questions, Payton, as you can imagine,' Gilchrist said, getting to his feet. The other methics looked at him with respect and appreciation. He would be Jenipher's successor, Payton suspected. He was kind and trustworthy and wise.

'I think it's best we begin with your arrival at Queen Cleo's.'

Payton gave as honest an account as she could. She explained about getting caught in the Blood Library; how Jenipher discovered that she was a gwaidmesur and trained her; what she'd discovered at the Observatory; Jenipher's outburst after Estlin blew up the Eye and ruined her supply of anghofio flowers.

'Nobody has told me what has happened to her. I know she was . . . what she did was terrible, but . . . she was my teacher,' Payton concluded.

'Methic Blake has returned to Queen Cleo's. As a patient,' Gilchrist informed her. 'It is the only hospital with the facilities to protect people from an incendiary disease that severe. She is being cared for by her own methics.'

Payton nodded, grateful to know.

'We have been discussing what to do with you. The first gwaidmesur in generations. It is a dangerous power, Payton.'

'*Too* dangerous,' the oldest of the methics apart from Gilchrist growled this clarification. Payton saw a few of the others nod.

'It's an opportunity,' said the grey-haired woman. 'A tool we haven't had since the first days of the Turn. If we'd had a human gwaidmesur, this mess with Blake could have been avoided.'

'As you can see, it is not an easy matter for the guild to resolve,' said Gilchrist. 'But it is a matter for the guild. And in that light . . .'

He tugged something from the back of his chair. It was a set of blue robes.

'These are for you.' He held them out to her.

Payton hesitated. To her, they were worth a hundred of her purple robes.

'Are you sure?'

'You will sit your Trials like any other methic. If you pass, you will join our junior methics. Until then, you may not treat patients; you may only shadow other methics.'

She nodded.

'And you will not read blood. If you join our guild, your gift belongs to us all. We should all agree on how to put it to use.'

'I understand.'

'Take them, then, girl,' said the bearded methic, with a booming laugh. 'They don't bite.'

Payton took the robes from Gilchrist and slipped them over her shoulders. She looked down at the cascade of blue fabric.

'Welcome to the Guild of Medicine,' Gilchrist said, with a small bow of his head.

'Thank you.' She took care to look each one of them in the eye. 'I won't let you down.'

'You and your sister will stay here,' said Gilchrist, sitting back down. 'This is your home.'

'About my sister . . .' Payton ran her hands over the blue fabric. 'I need to tell you. She was on the brink of developing spark breath for years. My father gave her medicine to keep it in check, but nothing could help her control her feelings. Then she stayed in Hyde Gardens. My understanding is that a couple live there – they are descended from wilders – along with Estlin.'

'Who?' somebody asked.

'The boy with the lightning treatment,' Gilchrist supplied.

'Yes,' said Payton. 'And Ani says . . . well, she says the Wild healed her. I know it sounds mad, but I read her blood and her anger is gone. I can't explain it, but I think it's an area we should research.'

Gilchrist smiled kindly.

'We will take it under consideration.'

'Thank you.'

'Goodnight, Methic Darke.'

'Goodnight.'

Payton hurried down the steps to the Inertia Ward. She knew her mother wouldn't be able to see her blue robes, but she wanted to tell her anyway.

When she rounded the corner into the cellar, she stopped in her tracks.

Ani was standing in the gloom next to their mother's water chamber.

Payton paused on the threshold, watching the hunched shape of her sister – it was the shape of tears.

Payton chose to melt into the shadows and tiptoe back up the stairs. She let Ani have her reunion.

CHAPTER TWENTY-SIX

It was the middle of the night at King Jude's Hospital. The anghofio patients were settling into their new ward. In the dim Inertia Ward, Iona Darke still lay underwater in an artificial, eternal sleep to protect her from her own grief. Most of the methics and nurses were asleep or on their night rounds.

All was at peace.

Ani Darke strode through the long, tangled grass behind the operating theatre. The summer night smelt of earth, the ground releasing the heat it had absorbed during the day. The papers she was carrying rustled in her arms – the only sound this far away from the main buildings of the hospital.

She spotted Estlin's twitching outline next to the dark mound they had spent the night building.

'There.' Ani let the armful of papers fall on to the pile. She wiped her hands, smearing the ink that was smudged on her skin. 'That's the last of it.'

'Can we start?' Estlin asked.

'We need to wait for Payton.'

Ani and Estlin were both tanned from days spent in the sun in Hyde Gardens. They came back to King Jude's most evenings to visit Payton and Kitt, to enjoy the food from the kitchens and make mischief on the wards.

'Wait – do you hear that?' Ani asked.

A twig snapped and the grass whispered as Payton rounded the corner of the theatre. Kitt was with her, still in his hospital pyjamas and mitts. Once again Ani was struck by how grown-up her sister looked in her blue robes.

'Sorry I'm late,' Payton said. 'I had a little trouble sneaking him past his nurses.' She nodded at Kitt.

'I had to see you,' Kitt explained. 'I'm leaving tomorrow. They're taking me to the Guild of Finance.'

'What? You can't go there!' Ani recalled the eerie gaze of the Guild Master.

'But I want to,' he said to her. 'Methic Gilchrist says they'll let me join the guild one day. Can you imagine? Me! A financier! It wasn't so long ago I was stealing from market stalls.'

'Just steer clear of the badgers,' Estlin muttered.

'Is this everything?' Payton looked at the mound of papers.

'Every last scrap.'

'What is it?' Kitt asked, scooping a page from the pile with his mitt.

'Our father's research.' Payton took the page off him and cast it back on to the mound. 'It's to protect Ani. Once we burn this, we're the only ones in the world who know what her blood could do.'

The four of them looked at the pale sheets of paper over dark, crisscrossed wood: Neel Darke's life's work.

Ani hugged Payton, who stood stiffly and didn't move into the embrace, but bent her head towards her sister, which was how Ani knew it was appreciated.

'Come on. Let's put an end to this.'

Ani had the matches. The sisters stood together as she threw the first one on to the bonfire. It caught quickly. Their father's handwriting glowed at them before turning to ash, and his cure for water fever vanished for ever.

Their faces were bathed in orange light. Only the moon and a sparse scattering of stars watched them.

'Only we know?' Ani asked Payton as they watched it burn.

'Only we know.'

Ani squeezed her hands into fists. She could feel the pulse of her blood. She thought about the cure that was hidden inside her.

'I'm sorry,' she said suddenly.

'For what?'

'I feel like I've taken the one thing that could cure Mother and locked it inside my veins. Weren't you tempted?' She searched her sister's profile for a clue to her thoughts. 'Didn't you want to try?'

'It would have killed you.'

'You could have taken the risk. You always wanted to cure water fever.'

'I will cure water fever.' Payton turned to look at her, her face flame-washed. She took Ani's hand – the old turquoise cloirias burn covered by her clasp. 'The right way. As a methic should. I'll bring her back to us. I promise.'

The bonfire spat and hissed.

As it roared upwards and then burnt softer over the course of the night, the four of them sat on the grass and began to talk. Of nightmare vapour and lightning and anghofio at first, but eventually they lightened into jokes and laughter and talk of the adventures that would soon take them out into the ever-changing world. The sun came up as the fire died, and they slept like children.

A NOTE FROM THE AUTHOR

I began writing *Once Upon a Fever* in January 2020. A story where magic and medicine and mystery intertwine in an alternate London had been taking shape in my imagination for some time. But I never could have imagined that only a few weeks into writing it, my own beloved London would be locked down as COVID-19 threw the world into chaos.

At the time, I didn't know if I should continue with this book. My story about medicine, hope and corruption felt meaningless against the reality we were all living. Fortunately, I had people in my life who convinced me that fantasies can always offer us meaning, even in the darkest of times.

Those people are the reason you are holding this book today. They kept me going.

So that's who I'd like to acknowledge on this page: the people who simply kept us going.

And, above all, I'd like to thank the healers.

THE ASH HOUSE

A new boy arrives at the Ash House. He can't remember his name – or why he's been sent there.

Dom greets him, remembering the importance of Nicenesses, and the rules made by the Headmaster before he left them on their own. Dom gives the boy a new name – Sol, for Solitude. With nowhere else to go, and troubled by a mystery pain that no medicine can cure, Sol joins the gang of children living in the shadows of the secretive house, with its walls that seep smoke into the air. They do what they can to survive.

Soon, however, there's more for the children of Ash House to face – unless Dom and Sol's new-found friendship can defeat the darkness that descends with the arrival of the Doctor ...

'A mesmerizing other-worldly story that got deep under my skin – I couldn't put it down.'

JASBINDER BILAN

Paperback, ISBN 978-1-912626-97-7, £7.99 • ebook, ISBN 978-1-913322-58-8, £7.99

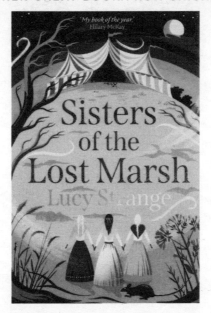

SISTERS OF THE LOST MARSH
by LUCY STRANGE

Life is hard for Willa, Grace and Freya, and their three younger sisters. Six motherless girls working a farm, living in fear of their cruel father and the superstition that obsesses him – the Curse of Six Daughters.

With the arrival of the mysterious Full Moon Fayre, there's a chance for the eldest girls to steal a moment's fun, but the day the fayre moves on, Grace vanishes.

Willa goes after her, following a trail that leads into the dangerous Lost Marsh, where it is said a will-o'-the-wisp lures lost souls into the dark waters of the mire. If Willa is to survive and reunite her family, she will need to unravel the secrets her father has kept hidden, and face her own deepest fears . . .

'My book of the year.'
HILARY MCKAY

Paperback, ISBN 978-1-913322-37-3, £7.99 • ebook, ISBN 978-1-913696-36-8, £7.99

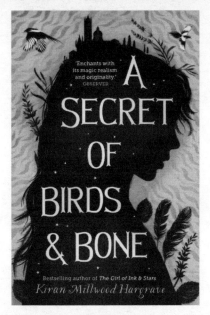

A SECRET OF BIRDS & BONE
by KIRAN MILLWOOD HARGRAVE

Sofia lives outside the city of Siena with her mamma, little brother Ermin, and their pet crow Corvith. Her mother is a bone-binder, famous for her keepsakes and charms.

But ever since an unexpected visit from a silver-veiled stranger, Mamma has not been herself. She no longer takes pleasure in her work, nor will she let Sofia help her.

When Mamma is arrested on Sofia's birthday, the children are taken to the city orphanage. It's there that Sofia decides she is no longer a helpless child. Clutching her mamma's gift, an intricate bone locket, she sets out to unravel the secrets that bind her family to Siena itself: its catacombs and towers, its birds and rivers. Its rulers and people. A journey to darkness, danger, destiny – and hope.

'A dark and mesmerizing historical adventure . . .'
THE BOOKSELLER

Paperback, ISBN 978-1-913322-96-0, £7.99 • ebook, ISBN 978-1-913322-63-2, £7.99

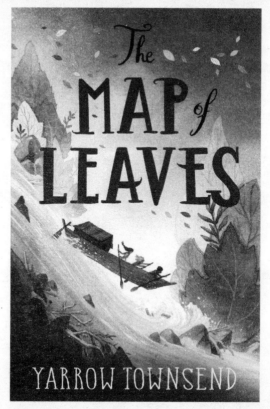

THE MAP OF LEAVES by YARROW TOWNSEND

Orla has lived alone since Ma died, with only her beloved garden for company.

When sickness comes and nature is blamed, Orla knows she must find a cure. Armed with her mother's book of plants and remedies, she steals away on a riverboat with two other stowaways, Idris and Ariana.

Soon the trio must navigate the rapids of the Inkwater to a poisonous place from which they may never return . . .

Paperback, ISBN 978-1-913696-48-1, £7.99 • ebook, ISBN 978-1-913696-66-5, £7.99